A
MERRY
MURDER

KATE KINGSBURY

BERKLEY PRIME CRIME
NEW YORK

BERKLEY PRIME CRIME
Published by Berkley
An imprint of Penguin Random House LLC
1745 Broadway, New York, NY 10019

Library of Congress Cataloging-in-Publication Data

Names: Kingsbury, Kate, author.
Title: A merry murder / Kate Kingsbury.
Description: First edition. | New York: Berkley Prime Crime, 2019. |
Series: A Pennyfoot Holiday mystery; 10
Identifiers: LCCN 2019020781 | ISBN 9781984805928 (paperback) |
ISBN 9781984805935 (ebook)
Subjects: LCSH: Christmas fiction. | BISAC: FICTION / Mystery & Detective /
Women Sleuths. | FICTION / Mystery & Detective / Historical. | GSAFD: Mystery fiction.
Classification: LCC PR9199.3.K44228 M47 2019 | DDC 813/.54—dc23
LC record available at https://lccn.loc.gov/2019020781

First Edition: October 2019

Printed in the United States of America
1   3   5   7   9   10   8   6   4   2

Cover art by Dan Craig
Cover design by Judith Lagerman

To my husband, Bill, for all the years of
listening to me whine, for celebrating the good
times with me, and for the unique understanding
of what it takes to be a writer. I love you.

ACKNOWLEDGMENTS

To my new editor, Grace House. I have been extremely fortunate to have had exceptional editors in my career, and I'm delighted to have yet another. Thank you for working so diligently on this book and for appreciating the discrepancies between Edwardian England and modern-day America. It is a pleasure to work with you.

To my agent, Paige Wheeler. Thank you for your support and great advice, and for your patience when faced with my grumbling. I value our relationship and look forward to future projects.

To Ana-Maria Bonner. Thank you for taking such good care of my books and for all your help with the tedious side of this profession. It's comforting to know I can rely on you.

To my good friend Ann Wraight. Thank you for keeping me in touch with England, and all the memories. I hope you know how much I appreciate it.

To my readers:

Six years ago, I closed the doors of the Pennyfoot Hotel. I felt I had gone as far as I could go with the characters. Those characters, however, were not done with me. They continued to

Acknowledgments

haunt me, popping into my mind while I watched TV, or waking me up in the night to remind me they were still alive and kicking. I ignored their pleas to reopen the hotel, but when you, my dear readers, kept begging me to write another Christmas Pennyfoot book, I could no longer resist.

You are the reason the Pennyfoot Hotel opened its doors again. Your loyalty, your support, and your messages mean so much to me, and I am excited to bring you another saga in the lives of the Pennyfoot clan. They thank you, and I thank you. I wish you all the merriest Christmas ever and another year of great books to read.

Doreen
aka Kate Kingsbury

CHAPTER

❋ 1 ❋

Pausing to catch her breath at the top of the backstairs, Gertie McBride shifted the pile of linens she carried higher in her arms. From the kitchen below, she could hear the clatter of pots and pans, and Michel's strident voice bitterly complaining in his stupid French accent that didn't fool anyone.

The volatile chef always got frantic at Christmastime, and today was no exception. Mrs. Chubb could be heard screeching at him to shut up. Shaking her head, Gertie thanked the heavens that, for a change, she wasn't the one on the business end of the housekeeper's wrath.

Breakfast had been served over an hour ago, but already the midday meal was being prepared. Gertie could detect a faint whiff of onions, but the smell was overwhelmed by the fragrant aroma of pine and cedar that wafted across the hotel lobby.

In just a few days it would be Christmas Eve. She cast a

1

glance at the grand curving staircase leading to the upper floors, where huge boughs of evergreens hung on the railings. Bright red ribbons decorated the wreaths as well as little silver bells that tinkled when Gertie's skirts brushed against them on the way down from the guest rooms.

In the far corner the magnificent Christmas tree glowed a welcome to the arriving visitors. Gold and silver stars covered the branches, while little white angels with silvery gowns and red and green balls sparkled in the light from the massive chandelier above. A couple of guests passed by the tree, pausing to admire the decorations before strolling on toward the staircase.

Heaving a sigh, Gertie stomped down the stairs. The sooner she got the linens down to the laundry room the better. Mrs. Baxter—or "madam," as everyone called her—would get testy if she saw her chief housemaid carrying dirty washing across the foyer.

The Pennyfoot's owner was always kind and considerate to the downstairs staff, as long as they obeyed the rules and minded their manners. She could be an ogre, however, if one of them did something to upset the hotel guests.

Normally the sheets and pillowcases would be sent down the chute to the downstairs hallway, but the upstairs door was stuck again and Archie would have to mend it. Thinking about the new handyman reminded Gertie of Clive, who used to have the job.

She tried not to think about Clive these days.

She had always loved this time of year. Besides the housekeeping, Mrs. Chubb also baked, and nothing spelled "Christmas" like the enticing smell of her mince pies and plum puddings. Unless it was the sound of Phoebe Fortescue's dance group practicing their horrible out-of-tune singing in the ballroom, or the decorations brightening the halls of the Pennyfoot, or the excitement in her own twins' faces as they eagerly awaited the visit from Father Christmas.

This year, however, was different. It didn't seem possible that it had been a whole year since Clive had proposed. She'd been so excited and happy. She's accepted on the spot, and by rights she should be celebrating the season with a new husband and father to her twins.

It was only three months later when everything fell apart. Clive—the gentle, considerate man she'd fallen in love with—had turned into a domineering, selfish bugger.

When she'd told him that after she was married she still wanted to work at the Pennyfoot, he'd thrown a bleeding fit. He'd told her no wife of his would be anyone's maid, and that her place was in the home, taking care of him and her children. He'd made it sound as if her work was too blinking beneath him to be worth anything. As if *she* wasn't worth anything.

Well, that did it. Just because he'd left his job as the Pennyfoot's handyman and bought that flipping toy shop didn't make him bleeding royalty. He was no better than she was, and she'd wasted no time in telling him that. They'd had a good old blowup and she'd told that snot to shove off.

Reaching the floor, she closed her eyes for a moment to picture the scene, as she had done so many times since the spring. She'd missed him at first, but she'd kept reminding herself that she'd had a lucky escape. He would have dominated her whole life, and no one dominated Gertie Brown

McBride. Still, the memories kept coming back to taunt her, making her wonder what might have been if she'd done what he asked.

In the next instant she heard a grunt of pain as she smacked into something soft.

Opening her eyes, she stared into the gaunt face of Lilly Green, one of the latest maids to have been hired at the Pennyfoot. Lilly was almost as tall as Gertie, who towered over the rest of the staff with the exception of Michel. While Lilly was as skinny as a rake, however, Gertie was fighting a tendency to balloon out of her clothes.

She was built like a bloody bull to begin with, but had always managed to keep everything in proportion until this last year. No matter how little she ate now, it all seemed to end up on her blinking hips. She'd soon be as plump as Altheda Chubb. The bossy housekeeper was always complaining that her corset was pinching her.

"You smacked me in the stomach with those," Lilly said, frowning at the linens in Gertie's arms.

"Sorry, luv. I wasn't looking where I was flipping going, was I." Gertie paused for a moment, silently chiding herself. She'd promised herself so many times that she'd try to stop the curse words that seemed to explode from her lips with no way to stop them.

She'd grown up hearing that language from her dad all day long, and sometimes all night, too, and it had become so much part of her speech, she didn't even know she was doing it until someone said something. Usually Mrs. Chubb, who was always on at her to talk like a lady. Some bleeding hope of that.

"Why weren't you?" Lilly seemed about to cry. Then again, Lilly looked like that much of the time. She'd been working at the Pennyfoot for over a year, and she still acted like she'd wandered into a house of mirrors and couldn't escape.

There was an air of desperation about her that Gertie simply couldn't understand. It had taken Lilly months to get used to the work, and at times she still turned her nose up at some of the tasks, as if the whole thing was beneath her. She was finicky about everything, and went out of her way to avoid contact with the guests. Especially the men.

Gertie tried to get along with her, but was irritated by such a lack of gumption. As for herself, she would tackle anyone or anything that got in her bloody way. Besides, it irked her that Lilly always had her cap on straight and the straps of her apron sitting firmly on her shoulders. Gertie, on the other hand, rarely accomplished either. "Why wasn't I what?"

"Looking where you were going."

"Oh!" Gertie frowned. "I was thinking about something, that's why. Where are you off to anyway? Aren't you supposed to be cleaning the silver?"

Lilly raised her hand to tuck her hair more securely beneath her cap. "Mrs. Chubb sent me to tell madam that she's baking the Christmas puddings. She wants to know how many madam wants her to make."

"Then you'd better get on with it, hadn't you." Gertie stepped past her, adding over her shoulder, "You don't want Chubby after you for loitering. She'll have your bloody guts for garters." *Bugger it*, she thought. She was swearing again.

She could hear Lilly's black patent leather shoes clicking on the stairs as she hurried up them. Shaking her head, Gertie headed for the laundry room. If she didn't get back to the kitchen right away, it would be *her* guts turning into bloody garters.

Mrs. Chubb was like a mother to her, and to the rest of the maids. Her sharp tongue, however, would give them all a lashing if they got behind in their work. Gertie grinned as she shoved the door open with her shoulder. Chubby didn't take no nonsense from anyone. Not even madam or Mr. Baxter. Gertie liked that. You knew where you was with her.

Stepping inside the empty room, she marched over to one of the sinks and dumped the linens into it. Three of the ironing boards were stacked against the wall, while a fourth stood a few feet from the window. One of the maids had forgotten to put it away.

Gertie was tempted to leave it there and get back to the kitchen. She had actually turned toward the door when habit, engrained by years of following the strict rules of the Pennyfoot Hotel, forced her to turn back and fold up the ironing board.

As she carried it over to its place against the wall, something caught her attention in the dark corner by the sinks. A bundle of dirty clothes. Someone must have been in a hurry, chucked them at the sink, and missed. She probably hadn't even noticed that they'd landed on the floor. Most likely it was the same bloody twit who'd left the ironing board in the middle of the room.

Cursing under her breath, Gertie stomped across the room to pick up the bundle. As she drew closer, however, cold shock slammed into her chest. It wasn't a bundle of clothes after all. It was a man, lying curled up on his side, his eyes open and staring blankly into space.

"Here!" Gertie demanded, backing up a step or two. "What the bloody hell are you doing in here? You'd better get out of here before I call the copper and have you thrown in the bloody clink."

The man didn't even twitch, and looking at the bloodless face, Gertie thought she knew why. This man wasn't getting up again. He was bleeding dead.

Upstairs in the lavish suite overlooking the bowling greens, Cecily Sinclair Baxter watched her husband settle into his comfortable armchair with the latest edition of the *Illustrated London News*.

It had been almost a year since a bout of pneumonia had come close to taking Baxter's life. Every time she looked at him, she felt again the anxiety and dread that had filled her very soul when Dr. Kevin Prestwick had turned to her in that dim, candlelit room, his face grave with concern. She had lost her first husband in that same room. She could not bear to lose another.

Baxter had survived, thank the good Lord, but the illness had left him weak and depressed for months. So much so that he had officially declined the position offered to him as a director of overseas acquisitions—work that would have taken them to all four corners of the world.

Baxter had declared one evening over dinner that he had come to the conclusion he was too old to be taking on such a monumental task. "I am much more suited to managing one hotel in one place, rather than chasing all over the world taking on one headache after another," he'd told her.

She'd pretended to be dismayed, but had fallen to her knees later that night and given thanks for this reprieve. The only reason she'd agreed to the opportunity in the first place was because Baxter had come close to being seriously hurt while aiding her in a murder investigation. She had decided they would both be on safer ground away from the Pennyfoot and her penchant for tangling with villains. The possibility of seeing her sons again, both of whom lived abroad, was also an incentive.

Even so, she'd hated the very thought of leaving her home and the staff, who had become as close as family to her. She had become even more overjoyed when Baxter had surprised her later with a suggestion.

"I think we should purchase the Pennyfoot from your cousin," he'd said, and for a long moment Cecily had stared at him, afraid to believe what she was hearing in case she was mistaken.

When she didn't answer him, Baxter had added, "We could turn it from a country club back into a hotel. The memberships have been dwindling in the last year or so, and with a hotel we would attract a more diverse and hopefully a more abundant clientele."

She had leapt at the idea with so much enthusiasm, Baxter had told her he wished he'd thought of the idea sooner.

So now that they were once again the owners of the Pennyfoot Hotel, Baxter seemed happy and content and, more important, healthy again. He had maintained his business in

London, though he had cut back a good deal of it and now did most of the work at home.

Christmas was less than a week away, and the aroma of seasonings and spice from the kitchen, blending with the fragrance of fresh greenery from the woods, filled the halls.

It was her favorite time of the year, and Cecily was so overjoyed, she felt a strong urge to hug her husband. She had actually stretched out her arms to do just that when a sharp rap on the door halted her.

Baxter sighed and rattled his newspaper as she turned toward the door.

"Come in!" Cecily seated herself on her gold Queen Anne armchair as the door opened and Gertie edged into the room.

"I'm sorry, m'm," she said, dropping a slight curtsey. "I got some bad news."

Baxter groaned, and lowered his newspaper. "What now?"

Gertie's gaze seemed to fix on Cecily's face. "I was in the laundry room and I thought it were a bundle of clothes lying on the floor, but it weren't." She appeared to have something to add, but apparently had trouble getting it out.

Cecily was already getting a nasty feeling in her stomach. Every year at this time they seemed to have some kind of disaster. She called it the Christmas Curse, and for years the name had been whispered among the downstairs staff with the same dread that she felt right now.

She tried to sound calm as she gave Gertie an encouraging smile. "So, what is it, Gertie?"

Baxter, who had none of his wife's patience and restraint, growled, "Come on, girl. Spit it out."

Gertie swallowed, heaved air into her lungs, and announced in a voice hoarse with anxiety, "It were a dead body, m'm. Mr. Baxter. Mrs. Chubb has already sent for the police constable."

"Oh, Lord," Baxter muttered, folding his newspaper.

Cecily could feel her heart pumping. Not again. Not now. Just when they were beginning to see a large increase in bookings. They were already taking reservations for next year. They didn't need another calamity to frighten off prospective guests, or the ones still due to arrive for the holidays, for that matter. "Who is it, Gertie? Is it one of the staff? A footman? Could you tell how he'd died?"

Gertie shook her head. "I didn't look at him that much, m'm. I didn't recognize his face, though. It weren't one of ours."

Baxter groaned again. "So, it's one of the guests. Wonderful."

"Perhaps he had a heart attack or something," Cecily said, grasping at the fragile hope the death was caused by a medical event.

Gertie cleared her throat. "Dr. Prestwick is on his way, too, m'm. Mrs. Chubb rang him as well."

"Good." Cecily got up from the chair. "Well, I suppose I should go down and take a look."

"I'll come with you." Baxter stood, slipped off his smoking jacket, and reached for his dress coat. "What I want to know is what in blazes was one of our guests doing in the laundry room?"

"He must have been looking for something," Cecily said as she hurried to the door.

"Or someone," Baxter added darkly as he followed her out into the hallway.

"I'll go ahead and tell Mrs. Chubb you're on your way down." Gertie stepped past them and fled down the stairs.

Cecily followed her, conscious of her husband at her heels, willing her to go faster. Her thoughts, however, were firmly fixed on the body waiting for her below. Her hope that the cause of death was for medical reasons seemed doomed, considering the victim had been found lying in the laundry room. That was odd, and in Cecily's experience, odd meant a foul deed had taken place.

An elderly couple approached them on the stairs, and Cecily paused on the landing to let the guests pass. The woman was dressed in a fine purple satin gown beneath a navy blue coat. Blue and white ribbon roses decorated the wide brim of her hat, which almost hid her eyes. She swept up past them without a word, but the gentleman doffed his top hat at her and smiled as he turned the corner.

Cecily barely noticed. She was anxious to get down to the laundry room and find out what had caused the death of one of her guests. Picking up a fold of her black serge skirt to raise it above her ankles, she quickened her step down the rest of the stairs, with Baxter breathing down her neck behind her.

Mrs. Chubb was waiting for them at the foot of the staircase, her normally flushed face looking pale and drawn. The housekeeper had to be quite agitated, as she had forgotten to remove her white apron before entering the lobby. "I'm sorry, m'm," she murmured, nodding at Baxter. "This is a nasty surprise, to be sure. Rest assured, Dr. Prestwick and P.C. Northcott are on their way."

A small group of visitors stood by the front doors, apparently deciding on their activities for the day. A couple stood by the Christmas tree, holding the hands of two young boys to prevent them from reaching for the inviting decorations.

Cecily gave them no more than a passing glance as she stared at her housekeeper. "P.C. Northcott? He didn't go to London for his annual Christmas visit to his wife's relatives?"

"No, m'm. He didn't. From what I heard, his wife has been ill and they decided not to go this year."

"Oh, I'm sorry to hear that." While her sympathy lay mostly with the constable's wife, Cecily was none too happy that she would have to deal with the bumbling policeman again. That meant the brunt of the investigation would fall on her shoulders once more—something she'd hoped to avoid.

Then again, the alternative would be an encounter with Scotland Yard inspector William Cranshaw. Cecily shuddered at the thought. She'd rather walk barefoot on hot coals.

"Did you want to wait for the constable before you take a look in the laundry room?"

Mrs. Chubb had sounded anxious, and Cecily gave her an encouraging smile. "No, I think we'd like to inspect the scene before he gets here. Come, Baxter." She started for the backstairs with Baxter behind her and the housekeeper scurrying at his heels.

Moments later she pushed open the door of the laundry room and peeked inside. The room was empty, and she made straight for the corner where the dead man lay. Baxter followed her, while Mrs. Chubb still hovered outside in the hallway, obviously reluctant to view a corpse.

Staring down at the still figure at her feet, Cecily's heart sank. A blue silk scarf, delicately embellished with purple blossoms and pale green leaves, had been tied around the man's neck. A very feminine scarf. Obviously, it belonged to a woman. The incongruous article of clothing confirmed her suspicions. "I do believe," she murmured to no one in particular, "that we have another murder on our hands."

"Oh, good Lord," Baxter muttered. "Will this never end?"

Mrs. Chubb cleared her throat from the doorway. "The constable is here, m'm."

"Oh, send him in, please." Cecily turned to greet the portly policeman as he pushed the door open wider to make an entrance. "Good morning, Sam. How is your wife feeling? Better, I hope?"

"Not too bad, m'm, thank you." Northcott pulled his helmet from his head and tucked it under his arm, then raised his hand to smooth imaginary hair back on his balding head. "I see we 'ave another stiff'un."

Cecily winced, and frowned at Baxter, who was rolling his eyes. "I'm afraid so."

"One of your guests again?" The constable approached the body and stared down at the dead man's face. "Looks like he's been choked with that scarf there. Happens a lot, don't it. You 'ave his name?"

"I'm sorry, Sam. I don't recognize him at all." Cecily peered at the stone-white face. "Then again, I don't meet every guest who stays here."

Northcott nodded. "Well, someone from your staff must recognize him. We'll have to get 'em all in here to look at him."

"Oh, marvelous," Baxter muttered.

The constable gave him a sharp look. "You have a problem?"

Cecily instantly read her husband's expression. The two men had been enemies ever since their young days, when the constable had apparently stolen the girl Baxter had hoped to marry. Cecily had never really learned the whole story, since her husband was not one to elaborate on anything, but the situation had angered Baxter deeply enough for him to carry a grudge to this day. Right then he was glaring at the constable as if he would like to throw him through a window.

Hastily she intervened. "I could have one or two of the maids take a look, if you like. They are the ones most likely to recognize the man. My chief housemaid doesn't know him, but the others might." A sharp tap on the door turned her head.

The man who entered smiled at her. His fair hair gleamed in the glow of the gas lamps, and as always, he looked immaculate in a dove gray coat and trousers, and a dashing red cravat at his throat.

"It's Dr. Prestwick, m'm," Mrs. Chubb announced somewhat belatedly.

Cecily gave him a warm smile. "Kevin. How nice to see you again, though I wish it were in better circumstances. How is Madeline and little Angelina?"

"Both are in excellent health, thank you, Cecily." The doctor nodded at Baxter, then turned his attention to the dead man. "So, what do we have here?" He squatted down by the body, fingered the scarf, then turned the victim's head to the side. "Ah, here we go." He pointed to a large dark patch on the man's head. "He was struck with a heavy object. I imagine it's what killed him. I'll know more after autopsy." Gently he closed each of the man's eyelids.

"What about the choking?" Northcott demanded as Dr. Prestwick rose to his feet.

"He wasn't strangled, if that's what you mean." The doctor looked down at the victim. "The scarf isn't tight enough around his throat to do any damage. There are no visible marks on his neck, and no hemorrhaging of the eyes."

Baxter shook his head. "Then what the blazes was he doing wearing a woman's scarf?"

Dr. Prestwick shrugged. "Who knows?"

"I know." Northcott beamed with pride. "He was smacked on the old noggin by a woman. She thought he wasn't quite dead yet so she finished him off with her scarf."

Dr. Prestwick pursed his lips. "It's possible. Then again, it could have been put there by a man, to make it appear that the perpetrator was a woman."

"Or to cast the blame for the crime on the owner of the scarf," Cecily put in.

Dr. Prestwick smiled. "Of course. Trust the inimitable Mrs. Cecily Baxter to provide a logical explanation."

Baxter scowled, while Northcott grunted. "Well then, I 'ave to search the poor blighter before you take him away." The constable looked as if it were the very last thing he wanted to do.

"Of course." Prestwick turned to Cecily. "I shall need the assistance of a couple of your footmen to carry out the body."

"And you shall have them." Cecily turned to the door. "Mrs. Chubb? Are you still there?"

A faint, slightly embarrassed voice answered her from the other side of the door. "Yes, m'm." The housekeeper cleared her throat. "I was waiting to see if you needed me to fetch anything."

Cecily smiled. It was as good an excuse as any. "Very well. You can send two of the footmen in here to assist Dr. Prestwick. You can also tell Charlotte and Lilly to come here right away. I want them to identify this poor man. We need to notify his family."

"Yes, m'm."

"And Mrs. Chubb?"

"Yes, m'm?"

"Please see that this news doesn't reach our guests."

"Yes, m'm. Of course." Shuffling footsteps sounded in the hallway as the housekeeper hurried off to obey her orders.

Northcott laid his helmet down on a shelf and lowered himself to his haunches beside the victim. "I'll need to take the scarf for evidence."

He looked up at the doctor, who nodded his approval. Northcott gingerly pulled the scarf from around the man's neck. "Nice bit of silk, this," he murmured as he let the colorful fabric slide through his fingers. "My missus would like this."

"Not if she knew where it came from," Baxter said, looking a little appalled at the thought.

Northcott sniffed at the silky fabric. "Smells good, too. Expensive smellies, that." He tucked the scarf in his pocket, then started going through the victim's pockets, pulling out from the man's coat a folded white handkerchief, a small tin of snuff, a pack of playing cards, and a pipe.

Cecily kept close watch on him as he turned his attention to the trousers. Finding nothing in one pocket, he tucked his fingers into the other. "Aha! What's this, then?" He withdrew his fingers, which now held a small piece of paper folded in half. With a loud groan, he struggled upright, and unfolded the note.

He stared at it so long, Cecily felt like screaming at him. Finally, she could stand it no longer. "Well? For heaven's sake, Sam, tell us what it says!"

Obviously enjoying the tension he was creating, the constable looked at her. "Well, m'm, I'd say we have the crime solved already." He handed her the note. "There's your killer. Right there."

CHAPTER

❊ 2 ❊

Cecily took the note from the constable's pudgy hand and quickly scanned the scrawled lines. Shocked, she read it again, then jumped when Baxter barked, "Are you going to tell us what the dratted thing says or do we have to guess?"

"Oh, pardon me." She let out her breath on a sigh. "It's from Mazie. Apparently, the man's name is Percy. She asked him"—she paused, still unable to believe what she was reading—"she asked him to meet her here in the laundry room at midnight."

Baxter stared at her as if she'd lost her mind. "Mazie?" He shook his head in bewilderment. "*Mazie?* That meek little maid we hired two months ago? She doesn't look capable of killing a chicken, much less a man."

"I know." Cecily stared at the note, trying to equate her latest servant with the dreadful fate that had befallen the man at her feet. Mazie was little more than a child, not yet fifteen. Her parents were impoverished farmers who had sent her to work and live at the Pennyfoot.

It wasn't the first time Cecily had hired a servant out of pity and a sense of responsibility for the welfare of her new employee. Nor was it likely to be the last. Most of the time she had been vastly rewarded, surrounded by a happy and loyal staff that gave their best every day.

Only once in a while had one of them let her down. Never in a million years would she have placed Mazie in that category.

"There has to be a murder weapon somewhere around 'ere," Northcott mumbled as he wandered over to the shelves crammed with stacks of clean linens.

Cecily glanced across the room. Next to the ironing stove stood a small bureau, holding a box of starch, three kettles, three water bowls, and six heavy flatirons. One of the irons stood slightly askew, and she hurried over to it.

One glance confirmed what she had suspected. A dark stain covered the tip of the iron. "I think this might be the murder weapon," she announced.

Northcott muttered something she couldn't hear as he plodded over to her. "I have to ask you not to touch nothing, m'm. It's evidence, and I have to take it with me."

"Of course." Cecily stepped back.

"And I have to arrest your maid what done this."

She had been expecting as much, but she wasn't about to give up without a fight. "You don't really have enough evidence to arrest anyone yet, do you?" She smiled at the constable, who stood scowling at her with such intensity she knew she was already losing the battle. "I mean, all you have is a note. You don't really know for certain if Mazie met . . . er . . . Percy here. We don't even know for certain if this man is Percy. He could be someone else entirely."

"Well, m'm, I'm sure your maids can clear that one up for us."

Even as he spoke, a tap on the door announced the arrival of her staff. She turned to face them as they trooped into the room.

Lilly looked sick, her face white and drawn and seemingly unaware of the wisps of light brown hair escaping from her cap and floating in front of her eyes.

Charlotte, on the other hand, seemed more curious than disturbed by the sight of the motionless body on the floor. Sturdier in build than her companion, she was also made of sterner stuff. More like Gertie's indomitable spirit. Cecily had often thought that Gertie and Charlotte made an excellent pair together.

"We heard you had a dead body in here, m'm," Charlotte said as she bent her knees in a quick curtsey.

Lilly shuddered, and edged sideways behind the other maid.

"Do either of you two recognize the bloke?" Northcott demanded.

Lilly muttered, "Do I have to look at him?"

Charlotte moved closer to the victim and stared down at his face. "Yeah, I've seen him in the card rooms. I heard the other players calling him Percy, but I don't know his other name. He's not staying here at the Pennyfoot. I do know that."

"What?" Baxter's eyebrows had furrowed in annoyance.

"Then how the blazes did he get into the card rooms? They are off-limits to everyone except our guests."

Cecily sighed. Since they had changed the Pennyfoot from a country club back into a hotel, they were once more governed by the rules that forbade organized gambling of any sort on the premises. The games, however, were an integral feature of the hotel, and were one of the main reasons the Pennyfoot's guest rooms were filled practically all year round—unlike many of the other hotels that chose to obey the laws and therefore avoid risking closure of the premises.

The card rooms had long been a bone of contention between Cecily and her husband. An extension of the wine cellars beneath the floors of the hotel, the rooms had originally been accessed by a trapdoor in the hallway outside the ballroom.

When the hotel had become a country club, gambling was allowed on the premises, and the secret rooms were no longer necessary and were boarded up, until the Pennyfoot had once more been reestablished as a hotel.

Baxter had reluctantly agreed to allow the original rooms to be reopened as long as they were kept a strict secret to the outside world, and as long as they were not at risk of being discovered by the constabulary.

Unfortunately, P.C. Northcott had accidentally learned of their existence. He'd been sworn to secrecy, bribed by a constant flow of pastries and other such treats from Mrs. Chubb. It did not bode well to keep reminding him of the presence of the card rooms, however, since Northcott could not be trusted to avoid inadvertently blurting out mention of them in front of Detective Inspector Cranshaw.

The peevish inspector would be overjoyed to find an excuse to shut down the Pennyfoot, since he had long suspected that there were nefarious goings-on in the hotel, but so far had been unable to prove it.

Baxter seemed to realize his error, as he glared at Charlotte. The maid, however, was not looking at him. She seemed mesmerized by the body lying in front of her and blithely announced, "It must have been Mazie that got him into the games. I saw her in the ballroom with him when no one was there. They were having a bit of fun." She looked at Baxter and winked. "If you know what I mean."

Baxter looked horrified, and, clearly embarrassed, Northcott cleared his throat.

Deciding it was time to intervene, Cecily said hastily, "I think we should have a talk with Mazie. Charlotte, please find her and send her here at once. Lilly, you can return to your duties, and please, both of you, do not mention anything that you have seen or heard here to anyone. I'd like to keep this from the guests for as long as possible. At least until we have identified the man. We don't want to have a family member learn the tragic news in the form of gossip."

"Yes, m'm." Lilly lunged for the door, obviously desperate to get away from the ghastly scene, while Charlotte followed more slowly.

Cecily waited until the door closed behind them before turning to Northcott. "Sam, I would like to talk to Mazie in private before you question her, if that's acceptable to you?"

The constable folded his arms and rocked back on his heels. "Well, now, Mrs. Baxter, I don't think as how I can allow that. There are laws, you know."

"Oh, come now," Baxter said, his voice harsh with irritation. "I'm sure there's a law forbidding the acceptance of free refreshments from the kitchen, but you don't appear to have any misgivings about breaking that one."

Northcott visibly bristled. "It's not polite to refuse something that's offered in kindness. Then again, you probably wouldn't know about that."

"Gentlemen!" Cecily held up her hand, about to utter a rebuke, but at that moment another tap on the door heralded the arrival of the footmen.

Dr. Prestwick, who had remained a silent, if not exactly disinterested, observer for the past several minutes, now spoke up. "I must remove the body to my offices, where I shall conduct an autopsy." He looked at the constable. "You, sir, will have my report in the morning." He turned to Cecily. "I am sorry you have another unfortunate incident on your hands. I sincerely hope it will not disrupt your Christmas festivities."

"You should all be flipping used to it by now," Northcott muttered.

Baxter looked about ready to explode, and once more, Cecily had to step in.

After a warning glance at her husband, she turned to the doctor. "Thank you, Kevin. I shall see that you are informed of the identity of the deceased."

"Once your maid has told us who he is and what happened." Northcott fumbled in his chest pocket and finally withdrew a notebook.

Dr. Prestwick nodded his thanks, then directed the footmen to lift the body from the floor and carry it outside.

"I should like to accompany you," Cecily said as the doctor opened the door for the footmen and their burden. "I don't want our guests to see the body. If you don't mind, I would rather you leave by the back door, which means passing through the kitchen. I need to prepare the staff, however, before you do so."

The doctor appeared taken aback, while the footmen exchanged skeptical glances.

Baxter looked as if he were about to have heart failure. "Through the *kitchen*?" He apparently struggled to keep his voice down. "With all that food lying around?"

"He doesn't have the plague," Cecily said crisply. "It's preferable to upsetting our guests. She looked at the constable. "Please, allow me to speak with my maid before you arrest her. Perhaps you would like to accompany us to the kitchen. I'm sure Mrs. Chubb will have something sweet and delectable to offer you."

Northcott licked his lips. "In that case, Mrs. B, I will be happy to escort you to the kitchen. I s'pose I can spare you a minute or two to talk to your servant."

"Thank you, Sam. I appreciate that." She looked at Baxter. "Please keep Mazie here until I return. I shan't be but a moment."

Baxter sighed. "Very well."

Cecily stepped into the hallway ahead of the footmen and led the way down the hall to the kitchen. Pausing at the door, she said quietly, "Wait here until I alert the staff. I shall only be a moment."

As she walked into the spacious room, the steamy warmth seemed to fold around her like a blanket. The spicy fragrance of plum puddings baking in the oven made her mouth water. A large platter of freshly baked mince pies sat cooling on the side dresser, and she had a strong urge to trot over there and help herself.

Mrs. Chubb stood at the heavy scrubbed wood table, one hand brandishing a rolling pin, the other brushing flour from her ample bosom. She stared at Cecily, obviously taken aback to see madam appear unannounced. Gertie and Lilly swung around from the sinks when Cecily made her announcement.

"I'm sure you know by now that an unfortunate incident has occurred."

Gertie's cheeks turned pink, but she managed to hold on to an air of innocence as Mrs. Chubb murmured something unintelligible.

Cecily had no illusions about her chief housemaid's ability to refrain from blurting out the news to the kitchen staff. They, on the other hand, would not betray their friend, and indeed, everyone in the room gaped at Cecily as if they had not the slightest idea what she was talking about.

Michel had lifted a wooden spoon from the pot of soup he'd been stirring, and brown drops of liquid fell to the floor as he waved it at her. "What has happened, madam? It eez not good news, *oui?*"

"I'm afraid the news is not good," Cecily confirmed. "A gentleman has died, and we need to remove him from the premises with as much discretion as possible. Therefore, I have asked the footmen to carry him through here to the back door. Please open it for them, Gertie."

"Yes, m'm." Gertie rushed over to the door and flung it wide open, letting in a blast of cold, damp air from outside.

Michel quickly turned and slapped a lid on his pot of soup, while Mrs. Chubb shielded her pastry from anything that might blow in from the yard.

Lilly had turned her back on everyone, apparently determined not to set eyes on the horrible sight again.

Cecily beckoned to the footmen and they carried the body across the floor, past the shuddering housekeeper and a stone-faced Michel, while Gertie couldn't resist casting a glance at the victim before he was swept into the yard.

Northcott had followed the procession into the kitchen with his helmet tucked under his arm, and was now waiting with his tongue practically hanging out of his mouth in anticipation of his promised treat.

Cecily watched Gertie close the door again before saying, "I want to remind all of you how crucial it is that we do not spread the word about what has happened. Until we know the identity of the gentleman and have informed his family, this incident must remain a tightly held secret. Do I have your word, everyone?"

She looked directly at Gertie, who gave her a lopsided grin. "Yes, m'm." The housemaid drew her fingers across her mouth. "Mum's the word."

The rest of the staff murmured their assent, and only slightly reassured, Cecily glanced at the constable.

He nodded at her, then smiled at Mrs. Chubb. "Mrs. B said as how you might have a tasty morsel or two for me."

His bulging eyes stared at the plate of mince pies, and

the housekeeper briefly glanced at Cecily for confirmation, then headed over to the dresser.

Knowing that Northcott would not dawdle for long in the kitchen, Cecily hurried back down the hallway. She needed to talk to Mazie. The sooner they discovered the name of the dead man and informed his family, the better.

Opening the door to the laundry room, she stepped inside. Baxter stood by the window, his face a mask of gloom. One look at him and Cecily's spirits sank even further. All was not well.

Charlotte stood close by, biting her lip—a sure sign that she was about to deliver bad news.

Cecily looked at her husband. "What's happened?"

Baxter turned to Charlotte. "You might as well tell madam the news."

Cecily took a deep breath. "All right, Charlotte. What is it?"

Charlotte dipped a curtsey, muttering, "I'm sorry, m'm. I couldn't find Mazie anywhere so I went to her room. She wasn't there. Nor were her clothes. She's gone, m'm. Packed up everything and left."

Cecily puffed the breath out of her lungs. "I see. Then we shall have to find her. I'll send someone to her family's home. Perhaps she went there."

"Yes, m'm."

"You can go, Charlotte. Please do not say anything to anybody until we have found out exactly what happened here."

"No, m'm. I mean, yes, m'm." Looking flustered, Charlotte charged out the door, slamming it shut behind her.

The minute it closed, Baxter burst out, "What in blazes was Mazie thinking of when she got involved with that man? He had to be old enough to be her father."

Cecily sighed. "Judging from his clothes, he was obviously a man of means. When you're young, impressionable, and poor, a man like that paying attention to you is hard to resist."

Baxter fixed her with one of his looks. "I sincerely hope you are not speaking from experience."

Cecily smiled. "I was young and impressionable once, but I assure you, when I met my first husband, it wasn't his money I was interested in."

"Ah, yes." Baxter nodded. "I remember." His expression softened. "James Sinclair was a good man."

"He was indeed." She crossed the room and tucked her hand under his elbow. "My present husband is also a good man whom I dearly love and respect and whom, as I recall, had no great fortune when I agreed to marry him."

A patch of red spread across Baxter's cheeks. "I was well established in a profitable business when I proposed to you."

Cecily laughed. "You were, my love. But I would have married you if you had been as poor as a church mouse. There are more important things than money to make a marriage as joyful and fulfilling as ours. Now, do you think you could check on today's reservations with Philip while I talk to Sam and find out what he intends to do about Mazie?"

Baxter dropped a swift kiss on her cheek. "As you wish, my dear. Though must I talk to Philip? The man is a doddering old fool who can't find his nose to put on his glasses. I don't know why you keep him behind that reception desk. Our new guests must wonder what kind of establishment they've wandered into when they arrive."

Cecily withdrew her hand to pat his shoulder. "Philip might be old and somewhat confused at times, but despite what you think, he's quite wonderful when he's greeting the guests and he does keep a good hand on the reservations. The guests like him and so do I."

"You feel sorry for him." Baxter walked with her to the door. "He's all alone and would be lost without this job."

"That, too." She waited for him to open the door. "But most of the Pennyfoot staff have been hired because they need us more than we need them. That's why we have the most loyal, dedicated, and devoted people working for us."

Baxter followed her out into the hallway. "You are quite right, of course, my sweet. After all, that was the reason we hired Mazie. Now, I shall brace myself for my consultation with Philip and allow you time to speak with that idiot policeman." He shook his head. "I still can't believe that child is capable of taking a man's life. It just goes to show one never truly knows another person, no matter how well they are acquainted."

"So true." She waved him on, and he climbed the stairs ahead of her to the lobby. *Poor Baxter*, she thought as she pushed open the kitchen door. He usually took his time in learning to trust someone, but despite his caution, now and then someone he cared about betrayed him, and it cut him deeply.

She was well aware that he'd had an instant vulnerability where Mazie was concerned. The girl had appeared downtrodden and defenseless, and although she had not admitted as much, Cecily was convinced Mazie had simply been kicked out of the family home because her parents could no longer support her and her five siblings.

Normally Baxter left the hiring decisions to his wife, though at times he was not above offering his opinion. In Mazie's case, the child had apparently touched a nerve. Having never had children of his own, Cecily suspected that Mazie had stirred Baxter's paternal instincts.

When she had demurred about hiring Mazie, hesitant that the young girl could handle the work, Baxter had sprung to Mazie's defense. He'd reminded Cecily of Gertie's inexperience and lack of decorum when she had first arrived on the hotel's doorstep. He'd suggested they give Mazie a chance, and Cecily had agreed, having already assured herself that she could not turn way such a fragile human being.

The aroma in the kitchen once more teased her appetite, momentarily banishing her concerns. The sight of P.C. Northcott munching on a delicious mince pie reminded her how long it had been since she and her husband had enjoyed breakfast.

She raised a hand to get the constable's attention, just as Mrs. Chubb declared, "My goodness, m'm, it's way past your mealtime. I'll have something sent up to your suite right away. Unless you'd rather eat in the dining room? We'll be starting to serve the midday meal in an hour."

"Baxter and I will take our meal in our suite, Mrs. Chubb. Thank you." She looked at Northcott. "If you are ready, Sam? I need to speak with you."

"Yes, Mrs. B. Right away, m'm." Northcott swallowed the last of his mince pie, smacked his lips, and gave Mrs. Chubb a hearty slap on the shoulder that made her wince. "Best mince pies in all of Merry Old England, luv."

Cecily held her breath, but it seemed that the compliment outweighed the heavy hand and the somewhat impertinent appellation. Mrs. Chubb gave the constable a stiff smile and moved out of harm's way.

"In my office, Sam." Cecily glanced at the housekeeper. "I shall only be a moment, Mrs. Chubb. I will return to my suite shortly."

"Yes, m'm. I'll have the meals sent up right away." Mrs. Chubb turned to Gertie, who was loitering by the pantry, apparently waiting for her orders. "Take a tray up to madam's suite, Gertie, and be quick about it."

Satisfied that her next meal was taken care of, Cecily led the constable to her office.

No matter what problems were evolving in the hotel, she always felt a sense of peace when entering the room. This was her sanctuary, a place where she could spend a few minutes of her busy schedule alone, to reflect on the day's activities. She made most of her important decisions seated behind her desk and, when the necessity arose, solved many a complicated conundrum.

Here in this room, with its soft gray carpeting, the pale blue curtains at the lofty window, and the comfortable blue velvet armchair, she could free her mind of everyday distractions and concentrate on the matter at hand.

Which, right now, was the disappearance of her newest employee and the child's apparent hand in a brutal murder.

Sam, as usual, barely waited for Cecily to seat herself at her desk before depositing his chubby body onto the armchair.

Laying his helmet on the table beside him, he said gruffly, "So where's the 'orrible maid what did that poor bugger in?"

Cecily took a moment to remind herself that Sam Northcott was an officer of the law and she must treat him as such. "I'm afraid I have bad news," she said. "It seems that Mazie has left the hotel."

Northcott attempted to hook his leg over his knee, winced, and lowered it again. "I see. So, when's she coming back?"

"It appears that she has no intention of returning. Charlotte informed me that Mazie's belongings have left with her."

The constable tutted and shook his head. "Blast it. Now I'll have to go and hunt her down."

"I'll send a footman to her family home if you like. She may have gone back there."

"Nah. Just give me the address and I'll go there myself." He gave Cecily a hard look. "If she comes back here, I want to know right away."

"Yes, of course." Cecily stood up and waited for Northcott to climb to his feet. "By the way, Sam, I was wondering about the scarf that was around the victim's neck. I doubt very much that it belonged to Mazie. She could never afford such an extravagance. If you could perhaps indulge me, I would like to keep the scarf for a short while in the hopes of finding out to whom it belongs. I will return it to you as soon as possible, of course."

The constable rocked back on his heels—something he always did when he wanted to appear official. "Well, now, the scarf is evidence, and I shouldn't let it out of my sight by rights."

"I understand that, Sam, but it seems to me that the scarf

33

might belong to someone in this hotel, and if I could hunt down its owner, it could possibly lead us to Mazie's whereabouts and save you a great deal of trouble."

The idea of lessening his labor apparently appealed to Northcott. After another moment's hesitation, he drew the colorful scarf from his pocket and handed it to her. "There you go, Mrs. B. Take good care of it. It's evidence, you know."

"I will guard it with my life," Cecily promised. "Thank you, Sam."

With a nod, the constable moved to the door. "Well, I'll be off, then. Be sure to give me a ring if that Mazie comes back here."

"I will, and Sam?"

He was already halfway out the door, but he turned back to look at her. "Yes, m'm?"

"I'd truly appreciate it if you would advise me of any developments in this case."

Northcott puffed out his chest. "I'll tell you what I can, Mrs. B. That's all I can promise."

"Then I shall have to be satisfied with that."

As the door closed behind him, Cecily sank onto her chair and held the scarf to her nose. Sam was right. The exquisite fragrance clung to the material as only really expensive perfume could do.

Running the silky material through her fingers, she tried to get her thoughts in order. No matter how it looked, she couldn't imagine Mazie ever having the gumption or the strength to pick up a flatiron and viciously strike another human being hard enough to kill him.

Despite what she had said to Baxter, neither could she

understand how Mazie could get herself intimately involved with a man so much older than herself. That whole scenario seemed preposterous. Staring at the filmy material, she shook her head. No, there was a lot more to this murder than what it seemed. She needed to talk to Mazie, and she needed to find the owner of the scarf in the hopes that it would lead to a more reasonable resolution. She was not about to allow Northcott to blast his way into a false arrest and conviction.

She would summon a carriage and pay a visit to Mazie's home. Knowing P.C. Northcott as well as she did, she was fairly confident he would take his time in continuing his investigation. The constable never hurried himself over anything, unless it was a visit to the Pennyfoot kitchen. If she could talk to the maid before Sam reached the girl, she might be able to find out exactly what had happened. Reaching back behind her, she tugged on the bell rope, then leaned back in her chair.

She had to admit, she was feeling a surge of anticipation. It had been a while since she had been on the trail of a killer. Despite the anxiety of upsetting the guests and ruining the Christmas festivities, it felt good to be tackling another intriguing mystery.

Cecily Sinclair Baxter was back in the hunt, and she could only hope that the outcome would be as fruitful in bringing a villain to justice as her past endeavors.

CHAPTER

❊ 3 ❊

Charlie Muggins leaned his shoulder against the railings of the stall and stared into the dark brown eyes of the horse on the other side. "There's still another hour or two to go before you get your feed, Champion, so you'll just have to wait."

As if the horse understood him, the sleek animal turned his head and slowly twisted around to face the wall.

Heaving a sigh, Charlie overturned a bucket and sat down on it. He missed Tess. Dogs were a lot more fun than horses. Dogs chased after balls, went on walks, and gave big sloppy kisses to show their love.

Charlie glanced up at the horse. He'd had a lick on the face from Champion once. The horse's tongue was so strong when it lashed him, he'd almost fallen on his arse. He'd steered clear of Champion's jaws after that.

Tess, now, well, that was a whole different ball of wax. He missed playing with the dog, burying his face in her soft fur, seeing her race toward him when he whistled, her tail thrashing back and forth like a fern caught in the wind.

Tess was gone now. Her owners, Pansy and Samuel, no longer worked at the Pennyfoot. They'd moved out into their own little flat, taking Tess with them. Charlie stared gloomily at his feet. He never thought he could miss something as badly as he missed that dog.

A slight movement in the shadows at the doorway to the stables caught his attention. Someone stepped out of the daylight and moved toward him—someone small and dainty and not in the least what a mechanic should look like.

Charlie shoved himself to his feet. Henry Simmons was something else that confused him. The boy was a good mechanic, knew his stuff, and was quick about it, too. There was just something about him that made Charlie uncomfortable, and try as he might, he couldn't put his finger on it.

It wasn't as if the lad was disrespectful or antagonistic. Quite the opposite, in fact. Henry always listened to what Charlie had to say, and was so polite about it, he sometimes made Charlie grind his teeth.

Maybe that was it. Maybe Henry was too persnickety and fussy. The lad needed to toughen up, to show some backbone, act more like a man.

Charlie stared at the slender boy as he drew closer. Maybe what Henry needed was some guidance—some good old-fashioned lessons in what it takes to be a man in a cruel world. He'd seen it all in his twenty-five years on earth, and he was just the chap to teach him. After all, as stable manager, he was Henry's boss and it was up to him to see that the lad received all the benefits of working with someone as worldly as Charlie Muggins.

Henry halted in front of him and ran a nervous hand over his thick, blond hair. His voice was high-pitched and held a quiver of anxiety when he spoke. "Madam sent me to tell you that she needs a carriage right away."

Staring into the lad's eyes, Charlie felt a familiar flutter under his ribs. Henry had the most expressive blue eyes. It was like looking into deep pools of warm, inviting water. In the next instant Charlie gave himself a violent mental shake. What the devil was he thinking? Why was it every time he looked into Henry's eyes, he got this strange shiver in his gut? What were his senses trying to tell him?

Realizing that Henry was waiting somewhat warily for him to answer, he cleared his throat. "Right you are, then. I'll see to it." He gestured toward the doorway with his thumb. "Meanwhile, you need to take a look at Lord Melton's motorcar. His lordship says it's making wacky noises."

"Yes, sir."

Charlie studied the young face for a moment. "You don't have to call me sir. I've told you before, everyone around here calls me Charlie."

"Yes, sir." Henry's cheeks turned pink. "I mean, Charlie."

"Good." Somehow the way Henry said his name made Charlie uncomfortable again. Once more he cleared his throat. "And where's your cap? Didn't I tell you you're supposed to wear it when you're working?"

"Yes, sir." Henry pulled a crumpled cap from his pocket and crammed it on his head.

Sighing, Charlie gestured again with his thumb. "Get

along with you, then. His lordship will be wanting that motorcar this afternoon."

"Yes, sir." Henry scurried back to where three motorcars sat parked near the entrance to the stables.

Charlie felt compelled to watch as Henry threw up the bonnet of the black Austin. Yes, he definitely needed to give the boy some lessons in becoming more manly. Heading over to the closest carriage, he began mentally creating the first lesson.

Walking. That was the first step. Henry walked and ran like a girl. That one would be easy to remedy. He'd start that very evening, right after he'd finished work.

Surprised at how much he was looking forward to the experience, he grabbed the shafts of the carriage and dragged it over to Champion's stall. He was anxious now to get the day over with and start turning Henry Simmons into a real man.

Having been informed that her carriage awaited her at the front steps of the hotel, Cecily made her way to the lobby, where she found her husband in a somewhat irritable exchange with the reception manager.

Philip Lamont had been hired against Baxter's unsolicited advice. "He's too old and senile," he'd told Cecily when she'd announced the hiring of the new employee. "He'll get confused and make a mess of the reservations, and we'll have too many guests to accommodate or not enough guests to fill the rooms."

"Philip managed a bank in London for forty years," Cecily

had informed him. "That should count for something. He intended to retire in Badgers End, where he grew up, but since he's never married, he got desperately lonely. He badly needs interaction with people, and he's a personable and intelligent man. I believe he will perform with excellence behind the reception desk."

She'd been a little too optimistic about Philip's competence, but so far he'd avoided any real catastrophes. He tended to nap at inopportune moments, and he was somewhat vague when questioned about the hotel's amenities, but he was polite and accommodating with the guests and kept an efficient set of books, and that was enough to satisfy Cecily.

Right now, the manager seemed a bit put out as he stared up at Baxter. One hand kept straying to his head, where he stroked the few white hairs he had left, while the other constantly shifted spectacles farther up his thin nose.

"All I asked you was how many more guests are due to arrive for Christmas." Baxter folded his arms and puffed out his chest. "It's a simple question, old man. You don't have to make a big performance out of it."

Philip tapped on the open hotel register. "It's all in there, sir. You can see for yourself."

"I don't want to see for myself. I want you to tell me."

Suspecting that her husband was testing the manager, Cecily smiled as she reached his side. "There you are, darling. Would you be a lamb and take a look at the ballroom? Madeline said she would be finished decorating it for the welcome ball tonight, and I want to make sure it's ready."

Madeline had already left the hotel, but it was the only

excuse Cecily could think of to rescue Philip from her husband's scrutiny. To her relief, Baxter looked only too happy to oblige. He was halfway across the lobby before she realized she hadn't told him of her plan to visit Mazie's home.

Shrugging off her concern, she smiled at Philip, who was still looking disgruntled. She pulled the scarf from her pocket and dangled it in front of him. "Someone must have left this behind," she told him. "Most likely one of your guests. Do you happen to recognize it?"

Frowning, Philip peered through his gold-rimmed spectacles. "Well, now, m'm. It does seem to me that I've seen that scarf somewhere before."

Cecily's pulse quickened. "You saw it on a guest?"

"I think so, m'm." Philip stretched out a hand. "May I have it for a moment?"

Cecily handed the scarf to him and watched him run it through his fingers. Then he lifted it to his nose. "Mmm. It smells divine."

"Yes, I had noticed that. Do you remember to whom it belongs?"

Philip seemed engrossed in the material's fragrance and didn't answer right away.

Cecily raised her voice. "Philip?"

He lowered the scarf and gave her a look of reproach. "I'm thinking, m'm. I'm thinking."

"Well, try to think a little faster. I have a carriage waiting for me outside."

Philip sniffed at the fabric once more and handed it back to her. "I think I remember someone leaving it on my desk the other day. I was going to give it to you, but then some guests arrived and I don't remember seeing it after that."

"Do you remember who left it? Can you describe this person?"

Philip rubbed a sparse eyebrow with trembling fingers. After several aggravating seconds he murmured, "I'm sorry, m'm. I can't remember." He brightened a little. "It was a woman! I do remember that."

Cecily tucked the scarf back into the pocket of her skirt. "Thank you, Philip. I shall bear that in mind when I'm searching for its owner." Resisting the urge to shake her head, she walked briskly across the lobby and out the doors.

The cold breeze from the ocean hit her in the face as she descended the steps to the street. Charlie stood at the curb, engulfed in a red and white striped scarf that covered the lower half of his face. He removed his cap as she approached and sprung forward to open the carriage door for her.

"Bit brisk this morning, m'm," he said, his voice muffled by the scarf. "Looks like it's trying to snow."

She smiled at him as she stepped up into the carriage. "Well, I hope it waits until we have returned."

"Yes, m'm. So do I." He shut the door and climbed up onto his seat. Picking up the reins, he clicked his tongue at Champion and the horse started forward, jerking the carriage behind him.

Cecily always enjoyed the ride along the Esplanade, in spite of the snowflakes dancing in the wind. Fortunately, it was not quite cold enough for the snow to settle, and Champion trotted briskly along the seafront, while the carriage rolled smoothly along with just the slightest rattle of its wheels.

In the summer the beach would be crammed with deck chairs, where ladies lounged with parasols and some gentlemen draped knotted handkerchiefs over their heads to protect themselves from the sun. Children would be racing in and out of the crowds, chasing balls or flying kites, or squatting in front of the Punch and Judy show.

Cecily smiled at the memories. How she loved the seaside in summertime. Everyone seemed to be so carefree and relaxed, enjoying the fresh air and sunshine. Once the cold weather arrived, the beach stretched out toward the towering cliffs, bleak and lonely, with only the seagulls and oystercatchers to give it life.

Today the heaving ocean reflected the gray skies, and a lonely seagull circled above the deserted sands, hoping to spot a morsel of food. Cecily watched as the frothy waves raced across the sand, depositing seashells and seaweed before retreating back into the ocean.

The wind jolted the carriage, and she drew her navy blue cloak closer around her throat. Thank goodness she had securely fastened her hat with pins; otherwise the wind would catch the wide brim and toss it from her head.

Mazie's family farm lay on the other side of town, and Cecily had instructed Charlie to take the route through the High Street. Normally he would have taken the longer road over the cliffs to avoid the traffic, but this was Christmastime, and Cecily loved to see the shops all decked out in their holiday finery.

Gazing out the window as they trotted down the busy

street, she admired the boughs of holly and cedar hanging on the doors, some decorated with red ribbons, others with brightly colored balls and stars. Ducks and geese hung by their feet in the butcher's windows, and an elderly man stood on one corner, offering hot chestnuts from his can of burning coals.

Every shop window celebrated the Christmas season, with decorations and toys, snow made of cotton wool, and small trees covered in baubles and glitter. Housewives trudged along the pavements, carrying baskets loaded with packages tied with red or green ribbon, bags of food, and bottles of spirits.

Leaning back, Cecily let out a sigh. There could be no brighter time of the year than the celebration of the birth of Jesus. Now, if she could just solve this murder, and get all that nonsense out of the way, she could relax and enjoy the coming festivities.

A short time later the carriage drew up outside a rather dilapidated fence. Charlie jumped down from his perch, walked around in front of Champion's head, and opened the gate. They drove through and halted again on the other side while Charlie closed the gate behind them, then proceeded up the rutted pathway to the farmhouse.

The house itself was rather small, compared to most farms Cecily had visited. There were three outlying barns, and a couple of bedraggled fields beyond, while a noisy henhouse sat a few yards away. Faded curtains hung at the windows of the farmhouse, and the door needed a coat of paint.

By the time Cecily had stepped down from the carriage, a worried-looking woman wearing a checkered apron over her gray frock stood in the open doorway.

Charlie's face also reflected concern as Cecily stepped forward and called out, "Mrs. Clarke? I'm Cecily Baxter, owner of the Pennyfoot Hotel. I'd like a word with you concerning your daughter, Mazie."

The woman hurried forward, one hand covering her heart. "Is she all right? She's not ill, is she? Hurt?" She shook her head. "I told Walter she was too young to go to work. He wouldn't listen to me."

Cecily's spirits sank. Her hopes of clearing things up with Mazie were fading fast. "She's not here with you?"

Mrs. Clarke's eyes grew wide with fear. "No, she's not. Where is she? What's happened?"

Taking the woman's arm, Cecily began leading her back to the house. "Let us go inside and I will explain everything."

Once inside, Mazie's mother led her visitor to a small parlor, sparsely furnished with a narrow settee and an armchair, and not much else. A few pictures hung on the wall, as well as a photograph of Mrs. Clarke and a rather grim-looking gentleman, while five young children sat in front of them with varying degrees of discomfort mirrored in their faces.

Cecily recognized Mazie as the eldest of the children. A shiver of apprehension attacked her spine as she prepared to give this unfortunate mother the bad news. Declining the woman's offer of tea, she motioned for her to sit down.

Mrs. Clarke's face was tight with apprehension as Cecily sought for the right words to begin. "I'm afraid we've had a spot of trouble at the hotel," she said, holding up her hand when Mrs. Clarke answered with a cry of fear. "As far as we know, Mazie is unhurt. She has, however, left the hotel, and as of now, we don't know where she may be."

Mrs. Clarke lifted a trembling hand to her throat. "What kind of trouble, m'm? She's not done nothing wrong, has she? She was giving me money. A lot more than what she was earning. I asked her where she got it but she wouldn't tell me. She wasn't stealing, was she?"

Cecily heaved a sigh. "Not as far as we know. A gentleman was found in our laundry room. He'd been hit over the head. He had a note from Mazie in his pocket, asking him to meet her there."

The other woman raised her chin. "My Mazie with a man? She's not old enough for that. Besides, she's not that kind of girl. I bring my children up proper, Mrs. Baxter. Mazie would never get herself into that kind of trouble."

"I'm sure you do," Cecily said carefully. "However, there is this note that was found in the victim's pocket. It does appear to have been written by Mazie."

Mrs. Clarke's eyes widened in her ashen face. "Victim? He's dead?"

She had barely whispered the questions, and Cecily took a deep breath. "I'm afraid he is."

Mrs. Clarke let out a wail of despair, and Cecily quickly added, "I must tell you, I have a great deal of trouble believing your daughter is guilty of the crime. I do think, however, that she discovered the body and the shock sent her running for her life."

Mazie's mother covered her mouth with her hand, while her pale blue eyes stared into Cecily's face.

She seemed unable to answer, and Cecily leaned toward

her. "I will do everything I can to help Mazie, but I must talk to her to find out exactly what happened. Do you have any idea where I might find her? Anyplace she might have gone to hide?"

The woman shook her head, then eventually lowered her hand. "I can't think of anywhere right now, m'm. I can't even think straight."

"I understand." Cecily rose to her feet. "If you do think of something, or if Mazie should return home, please send me a message as soon as you can. The only way I can help her is to talk to her."

Mrs. Clarke got up slowly, nodding her head. "I will, m'm. Thank you."

"I have to warn you," Cecily said, feeling awful that she had to add to the woman's anxiety, "P.C. Northcott will be paying you a visit. He wants to find Mazie, too. Don't let anything he says upset you. We will get to the bottom of this, I promise you."

A faint light of hope crept into the other woman's eyes. "Thank you so much, m'm. If I find out where my girl is, I'll be sure to let you know."

Praying that she was right about Mazie's innocence, Cecily returned to the carriage. The news that Mazie had money to give to her mother was troubling. Perhaps she'd been wrong about the girl. Could Mazie possibly have killed that man to take money from him?

No, she assured herself in the next breath. She just couldn't imagine that young, fragile girl beating someone over the head to steal from him.

She was still wrestling with the problem when they

reached the gate. As they pulled out onto the road, the constable appeared on a bicycle, pedaling around the bend. His face was hidden by his helmet as he bent his head against the wind, and his knees pumped up and down in a vigorous attempt to make headway.

Cecily kept her own head down as they passed by him on the road. That was a little close for comfort. He would learn soon enough that she had visited Mazie's mother. She could only hope that she could question Mazie before Northcott found the maid. That is, if some terrible tragedy had not befallen her.

Cecily had not mentioned that possibility to her mother, but the feeling of dread that had plagued the pit of her stomach ever since she'd learned of the maid's disappearance had intensified, and she was very much afraid that this particular situation was not going to end well.

If Mazie was still alive, however, she must find the child. As long as Mazie was employed by her, she was responsible for the girl. It was up to her to sort out this puzzle and make sure, if Mazie was innocent, that she received the best help possible in clearing her name.

Or the best professional advice if she had indeed killed the stranger in the laundry room. There was always the possibility of self-defense if that were so.

On the other hand, if her worst fears were realized, and some dreadful mishap had happened to her servant, then she would be there to comfort the family and make suitable arrangements for her burial.

She had instructed Charlie to take the longer route over the cliffs, and a shudder shook her body as she gazed down at the angry ocean. She could not dismiss the vision of Mazie's scrawny body hurtling to the rocks below.

Turning her face away from the view, she prayed again for the child's safety. She had to find Mazie alive, or she would never forgive herself. If she had not hired her, Mazie would not be in this predicament now. She must find her and get to the bottom of the puzzle as soon as humanly possible. At the moment, however, the chances of achieving that seemed pretty slim.

Gertie stood back from the table and studied her handiwork. Like the rest of the tables in the dining room, she had covered it with a fresh white tablecloth. She'd set the silverware in the correct pattern on either side and at each end of the embroidered table runner. Aperitif glass, wineglass, and brandy glass had all been placed neatly upside down on the right side of the setting. Red candles nestled in silver candlesticks waiting to be lit, and an arrangement of holly and mistletoe with a bright red ribbon bow finished off the display.

Nodding with satisfaction, she picked up the tray of silverware and turned to move on to the next table. Charlotte suddenly appeared in front of her, taking her by surprise. "Blimey," Gertie blurted out, "where'd you flipping come from?"

Charlotte grinned. "Watcha doing? Admiring your own work?"

Gertie sniffed. "It ain't a crime to take pride in what I'm doing. Better than trying to duck out of work like some people I know."

Charlotte tossed her head. "I do my share. More than Lilly does, I know that much." She looked around the room. "It looks very nice. You did all right."

"Thanks." Somewhat mollified by the faint praise, Gertie added, "Wanna help me? This is the last one, then we can go down to the cellar to fetch the wine."

Charlotte shivered. "I hate going down there. It gives me the creeps."

"It's a lot better since madam got it done up." Gertie started laying out the solid silver utensils. "It were a mess for a long time—full of cobwebs and spiders and Gawd knows what else. Now that they've opened the card rooms again, the housemaids have to keep it a lot cleaner."

"I've just been talking to Archie." Charlotte giggled. "He's a bit of all right, he is."

Gertie tried not to listen to Charlotte mooning over the new handyman, and concentrated instead on the proper order for the knives, forks, and spoons.

"I love the way he smiles, and he has the most gorgeous body—all muscles and—"

Gertie thrust a handful of silverware at her. "Here, lay these out for me over there." She nodded at the other end of the table.

For a moment, Charlotte looked as if she would refuse, then she shrugged her shoulders and took the utensils from Gertie's hands. "Anyhow, from now on, I'm going to be spending a lot of time finding excuses to see him."

"Yeah, well, you're probably wasting your time. I think he's sweet on Mazie."

"What? That little bugger? I don't believe it."

"I saw them together more than once," Gertie said with relish. She was beginning to enjoy the conversation now. "They had their heads together, talking and laughing. . . ."

"Go on with you. You're making it up."

"I'm not." For a second or two she wished she *were* making it up, then pulled herself together. "Anyhow, he won't have much time to dillydally. I heard Chubby talking to him about building a set onstage for the pantomime."

"We'll see about that." Charlotte peered at a fork, then polished it with the corner of her apron. "So, do you think our Mazie killed Percy?"

"What, that little midget? I don't think she could reach high enough to hit him on the head."

Charlotte carefully set down a fork. "I never thought of that. You're right! I wonder if madam and the constable thought of that."

"Then again, he could have been on the floor when she hit him."

"Right again. She just doesn't seem like a killer, though. She's such a quiet little thing."

"She's just a baby." Gertie gazed off into the distant past. "I was that age when I started working here. I was just like her."

Charlotte let out a burst of laughter. "Wot, you? Go on with you. You was never like her. Never in a million years."

"Maybe not on the outside, but on the inside I was scared out of my wits." Gertie placed a fish fork next to a pearl-handled knife. "I only pretended to be tough, ready and able to clobber anyone who looked at me wrong, but then I did it for so long, it started to be who I was, and I just grew from there."

"Strewth!" Charlotte's expression reflected her astonishment. "I never would have thought that."

"Well, don't tell anyone that." Gertie grinned. "I have a reputation to keep up."

Charlotte looked as if she wanted to say something, then apparently changed her mind.

Curious now, Gertie felt compelled to prompt her. "Go on, say what you want to say."

Charlotte glanced over her shoulder at the door, then moved closer to her. "I wasn't going to tell you this, but I've been thinking about it for a while now, and there's something I want to ask you."

Gertie was all ears as she leaned forward. "What is it?"

"Well . . ." Again Charlotte looked over her shoulder, then lowered her voice. "I've joined the Women's Social and Political Union."

"The suffragettes? When did this happen?"

"About two months ago. I went to one of their meetings and I got caught up in all the excitement, and before I knew it, I became a member."

Gertie groaned. "You have no idea what kind of trouble that can get you in. I used to go on protests and stuff and I know what I'm talking about."

"I know. Pansy told me. That's why I was hoping you'd go on a protest with me. There's going to be one in Wellercombe and I really don't want to go on my own."

Gertie took a deep breath. "Sorry, Charlotte, but you'll

have to ask someone else. I can't do that again. I nearly ended up in jail when I did it before and I have my twins to think about now."

Charlotte's face clouded with disappointment. "I thought you were strong on women's rights. You're always talking about it—how men take advantage of us, and don't treat us like human beings and stuff."

"Yeah, well, talking about it and going to prison about it are two different things." She lowered her voice for effect. "Did you know they punch up suffragettes in prison? And if you don't want to eat the slop they give you, they force it down your throat in a tube."

"Then I'll just have to make bloody sure I don't get dragged off to the clink, won't I."

"Yeah, and the best way to do that is to stay away from those protests."

"All right, Gertie McBride. If you're too afraid to go with me, then I'll just have to go alone." She started for the door, throwing over her shoulder, "But I thought you had more guts than anyone else around here. Obviously, I was mistaken."

Gertie felt a harsh rebuttal rising in her throat and fought to keep it down. Maybe Charlotte was right. Maybe, after everything that had happened to her, she had lost some of the fire and fury that had landed her in so much trouble back then. But she was older now—and a mother of twins.

It was all right for Charlotte—she was a lot younger and didn't have no family to worry about. Gertie picked up the empty silverware tray. As for herself, she had more to lose, and no matter how strongly she agreed with the suffragettes' fight, she had to put her children first.

Having reassured herself that she was doing the right thing, she followed Charlotte out into the hallway. Though she couldn't quite suppress a tinge of regret for the rebel she used to be.

CHAPTER

❊ 4 ❊

The first thing she needed to do, Cecily told herself as she entered the Pennyfoot's lobby, was find out the full name of the dead man. If she could learn more about him, then maybe she could piece together exactly what had been going on between him and Mazie.

Glancing up the winding staircase, she spotted a gentleman on his way down. He was dressed fashionably in a checkered coat and trousers, with a red velvet vest and a black bow tie under his starched white collar. In spite of his protruding belly, he descended the stairs with alacrity, apparently on his way to an appointment of some kind.

Cecily recognized the gentleman as Edwin Coombs, who had something to do with engineering, if she remembered correctly. He had arrived alone and been joined by a stylish young woman shortly after. At the moment, however, his companion appeared to be elsewhere. This would be a perfect opportunity to question the guest. She always had better luck digging up information when her target was alone.

Seizing the opportunity, Cecily met the gentleman at the foot of the stairs. She would have to tread delicately, she warned herself, so as not to divulge that Percy was deceased. "Good afternoon, Mr. Coombs," she said as he doffed his cap at her. "I trust you are enjoying your visit to the Pennyfoot Hotel?"

Her guest seemed ill at ease as he paused beside her. "I am, Mrs. Baxter. Very much so."

"I'm so happy to hear that." She peered up the stairs. "And your . . . er . . . companion? I trust she feels the same way?"

Edwin Coombs cleared his throat and ran a finger under his collar. "Yes, indeed, madam."

"Wonderful!" Cecily gave him a bright smile. "We try our best to keep our guests entertained. I was talking to another gentleman earlier, and he mentioned that he especially enjoyed the card games. Do you play cards, Mr. Coombs?"

"Er . . . yes, I do." He gazed across the lobby as if seeking a way to politely escape.

Cecily shifted her position a little, making it difficult for him to get past her without bumping into her. "Then you probably know the gentleman." She pretended to think. "His name escapes me at the moment. Percy something or other."

The guest's expression surprised her. His face darkened, and a slight flush spread across his cheeks. "Yes, I know the chap. Nasty piece of work, if you ask me."

Cecily raised her eyebrows. "I beg your pardon?"

As if realizing he had misspoken, Coombs doffed his cap

again. "If you will excuse me, Mrs. Baxter? I have an urgent appointment I must keep."

Cecily stood her ground. "Mr. Coombs, if one of my guests has upset you, I am obligated to know why, in that I might be able to do something about it."

Coombs held up his hand, which shook with agitation. "No, no, it is nothing. We had a slight altercation, that is all. He accused me of cheating when I won a sum of money from him, and I took umbrage at that. I have never cheated in my life." He hesitated, coughed, then added, "Not at cards anyway. Now, I really must be on my way."

He moved toward her, and there was nothing more she could do but stand aside. As he passed her, however, she asked, "I seem to have trouble remembering Percy's surname. Can you enlighten me?"

He paused again and gave her a dark look. "I cannot. He didn't mention it and I didn't ask for it. I don't think he's a guest in this hotel, which made me wonder how he was at the card tables in the first place. I do remember seeing him at a gentleman's club a few weeks ago. He was being loud and obnoxious, as he was here in the card room. I noticed Sir Clarence Oakes frowning at him as well. If you wish to know Percy's last name, I suggest you ask Sir Clarence. He attends the same gentleman's club."

Picturing the rather austere aristocrat she had met earlier, Cecily felt reluctant to approach Sir Clarence, or his wife for that matter. Lady Penelope Oakes seemed rather distant and somewhat disparaging of her surroundings, which did not sit well with Cecily at all. The woman's husband wasn't much better.

Then again, Cecily reminded herself, if she were to discover Percy's identity, a brief conversation with Sir Clarence seemed necessary.

She watched Edwin Coombs stride across the lobby toward the front doors, his words still ringing in her ears. It appeared that Percy had acquired at least one enemy. Judging from the opinion Mr. Coombs had of the dead man, it seemed entirely possible Percy had upset more than one person. Who was this man? Where had he come from? What was he doing at the Pennyfoot and why was Mazie planning to meet with him?

Cecily sighed. She would have to hunt down Sir Clarence Oakes. Hopefully, he would be able to supply her with at least some of the answers.

After venturing fruitlessly into the library and the conservatory, she peeked into the bar as a last resort. There she was rewarded. Sir Clarence sat alone at a corner table, enjoying a glass of ale.

At least, she assumed he was enjoying it. It was hard to tell from the ferocious scowl and clenched fingers around his glass.

She rarely entered the bar. Women generally were not allowed in there, and only her position allowed her the privilege. Even so, there were some gentlemen who felt uncomfortable with her presence, and she avoided the room unless she had an urgent reason to enter.

Deciding that her desire to speak with Sir Clarence was not reason enough to upset her guests, she retreated to the lobby, where she was immediately hailed by a shrill voice.

"Cecily, dear! I'm so happy to see you. I have an urgent request and it simply won't wait."

Cecily halted as a slight woman dressed in a royal blue coat sailed toward her. Phoebe Fortescue's hat almost hid her face, its extensive brim loaded down with an assortment of blooms, ribbons, and two stuffed doves.

Reaching Cecily, she stretched out a gloved hand. "I need the ballroom tomorrow to rehearse our Christmas pantomime. The church hall simply isn't big enough, and we have only a few days left to prepare." She fluttered her hand in front of her face. "I'm quite sure I don't have to remind you how troublesome the dance troupe can be at times. They become quite difficult when they don't have enough space to perform."

Cecily winced at the memories Phoebe's words conjured up in her mind. Her longtime friend had presented many recitals at the Pennyfoot over the years. She engaged several young women from the village of Badgers End, most of whom were lacking in talent and, in some cases, intelligence.

Cecily could not remember a single performance where some kind of calamity had not occurred. Performers falling, sets collapsing, enraged players storming off—it had all happened more than once. There was the matter of the escaped snake that terrified the audience, and one horrified matron had almost been stabbed by an errant sword tossed from the stage.

Fortunately, there had never been any serious injuries, though one young lady had her arm encased in a sling for six weeks, and another had a limp that lasted for months. Mostly, though, it was a matter of bumps, bruises, and a heavy dose of hurt pride.

Baxter had often hinted, rather darkly, that it might be better to forgo Phoebe's valiant attempts at entertaining.

Apart from the fact that Cecily could not possibly offend such a close friend in that manner, there was also the fact that the audience actually enjoyed the disasters. They appeared to gleefully anticipate the moment when the mayhem occurred. Cecily would even go so far as to say that was the reason the seats were always filled to capacity.

"We're doing *Aladdin* this year," Phoebe prattled on, oblivious of the glances cast her way as her raised voice penetrated to the walls. "We have an enormous set that we absolutely must start building tomorrow."

"Of course." Cecily frowned. "I have already informed Archie he is to help you."

Phoebe peered up at her from under the brim of her hat. "Archie? I'm not familiar with that name."

"Archibald Docker, our handyman."

"Oh." Phoebe frowned. "What happened to the other one you had? Jacob something or other."

Cecily hesitated. She didn't like to remember what had happened to her previous handyman. "He . . . er . . . passed away, about this time last year."

"He did?" Phoebe actually looked relieved. "Well, thank goodness."

Cecily raised her eyebrows. "I beg your pardon?"

"Oh, well, I'm sorry for him, of course." Obviously agitated, Phoebe withdrew a lace-edged handkerchief from her sleeve and patted her forehead with it. "But, I have to admit, I'm not sorry he's gone. He was absolutely useless at building sets. Do you remember the horrible mess he made of the stage for our last pantomime? I've never been so ashamed of a performance in all the years I've been presenting them."

Cecily had to swallow hard. In her humble opinion, it seemed that Phoebe had far more to be ashamed of than a shoddy stage set.

"However, one should not speak ill of the dead. What did the man die of anyway? He was quite young, wasn't he?"

Again Cecily paused to ponder. Apparently, Phoebe had forgotten about the incident, or perhaps she had missed the account of it in the newspaper. Cecily herself had never spoken of it to anyone after the dust had cleared.

Phoebe stared at her, obviously intrigued by her silence, and Cecily made an effort to carefully phrase her words. "Jacob met with an . . . accident, while working on the cellar wall last year."

"Oh, my. How unfortunate. That must have been uncomfortable for you."

That was putting it mildly, Cecily thought, considering that Jacob was actually stabbed in the chest by a gang of thieves who were using the tunnel beneath the hotel to store their ill-gotten gains. She wasn't about to upset Phoebe with that news, however, and thankfully, her friend accepted the explanation without any more questions.

"So, what about this new handyman, then? Who is he? Is he capable? Will he be able to build me a set as per my instructions?"

"I'm quite sure you will find Archie not only capable but extremely pleasant and accommodating. He only joined us recently. The fellow we hired after Jacob died was incompetent and we had to get rid of him. We found Archie about a month ago and he seems to be working out very well. He's taking care of the gardening as well as the maintenance, so he's living in the caretaker's cottage on the grounds."

Phoebe nodded. "Well, I hope he turns out to be a better employee than your last maintenance man. You don't seem to have had much luck with them since Clive left."

"Indeed, but I feel confident we've picked a good one this time. I will instruct him to meet you in the ballroom tomorrow morning."

Phoebe nodded. "Thank you, Cecily. I'm much obliged. We shall need three changes of sets, so I hope your handyman has plenty of energy."

Cecily was already feeling sorry for her new servant. Phoebe could be quite unmanageable when she was under stress.

She was about to make her excuses when a loud voice hailed her from across the room.

"Cecily, old girl! Haven't seen you in quite a while. You're looking dashing today. Must have something special going on, what? What?"

"Thank you, Colonel." Cecily smiled at the white-whiskered gentleman striding toward them. Phoebe's husband, Colonel Frederick Fortescue, was always lavish with his praise, whether deserved or not, which in Cecily's opinion was not necessarily a bad thing.

The colonel reached Phoebe's side and gave his wife a hefty nudge that almost toppled her off-balance. "What are you up to, my little peacock? Hatching nefarious plans, no doubt, what? What?"

Phoebe gave him a scathing glance that would have

floored a more astute gentleman. "Freddie, dear, please do refrain from bellowing my business for all ears to hear."

Blissfully ignoring that, the colonel looked at Cecily. "All ready for Christmas, are we, old bean?"

"We're getting there," Cecily told him. "This is always a busy time of the year for us."

"Yes, yes, of course it is." The colonel twirled one side of his luxurious mustache. "Preparing for Christmas can be utterly exhausting. I remember when I was in India, I—"

"Oh, for heaven's sake, Freddie," Phoebe muttered, rudely interrupting him. "You're not going to launch into another of your eternally long, boring stories, are you?"

Totally ignoring her, the colonel continued, "It was Christmas Eve, and the chaps wanted a tree. Couldn't find a blasted fir tree anywhere, so we put one together with brooms and brushes, hung tin mugs on it, and draped it with string."

Cecily smiled. "Most admirable, Colonel. Now, if you'll excuse me—"

"You should have seen it, old girl." The colonel twirled his mustache again. "Dashed magnificent, if you ask me. You can't beat the genius of the king's army, by George!"

"Freddie."

Once more he ignored the warning in his wife's voice. "Anyway, there we were, all standing around the tree, knocking back the gin and singing carols with as much gusto as we could muster, when someone fell over the bucket of coal by the fireplace." The colonel smacked the air with his hand. "Coal dust everywhere. One chap grabbed one of the brooms to sweep it up and the whole blasted tree came down, raining tin mugs everywhere. You never heard such a racket in your life. I—"

"That's *enough*, Frederick!"

The colonel shut his mouth and gave Phoebe a reproachful look. "What's the matter, old bean? Feeling a bit liverish this morning, are we?"

Phoebe's cheeks burned with indignation, and at that moment Cecily caught sight of Sir Clarence Oakes striding across the lobby toward the door.

"I'm sorry, Phoebe, I have to run. Do feel free to take over the ballroom tomorrow. Once the ball is over tonight, we shall have no use for it until your pantomime." Without waiting for an answer, she sped after the retreating figure of the aristocrat.

She reached him as he paused in front of the Christmas tree. Halting at his side and slightly out of breath, she frantically rehearsed how to phrase her questions. She wasn't quite sure why the man disturbed her. She wasn't easily intimidated by anyone, but Sir Clarence had a way of scrutinizing people when talking to them, as if he was delving into their innermost secrets.

Feeling decidedly at a disadvantage, she prepared to disarm the man. Maybe she could charm him into answering her questions. And maybe not.

Gertie huffed and puffed as she reached the top landing. It didn't help to settle her nerves. She was already on edge, given that the new handyman was directly behind her, apparently having no trouble with the climb.

She wasn't about to admit it, even to herself, but there was something about Archie that unsettled her. In a good way. This was the first time she was actually alone with him, and it was doing strange things to her stomach.

Which was extremely disturbing, since she had sworn off all men after her breakup with Clive. The very last thing she wanted to do was to get cozy with another handyman. Besides, Archie was younger than her, and a lot more energetic—she didn't think the man had an ounce of excess fat on him. Whereas she had bulges everywhere.

Annoyed with herself for even thinking about him in such a personal way, she turned on him as he stepped up next to her. "I need the door to the chute mended right away. I don't want to have to carry all those linens down all those stairs again."

"Yes, ma'am." Archie gave her a cheeky grin that warmed her toes.

He was clean-shaven, which she liked. She never did care for all that fuzz on a man's face. His dark brown hair had gold streaks in it, and curled at the back of his neck. A deep dimple appeared in his cheek when he smiled, and he had a way of tilting his head to the side when he made a joke, which made it all the more amusing. She liked a man who could make her laugh.

Reminding herself of her resolution, she turned sharply away from him and marched down the corridor to the chute. "There it is." She pointed at the door. "It's stuck and I can't get it open."

Archie stepped in front of her, peered at the door, and stroked his chin. "Hmm . . . has it ever got stuck before?"

"Yeah, once or twice. But usually I can get it open."

Gertie grabbed the handle and heaved as hard as she could. "This time it's well and truly bloody stuck."

Archie grinned again. "Well, we can't have that, can we. We'll just have to see what we can do about it."

"Good." Gertie avoided looking into his eyes. "And be quick about it."

"Yes, m'm."

Something about the way he said it drew her gaze to his face. "You don't have to call me m'm, Mr. Docker," she said stiffly. "I'm only the chief housemaid here."

"And a very good one at that, I'm betting." He took a screwdriver out of his tool belt and walked over to the chute. "So, do I call you Mrs. McBride?"

"You can call me Gertie, like everyone else around here." She didn't know why she was talking so gruffly, but she couldn't seem to get her voice to sound normal.

"Thank you, Gertie, and please call me Archie." He fitted the screwdriver into one of the screws in the door hinge and started twisting it around. "And what about Mr. McBride? What does he do for a living?"

"Mr. McBride is dead." Aware that she'd sounded rather short, she added more calmly, "I'll leave you to it, then."

She was walking away when Archie called out softly, "Gertie?"

She turned to look at him.

He had a look on his face that melted all her resistance. "I'm truly sorry. About Mr. McBride, I mean."

For the first time she gave him a genuine smile. "Thanks, Archie." After that, she flew down the stairs a good deal faster than when she'd come up them.

She reached the first landing and barreled around the curve. The elegant figure in the fur-trimmed velvet coat appeared in front of her without warning, but she was moving too fast to stop. With a sickening lurch of her stomach, she slammed into the woman, sending her into the wall.

The lady's hat tipped over her face, dislodging two large hat pins, and it was a moment or two before her hand jerked the extensive brim back into place.

Staring at the sharp features burning with rage, Gertie's stomach sank even farther. She was looking into the furious eyes of Lady Penelope Oakes.

Gertie stooped down to retrieve the pins and handed them to the woman. "I'm ever so sorry, your ladyship—" she began, but Lady Oakes cut her off with a haughty wave of her hand.

"Look where you're going next time. There are other people on these stairs besides you." With a toss of her head, she rudely pushed past Gertie and marched stiffly up the steps to the landing.

Gertie traipsed down the rest of the stairs, muttering under her breath, "Who the heck does she think she is? Bleeding queen of England?"

Vowing to make sure she never came close to that stuck-up toff ever again, she crossed the lobby and stomped down the stairs to the kitchen.

Sir Clarence Oakes was an imposing figure with his black curly hair and clipped mustache, but it was his eyes that caught attention—dark, mysterious, and unfathomable.

At that moment those eyes were focused on Cecily's face, and she had to gather her thoughts. The gentleman was apparently waiting for someone, most likely his wife, judging from the irritated glances he kept taking of his pocket watch.

Deciding to come straight to the point, she declared, "Sir Clarence, please excuse the intrusion, but I'm trying to locate a gentleman who is improperly attending the card rooms. I believe you are acquainted with him. His Christian name is Percy. I need to obtain his surname."

Sir Clarence continued to gaze at her in silence for a little too long before answering. "I regret that I cannot help you, Mrs. Baxter."

Disappointed, Cecily nevertheless persisted. "I heard that the gentleman in question had an altercation with Mr. Edwin Coombs. He mentioned that you were present at the time."

Sir Clarence narrowed his eyes a fraction. "Ah, yes. I do recall that instance. Most unpleasant."

"Mr. Coombs also mentioned that the gentleman was a member of your club in London."

Sir Clarence stiffened his back. "I am quite certain, madam, that the person to whom you refer is not a member of the Bond Street club. We are most particular about whom we accept as our patrons." He raised his chin, his gaze shifting to the lobby behind her. "Excuse me, Mrs. Baxter. My wife is about to join me."

Although Cecily had seen Sir Clarence upon occasion in the hotel, she had yet to meet his wife. Eagerly she turned around to see an elegant woman sweeping toward them from the stairs.

Lady Oakes wore a heavy blue velvet coat trimmed with white fur and carried a white fur muff. Swirling white feathers decorated her matching blue hat, and a white lace collar covered her throat. "Darling," she murmured as she reached her husband's side, "please forgive me. I was delayed by a servant on my way up to fetch my muff, and then had trouble finding it once I reached our room." She nodded at Cecily. "Good evening."

Cecily smiled at the newcomer. The woman was quite beautiful, with greenish brown eyes that appeared to have trouble focusing on one spot. "I trust you are enjoying your visit to the Pennyfoot?"

"Quite, thank you." Lady Oakes stretched out a hand to take her husband's arm, then apparently changed her mind and fidgeted with the folds of her coat instead.

"I was just asking your husband if he knew a gentleman by the name of Percy," Cecily said, ignoring Sir Clarence's fierce glare. "I wish to learn his surname. I don't suppose you know of him?"

Lady Oakes shot a glance at her husband. "The name sounds familiar. My husband may have mentioned him, but from what I hear, the gentleman was not the sort of person with whom we would care to associate."

Obviously annoyed with his wife, Sir Clarence coughed. "If you will excuse us, Mrs. Baxter? We are off to do a spot of Christmas shopping."

"Of course. If I may have just one moment more?" Cecily pulled the scarf from her pocket and dangled it in front of Lady Oakes. "Do you, by any chance, recognize it?"

The woman stared at it for a moment, then shook her

head. "I have never seen it before. It is not something I would care to wear."

Sir Clarence took hold of his wife's arm, sounding harsh when he said, "Come, Penelope. We must be off."

Cecily couldn't help noticing Lady Oakes wince at the contact. She tucked the scarf back in her pocket. "You have a carriage waiting for you?"

"Actually, we shall be taking my motorcar." With a curt nod at Cecily, Sir Clarence opened one of the doors and ushered his wife through it.

Cecily stared at the closed doors for several seconds before returning slowly to the staircase. If she wasn't mistaken, she told herself, Lady Oakes appeared to be nervous around her husband. In fact, she would even go so far as to say the good lady seemed fearful of him. They both appeared reluctant to admit they were acquainted with Percy, yet it was obvious they knew the man. Were they, perhaps, ashamed to be publicly included in Percy's circle of acquaintances?

There was something else—something that Cecily couldn't quite recall. Something Lady Oakes had said. She tried in vain to remember what it was that was poking her mind, and finally gave up.

It would come to her later. It always did. Most of the time, when she got a niggling notion in her head, it turned out to be something significant. She would just have to be patient and wait for it to surface.

CHAPTER

❀ 5 ❀

Lilly picked up the hem of her skirt as she walked across the courtyard toward the stables, her gaze fixed to the ground. Charlie was a good manager, and he kept the yard clean, but she never knew if he'd missed something and the last thing she needed was to step into horse dung. She'd done that once and it made her sick having to clean it off her shoes.

Tiny flakes of snow drifted down past her nose, and she wondered if they'd have snow on the ground by tomorrow. It always seemed more like Christmas when the pavements and trees were covered in white. She loved to see the branches bowing under the weight of the snow.

The horses didn't like it, though. They always snorted a lot when Charlie brought them out onto the cold, wet stuff. Lilly smiled to herself, picturing the horses stamping impatiently in front of the carriages. She'd stamp herself if she had to tramp through all that mess.

Reaching the stable door, she peered inside and wrinkled her nose. She wasn't fond of the smell of horses and dried straw. At first, she couldn't see anything but shadows, but then, as her eyes adjusted to the gloom, she saw Henry bending beneath an open bonnet of a motorcar.

She was about to call out when she noticed something else. Charlie was leaning against a stall, one hand in his pocket, the other clasping a rake. He was staring at Henry, and something about the way he was looking at the mechanic made Lilly's pulse quicken.

She stepped forward and called out, "Henry! Sir Clarence wants his motorcar right away. Mr. Baxter says to bring it around to the front steps."

At the sound of her voice, Charlie dropped the rake. Bending over to pick it up, he said gruffly, "Get a move on, Henry. Don't keep the bloke waiting."

Henry straightened and slammed down the bonnet. "Right away, sir!"

Lilly watched as Charlie carried the rake over to the rack and stood it up alongside the other utensils. Then he headed toward the door. As he passed Henry, Lilly heard him mutter, "I keep telling you. Don't call me sir. My name is Charlie."

Henry simply nodded, and without looking at Lilly, Charlie walked out into the courtyard and disappeared around the corner.

Henry moved toward the silver blue motorcar at the end of the row and pulled a hand crank out from the back of it.

Lilly hurried forward, calling out, "Henry, wait a minute."

Henry stared at her with wary eyes as she approached. "Watcha want?"

"I think you need to know something." Lilly lowered her voice and glanced at the open doorway of the stable before adding, "You know Charlie fancies you, don't you?"

"What?" Henry's voice had risen several octaves. "I don't know what you're talking about."

"I saw him watching you." Lilly checked the doorway one more time before adding, "He had that look on his face."

"What look?"

Lilly shrugged. "You know. That look a fellow gets when he's smitten."

The shock on Henry's face almost made Lilly laugh. "That's the stupidest thing I ever heard."

Lilly leaned forward and spoke slowly and deliberately. "It's the look that says he wants to grab you and kiss you."

Henry uttered a cry of protest. "Don't be daft. He never would dream of doing something like that."

"Oh, I think he's dreaming all right. Dreaming about you." Lilly crossed her arms. "You need to tell him the truth."

Henry's face paled. "I can't tell no one I'm a girl. I'll lose my job. That's why I haven't told no one but you. No one will hire a girl mechanic. My dad is ill and can't work. I need this job."

"I know." Lilly reached out and patted Henry's shoulder. "But if you go to madam and tell her all about your problem, I know she'll understand. Mr. Baxter might have a hard time with it, but madam will set him straight. She did that for me when I told her about my problem."

Henry's expression changed to one of curiosity. "What *is* your problem? I know you've mentioned it before, but why won't you tell me what it is?"

Lilly hesitated. Only madam and Mr. Baxter knew the truth about her predicament. She'd told herself it was safer not to tell anyone else, but keeping a secret like that was hard, and it would be so good to be able to share it with someone.

Someone like Henry, who was also struggling with a secret.

Once more she studied the empty doorway before lowering her voice and saying, "I have to ask you to keep it a strict secret if I tell you. You can't tell anyone. Not a soul. Promise?"

Henry eagerly nodded. "Course I promise. After all, you're keeping my secret."

"Okay, then." Lilly took a deep breath. "I was married once."

Henry looked disappointed. "Is that all? What happened to him? Did he die?"

Lilly shivered. "No, but I wish he would have. He beat me. Almost killed me. He told me if he couldn't have me, he'd cut up my face so badly no one would ever look at me again."

Henry mouth trembled. "Oh, Lord. I'm so sorry."

Lilly sighed. "I was terrified of him, but too afraid to leave in case he came after me. But then one day, after he'd slammed me against a wall, I decided I was going to die anyway if I stayed there. I waited until he was asleep that night and I left. I hitched a ride on a milk cart and eventually ended up here."

Henry nodded. "So how did you get this job?"

"I heard they were looking for maids here, so I asked for a job. I told madam what I'd done and she told me she and

Mr. Baxter would protect me." Lilly uttered a soft sigh. "They're good people, Henry. They would understand, I know they would."

Henry's mouth thinned. "No, I can't take the risk. And you can't say nothing. You promised!"

"I'll keep it, too," Lilly said, "but you need to watch out for Charlie. Sooner or later he's going to find out, and he'll go to madam. It would be better for you if you got to her first."

Henry's eyes filled with despair. "I'll think about it." One thin hand reached up to pull the cap farther down. "Just don't say nothing to no one."

Lilly nodded. "All right. Now you'd better hurry up and get that motorcar over to the steps, or Sir Clarence will be complaining. He's a surly one, that one."

She watched Henry lean down to fit the crank into the front of the motorcar, then hurried out of the stable into the chilly courtyard. She'd already spent far too long talking to the mechanic. Mrs. Chubb would probably pounce on her the minute she got back to the kitchen.

Still thinking about Henry, she lifted her skirt and sprinted across the hard ground toward the kitchen door. It was only by chance she'd found out that Henry was really a girl in disguise, keeping up the pretense because she was convinced no one would hire a female mechanic.

Lilly just wished Henry would tell madam the truth, because she knew Charlie well. If he ever found out, he'd be so embarrassed and cross that he'd been taken in by a girl pretending to be a boy, he'd most likely sack her on the spot, and Henry would lose her job.

True, there weren't many people who would hire a girl to take care of their motorcars, but Henry knew all there was to know about them. She was as good as any lad at the job; madam would see that and keep her on, and Charlie would have no say in the matter.

Coming to a breathless halt at the door, Lilly wrestled with the problem. She'd promised Henry she'd keep her secret, but she knew madam and Mr. Baxter better than Henry did. Maybe she should tell them the truth about their mechanic.

It would be breaking her promise, true, but she would be saving Henry her job, and that's what mattered. Henry would have to forgive her after that.

Wouldn't she?

The orchestra at the Grand Ball was in full swing when Cecily arrived later that evening on the arm of her husband. Baxter looked suave and elegant in his formal black dress coat and gray striped trousers. He'd reluctantly agreed, at his wife's request, to forgo the usual gray vest, although he drew the line at substituting it with a red one. Instead he wore a dark green vest, trimmed with just a hint of gold braid, and finished off the ensemble with a black bow tie.

Cecily had chosen to wear her favorite blue silk gown, with white lace trim and sequins sprinkled here and there. She wore blue and white feathers in her hair, and diamonds sparkled from her ears.

She was delighted to see her friend Madeline Prestwick seated near the windows and talking quite earnestly with her husband, Dr. Kevin Prestwick. Madeline was dressed unconventionally in a simple flowing gown in a vivid pattern of roses, violets, and numerous other blossoms. As usual, her feet were bare, encased in open-toed gold sandals. Her unbound dark hair hung over her shoulders, with a sprig of holly to hold the heavy strands away from her face.

It was no surprise to Cecily to see some of the scandalized glances cast her friend's way from the fashionably clad ladies circling the floor, though for the most part, some of the gentlemen seemed fascinated by the aura of abandonment.

Cecily smiled as she made her way around the room while Baxter paused to exchange a few words with one of the footmen. The young man, apparently bemused by the spectacle of so many stately aristocrats in his presence, was neglecting his duty. Instead of serving the guests with his loaded tray of hors d'oeuvres, he stood staring at the dancers as if mesmerized.

Cecily had no doubt her husband would set the footman straight, and left him to do just that as she headed toward Madeline's table.

Her friend broke off her conversation and looked up with a smile as Cecily reached her. "My dear Cecily!" She held out a slim hand to touch Cecily's arm. "You look magnificent."

"Thank you, and you look exquisite, as always."

The doctor had sprung to his feet at the sight of her and, with a smile and a nod, offered her an empty chair.

Cecily seated herself, murmuring, "This music is so lively. I'd like to dance, but I'm not sure I could keep up with the rhythm of it."

Madeline's tinkling laugh rang out. "Why, Cecily, you

have more energy than most of these privileged damsels put together. Only you could suffer all the trauma of running a hotel and still look fresh and vigorous at the end of the day." Her expression sobered. "By the way, I'm so sorry you have another unfortunate incident on your hands. Kevin told me what happened today. I do hope it won't cause too much chaos for the Christmas season."

Cecily sighed. "It's not as if we're a stranger to upheavals like this, but I do wish it wouldn't happen so close to the festivities." She glanced at Kevin. "I don't suppose you've heard from P.C. Northcott? I rang him earlier to tell him that our"—she paused, and lowered her voice—"that our mysterious guest had been seen frequenting the Bond Street gentleman's club in London. He told me he would contact them. I would have rung them myself but I doubt they would give me any information."

Kevin gave her a wry smile. "You're probably right. They are far more likely to talk to a police constable."

"I imagine he has also spoken with Mazie's family by now. I'm wondering if she's been located."

Kevin sent a quick glance around the room. "I haven't heard from him, but I'll finish conducting my postmortem tomorrow, and I'll speak to him after that."

"You will give me a ring if there is any news?" Cecily glanced at Madeline. "Sam is notoriously slow in giving me information."

"That's most likely because he knows you will take that information and charge off to do your own investigating."

Cecily was about to answer her friend when she saw Madeline's eyes clouding over. Sensing what was coming, she turned to the doctor. "Kevin, dear, would you be an angel and tell my husband I am waiting for some sustenance? I haven't eaten since midday."

"Of course." Kevin jumped to his feet and marched off with his long stride to where Baxter still stood quietly scolding the footman.

The second he was out of earshot, Cecily turned back to Madeline, who sat very still, her gaze focused on something far off in the distance.

Cecily knew that her friend was in one of her trances, and there wasn't much she could do except wait for whatever the woman had to say.

Most of the villagers of Badgers End were convinced that Madeline was a witch. She had extraordinary healing powers, using only herbs and wildflowers, much to her husband's discomfort. Her skills, pitted against the doctor's alliance with science, had been a bone of contention between them that had threatened their relationship at times.

Madeline's reputation for providing some of the male population with remedies for certain delicate matters did nothing to improve the situation. Add to that her propensity to foretell the future with alarming accuracy, and it was a miracle that the two of them had any marriage at all. As far as Cecily could tell, however, their union appeared to be on solid ground, no doubt aided by the birth of their daughter, Angelina.

"You must take extra care," Madeline said in a deep voice quite unlike her own.

Cecily jumped. "I usually do."

"All is not as it seems. You will face danger from an unexpected source."

Well, that was nothing out of the ordinary, Cecily reflected. Over the years she had faced many dangers, but had always managed to escape them relatively unscathed. "Can you tell me where or when?"

Madeline slowly shook her head. "That is why I say it will be unexpected. Even you won't know from which direction it will come."

"Well, thank you for the warning. I'll do my best to stay on guard."

"Beware of the beast that flies."

Cecily stared at her. "I beg your pardon?"

At that moment Kevin spoke from behind her, making her jump. "Your refreshments are on the way." He appeared at her side. "Baxter will join you shortly."

With Madeline's warning still ringing in her ears, Cecily glanced at her friend, who sat rearranging the holly in the gold bowl in front of her. She had apparently returned to her normal state as she smiled at her husband. "Kevin, my sweet, I would dearly love to dance."

"Of course." Kevin held out his hand to assist his wife to her feet. If he felt any qualms about taking the floor with such an unorthodox creature, he showed no sign of it. The doctor's love for his wife surpassed all concern for propriety, or the lack of it. Madeline was an individualist, and he embraced it with as much enthusiasm as he was able, considering his stature in the village.

Cecily greatly admired him for that. Not everyone could spit in the face of the aristocracy with such elegance and control. She had in the past rebelled herself against the rules of social conduct, and paid dearly for it at times. She envied

Kevin's cavalier attitude toward those who looked down on his choice of life partner, and heaven help anyone who voiced their opinion in his presence. He would leap in defense of his wife with all the fury of an enraged lion.

As had Baxter upon occasion, when his wife had received less-than-complimentary remarks on her attitude. Cecily glanced across the room and smiled as her husband approached, followed by the chastened footman bearing a tray of delectable treats from Mrs. Chubb's kitchen.

She had chosen well when she married her manager. When her first husband had died, she thought never to love again. Her romance with Baxter had grown slowly, but was all the more abiding because of it. He was everything to her, and she couldn't imagine life without him.

He reached her chair and touched her shoulder with his fingertips before seating himself. The footman offered her the tray, and she spent a brief moment deciding between a sausage roll and a shrimp canapé. Giving up the battle, she pointed to them both, and the footman deftly picked each one up with his tongs and deposited them onto the gold-edged plate in front of her.

"Thank you." She smiled up at him, and was rewarded with a nervous grin and a slight bow in return.

After placing Baxter's choices on his plate, the footman glided off to the next table, where a group of guests sat loudly laughing.

Baxter sent them a sour glance before reaching for one of the tasty morsels on his plate. "I saw you talking to Kevin," he said after he'd swallowed the canapé. "Did he have anything helpful to say about our predicament?"

Reminded once more of Madeline's warning, Cecily took a moment to answer. "He said he would contact me tomorrow if he had more news." She made an effort to dismiss her uneasiness. Baxter was perceptive, and would sense if something was wrong. The last thing she needed right now was a lecture from him on the dangers of delving into a case of murder.

Her husband, at that moment, was watching Kevin glide around the floor. Madeline, so light on her feet, always appeared to float above the ground. Several of the couples dancing gave them a wide berth. Madeline's dubious reputation had spread beyond Badgers End. It wasn't only the villagers who were unsettled by her presence.

Once more Cecily's mind was drawn to her friend's ominous words. She never took Madeline's warnings lightly. Paying heed to them had saved her life more than once. *Beware of the beast that flies.* It was an odd thing to say. Which made it seem all the more menacing. Cecily couldn't imagine what the phrase might mean, and her attempts to decipher it created such gruesome pictures in her mind, she hastily brushed them aside.

She would just have to be vigilant, and pray that her guardian angel would remain by her side.

The following morning Phoebe arrived at the Pennyfoot Hotel promptly at eleven o'clock. She made her way immediately to the ballroom, where she hoped to find her dance troupe ready and waiting, eager to begin rehearsals.

As always, her optimism exceeded the outcome. The

ballroom was empty, except for a young man squatting on the stage, wielding what appeared to be a folding measuring stick. Assuming this to be the handyman, she hurried forward.

Appreciative as she was that he was prompt and apparently willing, she had to set the standards from the very beginning. She had learned from past experience that allowing one chink in the armor of supervision could lead to a battle for control. Then it would be her requirements versus the handyman's lack of interest in the project, usually ending in some kind of disaster.

This time she was determined that nothing should go awry at this year's pantomime. Come what may, her set would be stable and perfect, her dance troupe would be competent, if not dazzling, and the audience would rise to their feet, loudly applauding the genius who had presented such an unforgettable performance. Her reputation as a brilliant producer and director would be broadcast far and wide.

It was her favorite dream, and she took a moment to indulge in it.

"Mrs. Fortescue, I presume?"

Rudely awoken from the fantasy, Phoebe blinked up at the stage. She had to tip her head way back to see the young man from under the brim of her hat. He stood looking down at her with a rather disrespectful grin on his face, and appeared even younger than she'd first thought.

"I assume you're Mr. Docker. How much experience do you have in building stage sets?" she demanded.

The handyman looked somewhat taken aback. "Er . . . I am, and not much, I confess, but I'm good with my hands."

His expression lightened. "Just tell me what you want and I'll do everything in my power to see it's done and done right."

Somewhat mollified by the man's enthusiasm, she nodded. "Very good, Mr. Docker. Wait there a moment and I shall join you."

"Yes, m'm. And it's Archie, m'm."

Unwilling to be that familiar with the handyman, she refrained from answering him. Instead, she made her way to the side of the stage and pushed open the door to the wings.

When she arrived onstage, Archie was once more squatting on the floor with the measuring stick stretched out in front of him.

Curious, she halted a yard or so behind him. "What are you doing?"

He turned his head to look up at her. "Measuring the stage, m'm. Mrs. Baxter couldn't tell me the dimensions, and I don't want to guess."

Impressed in spite of herself, Phoebe nodded. "I see. Well, that can wait for now. I want to give you an idea of what I need."

Archie got to his feet and folded up the measuring stick. Sliding it into his belt, he looked up and down the stage. "You're doing *Aladdin*, is that right?"

In answer to her nod, he waved an arm at stage left. "I believe you'll want a cave over there, and a palace over here." He waved his other arm at stage right. "Unless you have a revolving platform, which would make things easier."

Phoebe's eyes lit up. "A revolving platform? Can you build one?"

Archie frowned and rubbed his chin. "Well, I suppose I could, but we don't have much time before the performance. I might need some help with it."

Phoebe's hat trembled on her head in her excitement. "Oh, I'm sure that can be arranged. I'll ask Mrs. Baxter to provide us with one or two footmen. There's just one thing. I'll need three sets. One for the cave, one for Aladdin's palace, and one for Mustapha's desert home."

"Hmmm." Again Archie rubbed his chin. "How about this? I build the palace, and we change some of the furnishings in it to turn it into Mustapha's home."

"Oh, splendid!" Phoebe actually forgot herself enough to clap her hands. "I can see that I finally have someone capable of creating exactly what I want. I'm so happy Mrs. Baxter found you."

She was intrigued to see a dimple flash in his cheek. "So am I, Mrs. Fortescue. Believe me, so am I, and I'm looking forward to working with you on this pantomime."

For once, Phoebe was speechless. No one had ever said those words to her before. Not even her ungrateful dance troupe, who should be going down on their knees giving thanks to her for providing them with such a marvelous opportunity to display their talents.

As if her mind had conjured them up, the doors flew open and a group of women entered, all cackling and giggling like silly schoolgirls. Pushing and shoving one another, they stood just inside the room, completely ignoring their director.

Phoebe drew herself up as high as she could manage and took a deep breath. "Ladies! Let us have some decorum, please! Quieten down your noise and get up here onstage at once. We have no time to waste."

A great deal of mumbling followed her words, and one shrill voice could be clearly heard declaring, "Better get moving, girls. The old biddy is on the warpath again."

Phoebe winced, and stole a look at her handyman.

"Blimey," he muttered, "you've got your hands full with that lot."

Phoebe sighed. "You don't know the half of it." She turned back to glare at her wayward performers, but not before she'd seen the grin on Archie Docker's face. Somehow, she thought, as she watched the women saunter across the room, she had the impression she was going to enjoy working with Archie Docker. And that, indeed, would be quite remarkable.

CHAPTER

❋ 6 ❋

Cecily received the call from P.C. Northcott soon after she entered her office that morning. She had just settled down to examine Mrs. Chubb's list of needed supplies when the jingle of the telephone abruptly scattered her thoughts.

She reached for the receiver and lifted it off the hook, then pressed it to her ear. She still couldn't get used to talking on the dratted thing, but she had to admit, it made life so much simpler. Before they had the telephones installed, if she wanted to exchange messages with someone, she had to rely on footmen to carry them back and forth. It all took so much time, and now she could get things done so much faster.

Speaking loudly into the mouthpiece, she said, "Yes, Philip?"

Philip's quavering voice answered her. "I have a telephone operator on the line for you, madam."

"Thank you, Philip. You may hang up now."

"Yes, m'm."

A loud click vibrated in her ear, then a shrill voice demanded, "Hello? Hello?"

"Yes," Cecily answered, slightly irritated. "This is Mrs. Baxter."

"Police Constable Northcott is on the line. Do you wish to take the call?"

"I do."

Another click announced the presence of the constable. "'Allo? Police Constable Northcott here at your service. Is that you, Mrs. Baxter?"

"It is, Sam." Cecily pressed the receiver closer to her ear. "You have news for me?"

"Yes, m'm. I've learned the identity of our murder victim. His name is Lord Percival Farthingale, and he is a member of the Bond Street gentleman's club."

Obviously, Sir Clarence was mistaken about the caliber of his fellow club members. "So, he lives in London?"

"Yes, m'm. I've been trying to reach his wife, but she doesn't appear to have a telephone. In any case, it would be better if she was informed of her husband's death in person."

"Of course." Cecily thought quickly, then added, "Sam, I know how busy you are with this investigation. I have to go to London to do some Christmas shopping. Why don't I call in on Lady Farthingale and give her the sad news?"

The constable sounded vastly relieved when he answered. "That would be really helpful, Mrs. B. Since it's not strictly police work, you wouldn't be breaking any rules, so to speak, and it might be easier for the widow to take the news from another woman." He gave her an address in Eaton Square and added, "Please offer the poor lady my condolences, and give me a ring when you get back."

"I will, Sam. Now I must go. I will speak with you later." Cecily quickly replaced the receiver on its hook before Sam could realize that speaking with the dead man's widow could be helpful in his enquiries.

Leaving the supplies list until later, she went in search of her husband. She found him in the boudoir, where he had set up his desk. He looked up when she entered, his face lighting up at the sight of her.

Putting down his pen, he leaned back in his chair. "To what do I owe this most delightful intrusion?"

She laughed. "How important is your work at the moment?"

"Never too important to pay heed to you, my love. What can I do for you?"

She still had trouble reconciling this new version of her husband with the old. His attitude had changed a year ago, and she had never been able to understand what had brought about the transformation.

Baxter had always been attentive and caring toward her, but for the most part his manner had been rather crotchety and uncompromising. She had put it down to the demands of his business, coupled with her constant absence from his side while she managed the hotel and, worse, embarked on questionable pursuits of criminals. He had never been comfortable with that.

Then, seemingly out of the blue, everything had changed. He had become more affable, more interested in assisting her, to the point where he'd come very close to serious danger. After that they had drawn even closer, and she no longer questioned the reason. It was enough that he had reformed, and she couldn't be happier about it.

Realizing that her husband was watching her with a quizzical expression, she said quickly, "I was wondering if you might spare some time for a quick visit to London. I would like to do some Christmas shopping, and I thought you could use the opportunity to review your business affairs."

Baxter raised an eyebrow. "This is rather sudden, isn't it? Don't you usually plan these shopping trips in advance?"

She might have known she couldn't fool him for long. "Oh, very well. Sam told me that our dead man is Lord Percival Farthingale. I offered to go to London to give his widow the sad news. Sam thought it would be less difficult for her if a woman gave her the news."

"Hmmm. And I don't suppose it occurred to him that you could also investigate into Lord Percival's life and perhaps discover a motive for his murder?"

Cecily walked around his desk and deposited a swift kiss on his cheek. "I knew you would understand, darling. I'm overjoyed that we are now partners in crime-solving instead of always being at loggerheads over it."

Baxter sighed. "It was either that or suffer an attack of my heart for fear of your safety. Not exactly a valid choice."

"Well, I won't be needing your assistance for my visit to Lady Farthingale. I don't expect to stay for long, and I would like to do some shopping in Harrods."

Baxter raised his eyebrows. "You have expensive tastes, my dear."

She smiled. "Nothing is too good for my loving husband."

"You always did know how to placate me. Very well. When did you wish to go?"

"Right away! We can catch the noon train and return by this evening."

He thought about that for a moment, then rose from his chair. "I'll go down and order the carriage."

"I've already taken care of it. Charlie will be waiting for us at the front steps."

"You were so sure I'd agree?"

"Of course, my love!" She didn't feel the need to add that had he hesitated about joining her, she would have gone alone. She had a feeling that her conversation with Lord Percy Farthingale's widow could be very interesting, and she couldn't waste a minute to get there.

Charlie drove back from the railway station with one thing on his mind. He hadn't eaten since six o'clock that morning and his stomach was growling at him, demanding food. Before he could eat, however, he would have to unhitch Champion and settle him in his stall. Then he had to put the coach away and order one of the stable lads to clean it before he could go to the kitchen for his midday meal. By that time his stomach would be protesting so much, everyone within a mile of him would be able to hear it.

His sour mood didn't improve when he pulled up outside

the stables just in time to see Lilly turn away from Henry and hurry across the courtyard toward the hotel. Apparently, the maid had been chatting with his mechanic instead of letting him get on with his work.

Jumping down from his perch, he called out, "Did you find out what's wrong with Lord Melton's motorcar yet?"

Henry had already disappeared into the stables and must not have heard him. Grumbling to himself, he led the horse up to his stall and began unhitching the carriage.

He tried not to notice Henry bending over the bonnet of the Austin. Instead, he kept his gaze firmly on the harness as he removed it from Champion's neck. In spite of all his efforts, however, he was uncomfortably conscious of the slim boy's presence just a few yards away.

He'd planned to teach Henry how to walk and act more like a man, but the more he'd thought about it, the more unsettled he'd become. He didn't know why, but something was telling him that would be a big mistake, though he couldn't for the life of him understand why.

Frowning, he opened the stall gate and allowed Champion to trot inside. The more he'd thought about it, the more his suspicions had grown. The way the lad walked, the way he talked—it all added up. He'd finally arrived at the conclusion that Henry was one of *them*.

Not that there was anything wrong with that, he quickly reminded himself. In spite of what most people's thoughts were on the subject, he was open-minded enough to accept that some people were born different. What they did with their lives was their business and none of his. Live and let live, that was his motto.

Still, that didn't explain why he got the collywobbles every time Henry was around him. He'd always fancied girls. Never once had he had any inkling that he might be interested in boys.

Then why in heaven's name did he find himself unable to keep his eyes off Henry? There had to be something else going on in his brain. He just wished he knew what the heck was tormenting him.

"Sir?"

Henry's soft voice floated into his mind. Without turning around, he asked gruffly, "What is it?"

"I found the problem."

Hearing the boy's footsteps approaching, Charlie braced himself.

"It was the gasket. It was leaking. I replaced it and the engine is running smooth as silk."

Charlie made himself glance at the boy. Henry was looking at him with those alluring blue eyes that made him forget where he was. Hastily switching his gaze back to the carriage, he muttered, "Good work, Henry. I'll send the word to Lord Melton. Now this carriage needs cleaning, so take care of that, then you can get something to eat."

"Yes, sir." Henry turned away and walked over to the shelves to fetch a bucket.

It took a supreme effort for Charlie to avoid watching the lad. Gripping the shafts of the carriage, he gave it a mighty shove. This nonsense had to stop. What he needed was to find a girlfriend. He used to have one, until she went off with someone else. Since then he'd been wary of getting involved with the fair sex. He'd convinced himself that his work was enough, and he didn't need female company in order to be happy.

Well, obviously he'd been wrong about that. When he started getting hot under the collar over some boy, that was a warning that he needed to get close to a girl again. But how? He was kept busy at work and didn't spend much time away from the Pennyfoot.

He went down to the Fox and Hounds now and then to play darts and sink a couple of beers, but girls weren't allowed in the public bar. No, the only girls he came across worked right there at the Pennyfoot.

Charlie sighed. Well, it would just have of be one of them. Charlotte? Nah. Too aggressive. Definitely not Gertie. Lilly? He nodded. That was a possibility. He ran pictures of the rest of the maids through his head. None of them really appealed to him. So, all right, then. It would have to be Lilly.

Feeling only slightly better at the prospect, he started working out in his mind how to approach the housemaid and find out if she might be interested in going out with him. This wasn't going to be easy. But necessary.

Having settled that, he pushed the carriage into its slot in the corner.

Arriving at Victoria Station, Cecily parted company with Baxter and hailed a Hansom cab to take her to the address Sam Northcott had given her. Normally she would have dropped off a visiting card and followed up a day later, but this was an emergency, so to speak, and she hoped that Lady Farthingale would receive her upon a moment's notice.

To her surprise, a stout woman wearing the conventional black frock and white apron of a housekeeper opened the front door. Cecily had expected to see a butler, and it took her a moment to gather her thoughts.

"We do not entertain solicitors," the woman said stiffly, and began to close the door.

"Oh, I'm not selling anything." Cecily held up her hand to show she carried nothing but her handbag. "I realize I am intruding, but I have news for Lady Farthingale of an urgent nature. I should like to deliver it immediately."

The woman's suspicious stare made Cecily uncomfortable. "Give me the message and I'll see that Lady Farthingale gets it." The housekeeper shot out her hand in what Cecily considered a rather rude gesture.

"I prefer to deliver it in person." Deciding that some authority was needed, she stretched her back. "My name is Mrs. Cecily Baxter, and I am the proprietor of the Pennyfoot Hotel in Badgers End. I have news of Lord Percival Farthingale that his wife needs to hear."

At the mention of the dead man's name, the housekeeper's expression changed. She actually looked fearful as she drew back. "You may enter, but please wait here while I see if Lady Farthingale is available."

While she waited, Cecily studied her surroundings. The house was rather modest, considering it belonged to an aristocrat. Though, as Cecily had learned in the past, not all aristocrats were swimming in wealth.

It appeared that Lord Percival could be included in that company, judging from the lack of expensive furnishings. The chandelier in the hallway was of poor quality, and the blue-flowered carpeting had seen better days.

The house itself, though in a fairly decent locality, was not in the more select areas such as Belgrave or Grosvenor Square. Which was where Cecily might have expected a lord and lady to live.

When the ungracious housekeeper finally showed her into the drawing room, after announcing her name with a slight hint of distaste, Cecily was surprised to see this room looking closer to her expectations.

Heavy maroon velvet curtains hung at the tall windows, their cream lace edgings matching the cushions on the elegant gray settee. A fire danced and crackled in the marble fireplace, and on the mantlepiece sat a magnificent ornate clock. Its decorative pendulum swung slowly back and forth beneath a silvered dial, set between intricately carved satinwood panels.

Quite expensive, Cecily judged, and no doubt had originated in France. Turning her attention to the settee, she greeted the woman seated on it with a nod. "Please forgive the intrusion, Lady Farthingale. I have news of your husband, and I'm afraid it isn't good news."

The woman sighed, and waved a hand indicating that her visitor seat herself. "What has the fool done now?"

Cecily lowered herself carefully onto the embroidered seat of the chair. "If you don't mind me asking, when was the last time you saw your husband?"

Lady Farthingale narrowed her eyes. "Why, pray, is that any of your business?"

Cecily took a deep breath. "I am under the impression that you have not set eyes on your husband for some time, and must be wondering what has happened to him."

The woman stared at her for several long moments, then uttered a loud sigh. "I last saw Percy three days ago. We were staying at the Regency Hotel on the Esplanade. Percy was celebrating what he said was a lucrative business deal, though he wouldn't reveal the details. He actually wanted to stay at your hotel, but when he tried to book a room, he was told there were none available. We stayed at the Regency instead. My husband left our suite, saying he was going to explore the town, but I knew he proposed to attend your card games." She sniffed. "Which is why he wanted to stay at the Pennyfoot Hotel in the first place."

"I see." Cecily paused. This was going to be harder than she had envisioned. She took a moment to search for the right words. "Lady Farthingale," she said at last, "I'm terribly sorry to have to inform you that your husband was found in the Pennyfoot Hotel yesterday morning. I'm afraid he had passed away."

The aristocrat flinched, but her eyes remained dry as she looked at Cecily. "He's dead? Well, I can't say I'm surprised." She fished in her sleeve and drew out a lace-edged handkerchief. After dabbing at her nose, she stuffed the handkerchief back in her sleeve. "When he didn't return to the hotel after two days, I knew he was on one of his gambling excursions. It was nothing new. He disappeared often, sometimes for a week or more. Rather than wait for him to return, I packed everything up and returned home."

She looked down at her hands as Cecily murmured, "I'm very sorry."

"What was it? His heart?" Lady Farthingale shook her head. "I kept warning him that all that drinking and gambling would kill him one day. He never listened to me." Anger flashed across her face. "I'm sorry he's dead, of course, but I have to admit, I'm not sorry to see the end to all the anxiety. Percy was an obsessive gambler. He gambled away all our wealth, even borrowed from my father to cover his tracks and lost that, too. We already lost our home in Mayfair and had to move here. We had to get rid of our servants. I never knew if and when we would lose this home, too."

"That must have been difficult for you."

"It has been." The woman appeared to give herself a mental shake. Sounding determined now, she added, "I know this sounds heartless, but it's a relief, that's what it is. I shall sell the house, move in with my parents, and be done with this whole disaster of a marriage."

She actually sounded quite elated at the prospect. Cecily studied her for a moment. The lady wore a violet gown of fine quality, as far as one could tell. She had draped a blue scarf into the low neckline, and fastened it with a gorgeous dragonfly brooch that sparkled with diamonds and sapphires.

Cecily peered harder at the scarf. With its purple blossoms and green leaves, it looked very similar to the one she still carried in her pocket. "Excuse me, Lady Farthingale, and please excuse me if I'm being impertinent, but your scarf looks quite familiar." She drew the square of silk from her pocket and shook out its folds. "It looks remarkably like this one."

Lady Farthingale studied it for a second or two. "It does bear a resemblance, yes."

Cecily sniffed at the soft fabric. "I do believe it also bears traces of the perfume you are wearing."

With a fierce frown, the woman reached out for the scarf. Holding it to her nose, she murmured, *"Mouchoir de Monsieur.* It's French for 'gentleman's handkerchief.' Very expensive, I'm afraid. My bottle is almost empty." She brightened. "However, now that I will be selling the house, I shall buy more."

Hardly able to believe her ears, Cecily said quietly, "So the scarf does belong to you."

"It does." Lady Farthingale met her gaze. "Where did you find it? How did you know it was mine?"

"I didn't, until this moment."

The lady sighed. "I must have left it on the counter of your reception desk. I was so disappointed that we weren't able to stay at your lovely hotel, so I stopped by to book a room for the summer. I was upset when I realized it was missing, so I purchased another. It's not pure silk, of course, but the pattern reminded me of this one." She held up the scarf. "It was a gift from a very good friend of mine. He's dead now, and I was devastated that I'd lost the only tangible memory I had of him." She sniffed at the soft fabric. "Thank you for returning it."

Cecily held out her hand. "I'm sorry, but I have to take the scarf back with me. It's evidence in a murder case."

Lady Farthingale's face froze in disbelief. "Murder? I don't understand."

Cecily softened her voice. "I'm afraid your husband died from a blow to the head. This scarf was tied about his neck."

With one hand at her throat, the widow seemed at a loss for words. Finally, she murmured, "Percy must have found it where I had left it, and recognized it as mine. Who would want to do such a thing?" She held out the colorful silk for Cecily to take. "Then again, I can't say I'm surprised. Percy had a lot of enemies. I always knew he would come to a bad end."

"I'm so sorry." Somewhat confused by the lack of emotion displayed by the woman, Cecily added, "I can assure you we are doing everything in our power to discover who committed this dreadful deed."

Lady Farthingale gave her a sharp look. "'We'?"

"Yes, I'm assisting P.C. Northcott in his investigation. If there's anything else you can tell me that might help us find the culprit, I'd be most grateful."

"I'm sorry. I know nothing of my husband's personal pursuits. He wasn't in the habit of confiding in me."

Again there was that note of disgust in her voice. Pocketing the scarf, Cecily rose to her feet. "Very well. I must be on my way. I ordered my Hansom cab to return in half an hour. He is most likely waiting outside for me."

"Then I shan't keep you." The widow got up slowly. "Thank you for bringing me the news. It was easier to hear from you than from an officer of the law."

"The constable did ask me to convey his condolences. Rest assured, Lady Farthingale, I intend to discover who did this to your husband. The person responsible will be brought to justice. I promise you that."

Lady Farthingale reached for the bellpull. "You will return the scarf to me when you have no further use for it?"

"I'm sure that can be arranged."

"Thank you."

The door opened just then to reveal the housekeeper. With a nod at the widow, Cecily followed the servant to the front door.

Stepping outside, she saw the Hansom cab waiting at the curb, the driver impatiently swishing his whip. "Harrods, if you please," she ordered as he jumped down to open the door for her.

On her way to Knightsbridge, she would normally be gazing out the window, anxious to see the shop windows with their sumptuous displays of life-size reindeer and toy trains circling heavily laden Christmas trees.

She loved to watch the ladies in their elegant clothes bustling along the pavements, while the gentlemen tried to look dignified as they strode alongside carrying an assortment of gaily wrapped packages.

Today, however, her thoughts were squarely on Lady Farthingale and her rather cold acceptance of her husband's death. She had proclaimed that the scarf held great sentimental value to her, yet she had carelessly left it lying on the counter in the hotel. Surely she would have noticed it missing and returned for it?

Cecily replayed in her mind her conversation with the lady. The widow seemed unaffected by her husband's sudden death, even relieved to learn of her freedom. She had surmised that her husband had been carrying the scarf when he was killed—something that hadn't occurred to Cecily.

It was possible, of course. The killer could have noticed it in Lord Farthingale's pocket and decided to use it, either as a way to divert suspicion or, as Sam Northcott had suggested, to ensure that the victim was truly deceased.

Then again, the widow could have left the scarf on the reception desk, where anyone could have picked it up. It might be prudent to look at the hotel register, just to confirm that Lady Farthingale had, indeed, reserved a room for next summer, as she claimed.

Having decided that, Cecily settled back to enjoy the ride to Harrods department store, where she was looking forward to browsing the aisles. She needed to find something special for her husband's Christmas present, and she couldn't think of a more exciting place to shop for it.

CHAPTER
❀ 7 ❀

Standing at the kitchen sink, Gertie picked up a potato from the pile on the counter and began to chop the skin off it. Behind her, Michel was grumbling about the poor quality of the winter greens, which wasn't surprising, considering the lack of rain they'd had this year. The chef, as usual, took out his frustration on the stove, uttering explosive phrases in his phony French and smashing the lids down on the pots.

Mrs. Chubb was pounding bread dough on the kitchen table, shaking its legs until they rattled, while two of the housemaids argued about whose turn it was to empty the slops.

Gertie closed her mind to the racket, and concentrated on the aroma of roasting pork from the oven and apples for the sauce bubbling on the stove. The smell made her tummy rumble. She couldn't wait for supper. That was her favorite time of the day, when Daisy brought the twins to join her at the long dining table and they could all sit down with the rest of the staff and enjoy the end of another workday.

Smiling at the thought, she lopped off a corner of the potato.

"You keep doing that and there'll be nothing left of it," Charlotte remarked from behind Gertie's back. "You know they have gadgets to do that nowadays."

"I don't like gadgets." Gertie held up the knife. "You want to do it? I'll be glad to hand it over to you."

"Nah." Charlotte moved to Gertie's side. "I hate that job."

"You hate all the jobs." Gertie took another swipe at the potato.

"Yeah, I do. I should find meself a rich bloke, then I wouldn't have to work at all."

"Fat chance of that."

"Yeah, I know." Charlotte giggled. "I s'pose I shall just have to make do with someone like Archie."

A pang of resentment made Gertie blink. Rather than examine the reason for it, she said loudly, "I'm almost finished here, then I'll help you lay the tables for dinner."

"All right. I'm going to get started on them right now."

As if echoing her words, Mrs. Chubb's voice rang out across the kitchen. "Charlotte! What the devil are you doing gossiping at the sink when you should be in the dining room laying tables? Get up there this instant and don't let me see you dawdling again or I'll dock your pay."

"Yes, Mrs. Chubb." Charlotte made a face at Gertie, then flew out of the kitchen.

Gertie let out her breath. She didn't have much to do

with most of the housemaids, since her work was mostly in the kitchen. Charlotte, on the other hand, was also a kitchen maid, so they shared a lot of the chores. She liked Charlotte, a lot, but there were times when the girl was a bit overpowering.

At least the maid seemed to have given up on pestering her about going to the protest. Which was a huge relief. Still, she had to admire the girl's spirit and gumption. As she, herself, had before motherhood and life traumas tamed her.

Against her will, her mind was drawn back to the last conversation she'd had with Clive. She hadn't been so tame then, when she told him to bugger off. He argued, making demands and laying down the law like he was a magistrate or something. Telling her what she should and shouldn't do, and what he expected of her as a wife.

She suspected he'd gone back to drinking again. It had almost ruined his life once before, and he'd stopped it when he first came to the Pennyfoot. But, judging from the way he'd acted that day, she could almost swear he was sloshed.

Well, she'd soon told him where to get off. She wasn't going to be anyone's bloody slave, at his beck and call day and night. No, sir. She had done all right on her own for a good many years and she would be all right on her own again.

She'd left him still trying to order her about. So maybe she still had a bit of fire left in her. Feeling cheered at the thought, she dropped the last demolished potato into the pot of water, dried her hands, and headed for the kitchen door.

• • •

Cecily was pleased to find that she and Baxter had the train compartment to themselves as they rattled along the rails, heading for home. She was anxious to relay to him most of the conversation she'd had with Lady Farthingale and hear his thoughts on the matter.

"It certainly appears that the lady is not terribly heart-broken by the loss of her husband," Baxter remarked when Cecily's account came to an end. "I can't say I blame her. Lord Farthingale sounds like a rotter through and through."

"It's obvious they weren't enjoying a happy marriage." Cecily sighed. "I feel sorry that she'd had to put up with so much. Then again, I'm compelled to wonder if everything she told me was, in fact, the truth."

Baxter raised his eyebrows. "What are you saying? Are you suggesting she may have killed her husband?"

"Well, she does have a strong motive to be rid of him."

"Did she seem capable of cracking him over the head with a flatiron?"

"Physically?" Cecily pondered for a moment. "Yes, I suppose so. Mentally? I'm not so sure. Besides, why would she leave her own scarf at the scene of the crime?"

Baxter shrugged. "She would not expect anyone to find out it belonged to her. Maybe she used it to silence her husband while she finished him off with the iron."

Cecily shuddered. "That is so coldhearted and cruel."

Baxter's face was grave as he looked at her. "Murder is always coldhearted and cruel. And infinitely dangerous, which is why I am in constant fear of your safety."

"I know." She leaned forward to touch his hand. "But you know why I do this. I cannot stand to see a vicious criminal go unpunished, or worse, watch an innocent person wrongly imprisoned for a crime. Especially when it's a young girl for whose well-being I'm responsible."

"Yes, my dear, I do know that." He turned his palm upward and clasped her hand. "Which, while it pains me considerably, also makes me infinitely proud of my caring wife."

His words warmed her heart, and she smiled. "That's all I can ask of you. And that you love me."

"That I do, my love." He raised her hand to his lips. "Forever and always."

"As I do you." She slipped her hand from his and sank back on her seat. For now, she was content and at peace. Once she returned home, however, she must pursue this riddle and solve it, and hopefully, find Mazie so that they could all enjoy Christmas.

A soft hum of voices greeted them when she and Baxter arrived back at the hotel. Several of the guests were in the lobby, some standing in front of the Christmas tree, engaged in conversation, while others sat on the couches talking among themselves.

Cecily always derived a good deal of satisfaction from seeing her guests mingling with one another. This was how Christmas should be celebrated, with a joyful communion of strangers brought together in the festivities of the season.

She recognized Sir Clarence and his wife in the group by the tree. The aristocrat seemed surprisingly affable as he smiled at another guest's comment, while his wife remained somewhat aloof from the crowd.

Cecily crossed the lobby with Baxter following closely behind, to find Philip dozing in his chair. Her husband, as usual, rapped loudly on the desk, startling the receptionist so badly, he almost toppled off his perch.

As it was, his glasses fell to the floor, and he stared blindly down at his feet, clutching his chest as if he were about to suffer a heart attack.

Cecily gave Baxter a reproachful look before walking around the desk to retrieve the spectacles. Handing them to the confused gentleman, she said quietly, "I'm sorry if we alarmed you, Philip. I just need to look at the register."

She gave Baxter a meaningful stare, which he immediately interpreted.

"I shall be upstairs in my office if you need me," he said, and headed for the staircase.

"I'm sorry, m'm," Philip said, adjusting his glasses on his nose. "I must have nodded off for a moment. I don't know how that happened."

Cecily refrained from mentioning that his nodding off was a common occurrence, and she frequently had to wake him up. Fortunately, for some odd reason, he always became alert the moment a guest approached, as if he had a sixth sense.

Reaching for the register, she drew it toward her.

Belatedly remembering he was supposed to stand in her presence, Philip struggled to his feet. "Can I help you with something, m'm?"

Cecily briefly touched his arm. "Sit down, Philip. I shan't be but a moment."

"Yes, m'm. Thank you, m'm." Looking relieved, he sank down on his chair again.

Cecily turned the pages, scanning the lines, until she spotted the flowery signature of Lady Farthingale. Well, at least that part of the lady's story was true. She had booked a room for July of the following year.

Cecily closed the register and smiled at her receptionist. "Thank you, Philip."

"Yes, m'm." He frowned. "There's something I was supposed to tell you, but I'm dashed if I can remember what it was."

"Did you not write it down?"

"I don't think so." Philip started shuffling a pile of papers around. "Though maybe I did." He rubbed his forehead with the back of his thumb, dislodging his glasses again. "Mrs. Chubb came up to tell me something. She said to be sure and tell you when you returned."

"Very well. I shall go down to the kitchen and talk to her." Cecily walked out from behind the desk. "Don't worry, Philip. Mrs. Chubb can tell me whatever it is."

"Very well, m'm."

Cecily had taken only a few steps when Philip shouted, "Oh, now I remember, m'm! It's about the chap that was murdered in the laundry room. The police have arrested the perpetrator!"

For an elderly gentleman, her receptionist had a strong voice at times. She heartily wished this hadn't been one of those times. The sudden hush that fell over the lobby signaled the worst. There was no doubt in her mind that everyone there had heard Philip's words.

She noticed Sir Clarence staring in her direction, while his wife had turned her face away. Everyone else had their heads together, whispering among themselves like gossiping housewives. The news would be all over the hotel in short order.

Her housekeeper must have passed on the news to Philip, she thought, as she retraced her steps to the desk.

Her supposition proved to be correct when her clerk announced, "Mrs. Chubb told me not to tell anyone else, so I didn't."

Reminding herself that Philip was in desperate need of his job, Cecily leaned across the desk. "Philip, do not mention this again. To anyone. Not even a whisper. Do you understand?"

He raised his chin, obviously offended. "I do understand, madam. I assure you I can be trusted to keep my mouth closed."

"Thank you, Philip. I appreciate your discretion."

Looking appeased, Philip nodded. "My lips are sealed, m'm."

Cecily walked back across the lobby, trying not to notice the glances cast her way. She did see that Sir Clarence had left the group, and she was just in time to see him escorting his wife up the stairs before they disappeared around the curve.

As she reached the kitchen downstairs, she could hear Michel crashing his pans around on the stove. Apparently the preparations for dinner were not going well. She braced herself as she opened the door, inhaling a delicious aroma of herbs and spices that teased her stomach.

Mrs. Chubb was just emerging from the pantry, carrying a tray of cheeses. She hurried forward when she saw Cecily, and laid the tray on the table. "Is something wrong, m'm?"

At her words, a hush fell over the kitchen. Michel stopped bashing his utensils, the maids stopped rattling the silverware they were polishing, and Henry paused in front of the stove, where he'd been shoveling coal into the open belly.

Cecily nodded at everyone. "Carry on, please. I'm just here to have a word with Mrs. Chubb."

One by one, the staff returned to their work, though Michel was a great deal quieter as he turned his attention back to his cooking.

"Philip said you had something important to tell me," Cecily said as the housekeeper stared at her with anxious eyes.

"Oh, yes, I do." Mrs. Chubb wiped her hands on her apron. "I wanted you to know that Mazie has been found. P.C. Northcott stopped by here to let us know."

"Oh, thank God. Is she all right?"

Mrs. Chubb lowered her voice. "Yes, I think so, but she's been arrested for the murder."

"I expected as much." Cecily felt a deep sense of sorrow for the girl's plight.

"I knew Philip would probably be the first person you saw when you got back from London, so I told him to tell you that. He must have forgotten what I said."

Which he had, until he'd remembered and shouted it out, Cecily thought ruefully. She wished her housekeeper had found someone more reliable to pass on the news, but it was too late now. The damage had been done. "Well, thank you for letting me know."

Mrs. Chubb wore a worried frown as she stared at her. "What will happen to the girl? I still can't believe she killed that man on purpose. It must have been an accident, or something. Or maybe she was trying to protect herself from his advances." She shook her head. "You know what some men are. I heard that he'd been following Mazie around. Charlotte said they seemed more than friendly, if you know what I mean."

Charlotte, Cecily thought, was entirely too vocal with her opinions. She would have to have a word with the girl. "Well, let's not jump to conclusions. I will try to speak with Mazie and see if I can find out what happened." She raised her voice. "Meanwhile, I'd appreciate it if all of you would keep silent about this. Unfortunately, Philip announced to everyone far and wide that we have had a murder in the hotel, so I'm quite sure there will be questions. Say as little as possible. Insist that you know nothing about it and eventually the gossip will die down."

"You hope," Mrs. Chubb muttered. "What I don't understand is what Mazie was doing meeting that man in the laundry room at midnight. She must have been out of her mind."

"That's what I intend to find out."

Cecily was about to leave when Michel called out, "Mazie, she eez just a child. She does not know what she does. She did not kill anyone on purpose."

"Thank you, Michel." Cecily smiled at him. "I am quite sure Mazie would appreciate your belief in her."

"It eez not just my belief, *madame*. All of us here, we believe the same. *Non?*"

A chorus of voices answered him. *"Oui!"*

Cecily sighed. Now Michel had half the staff talking in

atrocious French. She headed for the door, calling out, "Thank you, everyone! The meal smells delicious, Michel! Keep up the good work!" She was out the door before she could hear his answer.

Instead of joining Baxter in their suite, she headed to her office, where she put in a telephone call to the constabulary. After a lot of clicks and buzzes, and the operator's voice assuring her she would be put through immediately, she eventually heard Sam Northcott's voice on the end of the line.

"'Allo! Police Constable Northcott at your service. What can I do for you, Mrs. B?"

Cecily came straight to the point. "I hear you have arrested Mazie Clarke for the murder of Lord Farthingale."

"Yes, m'm. We found her hiding with her belongings in the back of Dolly's Tea Shop, under the stairs. Dolly didn't even know she was there." He paused a moment before adding gruffly, "At least, that's what she says."

"Did Mazie tell you what happened?"

"She told us a lot of lies. That's what she told us."

"What exactly did she tell you?"

"That I can't say, m'm. I locked her up until the inspector can get down here and question her."

Cecily's pulse quickened. She needed to talk with Mazie before Inspector Cranshaw confronted her. Once Mazie was in that monster's hands, there would be no chance of her coming even close to her housemaid. "Sam, it's very important that I talk with Mazie immediately." She hesitated, then firmly added, "It could mean a matter of life or death."

"Oh, cripes, m'm. That does sound a bit dire. But—"

"No buts, Sam. I'm on my way. Please have Mazie

available for a private conversation." She hung up before the constable could answer her. She'd found that the best way to deal with P.C. Northcott was to take command. It confused him and she usually got her way before he realized what was happening.

Now, all she had to do was to keep up the pressure once she arrived at the constabulary. Hopefully she would be granted access to the prisoner, and with any luck, she would find out exactly what happened in the laundry at midnight.

Reaching the dining room, Gertie paused at the door. She could hear someone's voice speaking loud enough for the whole hotel to hear her. Whoever it was sounded agitated, like she was spoiling for a fight.

Gertie pushed open the door and walked in to find Charlotte standing in the middle of the room, her arm raised in the air, spouting something about standing up to the tyrants and showing the world that women mattered.

"Bloody hell, Charlotte!" Gertie charged over to her. "Keep your voice down or you'll have Chubby down on us like a ton of rocks."

Charlotte looked at the door. "She can hear me?"

"Everyone can flipping hear you. What are you doing anyway?"

"I'm practicing my speech. For the protest at the Christmas parade."

Gertie felt her jaw drop. "Wot! What Christmas Parade?"

"The one in Wellercombe. The suffragettes are going to march in it."

Gertie widened her eyes. "They're letting you march in the Wellercombe parade?"

Charlotte shrugged. "Not exactly letting us, no. We're going to take them by surprise and join them."

"Are you blinking bonkers?"

Charlotte looked offended. "That's what protests are, you ninny. You go where you're not wanted and you make them listen. You said you went on them, so you should know."

"I do know." Gertie shook her head in disgust. "Which is why I'm telling you you're bloody daft if you think you can just barge into one of the biggest Christmas parades in the country and not get into real trouble. You're dumber than I thought you was."

Charlotte tossed her head. "I never said I didn't expect trouble. But I'm telling you, if those bobbies think they can lay their hands on me, then they're in for a shock. I'll bash them over the head with my signboard. So there."

Now Gertie was really worried. It was obvious that the girl had no idea what she was letting herself in for, and if someone didn't stop her, Charlotte could end up in jail and maybe even die in there.

Short of telling Chubby, however, which would cause just as much trouble, she couldn't see any way to stop the girl. She knew determination when she saw it, and Charlotte's eyes were full of it. "How are you going to get time off to go? You can't tell Chubby where you're going. She'd put a stop to that right away."

"I'm swapping my afternoon off with Lilly. I told her I was meeting a friend in town."

Gertie felt defeated. There was only one thing to do. It

was the last thing she wanted to do, but if it kept her friend out of trouble, then she would do it.

"All right," she said quietly. "I'll try to get time off to go with you. But if I do, you have to swear to me that you will listen to what I say and do what I tell you to do."

Charlotte's eyes had lost their look of desperation as she grinned at Gertie. "Promise." She swiped a hand across her chest. "Cross my heart."

"And whatever you do, don't tell no one where we're going or what we're doing."

"All right, I won't." For the first time, Charlotte looked uneasy. "It'll be all right, though, won't it? I mean, the suffragettes have protests all over the country, especially in London."

"Yeah, and sometimes people get hurt." Gertie gave her a hard look. "If you want to change your mind, you'd better do it before we get there. 'Cos once we're there, it'll be too late to back out."

Again Charlotte raised her chin. "I'm not backing out of nothing. Someone's got to stand up for women's rights, and I might as well join them." She raised a clenched fist in the air. "Deeds, not words!"

Recognizing the motto of the WSPU, Gertie heaved a sigh. She didn't like the thought of marching with them at all, but someone had to keep an eye on Charlotte, and she was the only one she knew of who could do it. She only hoped they would both come out of it unscathed. "Well, right now," she said, "the only deeds you need to worry about is getting these tables laid for dinner."

"Speaking of deeds," Charlotte said as she arranged a

folded serviette in the center of a place setting, "what do you think about Mazie getting arrested for murder?"

Gertie shook her head. "We're not supposed to talk about it."

"Not when anyone's around, but we're on our own now." Charlotte plucked another serviette from the tray. "It looks like we were wrong about her being innocent."

"They haven't proved nothing yet." Gertie hated the thought of the housemaid behind bars. She hadn't had much to do with her, as Mazie spent most of her time cleaning and doing laundry, but the few times she'd talked to her, the young girl had been polite and respectful. She'd made Gertie feel important—something that didn't happen often. "I just hope they find out what really happened, and it turns out that Mazie didn't do it."

Charlotte paused, the serviette still held in her hand. "If Mazie really didn't do it, that means whoever did bump off that bloke is still hanging around, maybe waiting for his next victim."

Gertie dismissed that with a laugh that didn't sound too convincing. "Don't worry, whoever did him in isn't going after maids. He's going after the toffs, ain't he." She gave Charlotte a hard look. "And don't call them blokes. If madam hears you, she'll box your bloody ears."

Charlotte shrugged, and laid the serviette down on the table. "Well, I'm going to keep my eyes skinned anyhow." She looked up at Gertie. "You should, too. Any one of them footmen could be a killer and come after you. You never know who you can trust."

For a second or two the image of Clive flashed through

Gertie's mind. Shaking off the memory, she muttered, "Just let 'im try, that's all. I'll bloody clobber the daylights out of him."

Charlotte giggled. "I bet you could and all."

"Yeah, well, we'd better get these tables laid before *we* get the daylights bashed out of *us*." Gertie hustled over to the sideboard and picked up a tray of glasses, wincing as they rattled against each other. Charlotte's words had unsettled her nerves. She just hoped the bobbies found out who had bumped off the poor sod before he came after someone else.

Charlotte was right. She needed to keep looking over her shoulder. Shuddering, she took a glass from the tray and set it upside down on the nearest table. From now on, she'd be on her guard. Like Charlotte said, you never knew who you could trust.

CHAPTER

❀ 8 ❀

Cecily marched into the constabulary slightly out of breath and brimming with determination. The young constable on duty at the desk recognized her immediately and sprang to his feet.

"Mrs. Baxter! What a pleasure! What can we do for you?"

Cecily squared her shoulders. "Good evening, Albert. I am here to speak with your prisoner, Mazie Clarke."

Albert's freckled face turned pale. "Ah, I'm afraid that won't be possible, m'm. P.C. Northcott left strict instructions that no one be allowed to talk to her."

"I see." Cecily cast a glance around her. She had never felt comfortable in this room, with its bare floorboards and harsh faces peering out from the wanted posters pinned to the walls. The strong odor of soot from the potbelly stove in the corner irritated her nose, telling her the stove's chimney was in dire need of cleaning. As were the dust-covered cabinets against the far wall. It was a dismal place in which to work, and she felt sorry for the young man behind the desk.

Turning back to him, she demanded, "And where is P.C. Northcott? I'd like a word with him."

"Left for the day, m'm." The constable sent a meaningful look at the clock. "It's after hours now. I'm on night duty until the morning."

The dratted man had no doubt left before he would have to deal with her, Cecily thought, with a good measure of resentment. "My sympathies, Albert." She moved closer to the desk. "It's vitally important that I talk to Mazie. I am sure we can come to an understanding?"

Albert's expression reflected a sudden desire to flee. "I'm sorry, m'm. My orders, you know."

"Yes, well, we all know that orders can be bent a little. I won't tell anyone I spoke with my housemaid. She is still under my care as my employee, and I have a right to speak with her. I don't believe she has been formally charged yet, am I right?"

Albert backed up a step or two and started stammering. "I s'pose so, not until the inspector gets here anyway. But—"

"Ah-ah-ah!" Cecily held up her hand, palm facing out. "Not another word, Albert. Now open that door and let me through to the holding room."

Albert made one last attempt at restoring his authority. "I can't, Mrs. Baxter. I worked hard to be a constable. I don't want to lose my job."

"And you shan't. I'll make sure of that." Cecily walked around the desk and took up a stand at the locked door. "Open this at once, Albert, or I shall report you as being insubordinate."

Albert's eyes widened in alarm. "I'm only doing my job."

"Then do as I ask." She gave him a tight smile. "And all will be well. I promise. I shall only be a second or two, and no one will ever have to know."

For a moment she thought he would hold his ground. He stood staring at her as if conjuring up the courage to order her to leave.

Crossing her arms, she gave him her most commanding frown. "*Now*, Albert."

"Yes, m'm." To her relief, he opened a drawer and pulled out a ring of keys. Selecting one, he walked over to the door and unlocked it. "Five minutes, m'm," he muttered. "*Please.*"

"I swear," Cecily told him, "and thank you, Albert. I shan't forget this." Flashing a smile at him, she slipped through the door.

She found Mazie in one of the two holding cells at the back of the building. To her immense relief, the other one was empty, meaning she'd have privacy for her conversation with her housemaid.

Mazie lay on a disheveled bunk, fully clothed except for her shoes. When Cecily called out her name, she stirred and sat up.

Her eyes were red and swollen from crying, and her cheeks were so pale, Cecily feared for the child's well-being. The moment she saw Cecily, she burst into noisy sobbing that echoed through the barren walls.

"Shhh!!" Cecily touched her lips with her finger. "We don't want to bring in the constable. I'm here to help you, but you need to calm down and talk to me."

The ragged sobbing slowly subsided as Mazie gained control.

"That's better." Cecily drew closer to the bars. "Now, I don't have long, so quickly, tell me what happened between you and Lord Farthingale in the laundry room."

Mazie gulped, and shook her head. "Nothing. I mean, I didn't meet Lord Farthingale in the laundry room, and I didn't write no note." She drew a quick cross over her chest. "'Pon my heart, I didn't, m'm."

Cecily frowned. "Then why did you run away?"

Tears started spilling down the housemaid's cheeks again as she climbed off the bed and crept closer to the bars. "I went into the laundry room that morning to fetch the sheets and pillowcases for the maids' beds, and there he was, lying on the ground with his eyes wide open and staring. I was going to run and tell Mrs. Chubb about it, but then I started thinking about my arrangement with him and how people might think I done him in, so I ran." She gulped. "I know it was a stupid thing to do, but I was scared no one would believe me."

Cecily barely heard the last words. "Your arrangement? What are you talking about?"

"I unlocked the wine cellar door for him, m'm. I know he wasn't a guest and wasn't supposed to go down to the card rooms, but he gave me a lot of money to let him in and my mum needed the money so bad and . . . I wanted . . . to help her. . . ." She dissolved into more sobbing and returned to the bed, where she flopped down and covered her face with her hands.

"Listen to me," Cecily said firmly. "What you did was wrong, but I believe you when you say you didn't kill him. Now, how about the note? You say you didn't give it to Lord Farthingale?"

Mazie dropped her hands and raised her tearstained face. "No, m'm, I didn't. I really didn't. The constable showed me the note and I could never write fancy like that. My writing looks like a spider crawled all over the page. That's what my teacher told me in school. I kept telling the bobby I didn't do it but he wouldn't listen."

Of course. Cecily chided herself for not realizing that earlier. The hand that wrote that note certainly didn't belong to this child. The writing was bold, precise, and educated. A style that would, perhaps, belong to an aristocrat?

"I wished I hadn't done it afterwards," Mazie said between sniffs.

Confused, Cecily stared at her. "Done what? What are you saying?"

She was relieved when Mazie said quickly, "I mean letting him into the card rooms. I know it was wrong, but he gave me money to help him, and my mum needed it so bad and that's why I said I would, but I wish I hadn't now. He was really horrible to another gentleman in there."

"Horrible? In what way?"

"He lost at a game and accused the gentleman of cheating. They were both going at it hammer and tongs, and the other gentleman told Lord Farthingale that if he wasn't careful, someone would shut that revolting mouth of his once and for all."

Cecily leaned closer. "Do you know the name of the other gentleman?"

Mazie thought for a moment. "I think it's Cooper—no, Compton?" She shook her head. "No, it weren't that. Something to do with hair, I think. Combs?"

"Edwin Coombs," Cecily said quietly.

"That's it!" Mazie sighed. "He was really angry with Lord Farthingale. I thought it would come to blows between them, but then Mr. Coombs got up and left."

"Did Lord Farthingale leave then also?"

"No, m'm. He went on playing for a while."

"And this was the night before you ran away?"

"Yes, m'm." Mazie's lip trembled. "I never should have done that. I should've come to you instead."

"Well, if something like this happens again, you'll know better." Sending up a silent prayer that the child never had to experience anything so devastating again, she added, "Try not to worry, Mazie." She moved even closer to the bars. "I promise I will find out what really happened and we will soon have you out of here."

Mazie didn't look too convinced, but at least she had stopped crying. She sniffed, dashed her forefinger across her nose, and murmured, "Thank you ever so, m'm."

Cecily squinted into the shadowed cell. "Do you need anything? Is there anything I can bring you?"

Mazie shook her head. "Thank you, m'm. I don't need nothing, but if you could just call in on my mum and let her know I'm all right? She must be worried half out of her wits."

"I will do that. Stay strong, Mazie. I will get to the bottom of this, I promise." With that, Cecily hurried back out to the office. She hated leaving the young girl alone back there, but the best way to help her was to get on the trail of the real killer, and as soon as possible.

Albert shot to his feet, relief flooding his face as she

swept through the door. Without a word, he sprang over to lock it, then turned to look at her. "She's all right, isn't she?"

Somewhat comforted by his concern, she nodded. "At the moment, yes, but she's scared to death. She didn't do this, Albert, and I intend to prove it. Please tell P.C. Northcott when he arrives in the morning that I need to speak with him right away."

"Yes, Mrs. Baxter. I'll be sure to tell him."

"Thank you, Albert. Good night." She left the building, drawing her cloak around her as the bitter wind stung her cheeks.

Henry sat hunched up on his seat as she approached the carriage, his cap pulled low over his face. A sea mist had rolled in from the ocean, blanketing the flickering glow from the gas lamps and creating halos around the globes. The darkness made it difficult for Cecily to see Henry's face, but she could tell the lad was shivering with cold.

"Henry," she said as he opened the carriage door for her, "next time you wait for me like this, please seat yourself inside the carriage. There's no need for you to freeze out there on the box."

"Yes, m'm. Thank you, m'm."

His teeth were chattering, and Cecily felt guilty for not mentioning it before. Normally Charlie drove her carriage, but lately he'd been kept busy ferrying the hotel guests back and forth.

Ordering Henry to return to the hotel, she climbed up onto her seat and settled back for the ride. She had intended to stop by Mazie's home to have a word with her housemaid's mother, but that would have to wait until the next day.

Henry needed to get back to the Pennyfoot and into the warmth, and she could not delay their return another minute. The last thing she needed was a sick footman when they were in the midst of their busy Christmas season.

Already the lines of Henry's duties were blurred, considering he took care of the motorcars, as well as assisting Charlie in the stables. Henry was a little bit of everything—a mechanic, a groom, a footman, a coachman, and whatever else was needed at the time.

It would be a huge loss to the hotel if he should fall ill. As would any of her staff.

Such as Mazie, for instance. Frowning, Cecily recalled her discussion with the housemaid. Convinced beyond doubt that the child had nothing to do with Lord Farthingale's murder, she turned her thoughts to who might have had reason to dispose of Lord Percy Farthingale. Edwin Coombs, perhaps?

Falsely accusing the gentleman of cheating could have repercussions for Mr. Coombs. Other players would view him with a certain amount of suspicion, and if he were fortunate enough to win a large amount, there would be some dissention among his fellow players as to his integrity. They could even banish him from their midst, which would severely curtail his enjoyment of the holiday season, not to mention the possible further ostracism once he returned home.

That sounded like a strong reason to silence someone, or extract revenge for the damage already done.

Cecily stared out of the window as the carriage bounced and jolted along the Esplanade. It was too dark to see the ocean, except for a thin line of foamy waves reflected in the glow from the gas lamps. Once more, tiny snowflakes frolicked in the wind, melting as they touched the pavement. It was only a matter of time before the heavier snow arrived, covering the roads and making things difficult for the horses.

As the carriage rounded the curve, she caught a glimpse of sparkling lights in the distance. The glow from the windows of the Pennyfoot Hotel were calling out their welcome, and as always, the sight of them warmed her heart. She would soon be back in the comfort of her suite, discussing the day's events with her husband.

Now that Baxter had finally accepted her penchant for solving crimes, he had become a vital partner in her pursuit of justice. She had fought him hard and long to arrive at this enviable state of affairs. For so many years he had disapproved of her chasing after villains. Fearful for her well-being, he had done his very best to dissuade her, even to the point of forbidding her to continue her quests.

That had caused so much dissention between them, she had feared for the solidity of their marriage. She knew that was the reason he had even considered a position abroad. But then he'd announced that although he still didn't approve of her activities, he was prepared to help her in any way that he was able.

She had accepted the offer with delight, though not without reservations. Her husband was not as practiced as she with sleuthing, and she was concerned that he might land in trouble. Her fears were realized when he was attacked by a criminal, but thankfully he had survived. The experience had only strengthened his resolution to assist her, and although she still had qualms about it, she couldn't be happier.

Now she couldn't wait until she could tell him what she had learned from Mazie, and her theories about the murder. At the thought of it, she felt a delicious shiver of anticipation. Solving intricate crimes had become so much more enjoyable now that she had a viable partner with whom to share the experience. Leaning forward, she fixed her gaze on the approaching lights.

Charlie dropped the last armful of hay in the end stall of the stables and patted the horse standing nearby. "Don't gorge yourself or you'll be getting fat." He turned toward the gate and smiled as the horse nudged him in the back. "All right, Majesty, I'm going. Good night and sleep tight."

He closed the gate just as Henry appeared in the doorway, carrying a full bucket of water in each hand. The lad's shoulders were bowed with the weight of the buckets, and Charlie shook his head. Henry might be good at tending to motorcars, but he was useless with the heavier chores. He just didn't have the strength or stamina to keep up with them.

Walking toward the boy, Charlie frowned. He should toughen up the lad a bit, and build up those muscles. That would be a lot more helpful than teaching him how to walk like a man. Some weight-lifting might do the trick. He had seen a set of dumbbells stored in the coal shed. He didn't know who they belonged to, but since no one apparently was using them, it surely would be all right to borrow them.

He'd tried lifting them himself, but had quickly decided

his muscles were fine just the way they were. But Henry, now, well, he could certainly use a little help. Yeah, that's what he'd do. Start with the lightest one and build up. He'd have Henry swinging those pails around in no time.

He looked up and abruptly halted. Henry had lowered the buckets to the floor and was staring at him as if he'd gone bonkers. Realizing that he was grinning like a clown, Charlie straightened his face. "I'm off for the night. Make sure all the troughs have enough water before you go to supper."

"Yes, sir." With a heavy sigh, the lad bent over and took hold of the bucket handles.

Charlie wrestled with indecision as a strong urge to help the boy conflicted with the awareness that it was the assistant groom's job to fill the troughs and he wouldn't be doing Henry any favors by taking over his tasks.

No, the best way he could help the lad was to build him up, and that was exactly what he was going to do. Feeling satisfied with his decision, he nodded at Henry and headed out into the cold night.

Now his mind was concentrating on warming his insides with some of Michel's excellent cooking. A hot, savory stew, perhaps, or a large slice of steak and kidney pie. The thought of it made his stomach rumble and he quickened his step.

As he hurried toward the kitchen door, he saw the glow of a lamp swinging in the darkness, reflecting on the long skirt of a housemaid. He couldn't make out the girl's face, but he could see the coal bucket swinging in her hand. It had to be Lilly, since she usually filled the buckets at night.

For a long moment he struggled with his need to feed his

stomach against the opportunity to begin his courtship with the girl. Reminding himself that there wouldn't be too many opportunities to catch Lilly alone, he turned around and caught up with her.

"Need some help?"

He'd spoken from behind her, and she let out a shriek that would have scattered the seagulls if they hadn't already bedded down for the night. The bucket crashed to the ground, fell over, and rolled noisily across the bumpy gravel.

Shaken by the unexpected reaction, Charlie shot a look over his shoulder, expecting to see an anxious Mrs. Chubb barging out the kitchen door.

"What the heck are you doing, Charlie Muggins! You scared me half to death."

Charlie looked back to see Lilly's white face peering at him in the light from the lamp. "Sorry, luv. I just thought you might need some help." He leapt over to the fallen bucket and picked it up. "Here, I'll fill it for you." He bounced back to her side. "You just hold up the lamp so we can see our way."

Lilly just kept staring at him, as if she hadn't understood what he was saying.

Charlie shivered. The snowflakes were still falling, but they'd grown thicker, and in the reflection from the lamp, he could see the white specks beginning to settle on the ground. His light coat was no match for the biting wind from the ocean, and he could actually hear Lilly's teeth chattering.

"Do you want me to help you or not?" Hearing the irritation in his own voice, he cleared his throat. "Come on, luv, let's get to the coal shed and fill this thing."

"I'm not going to the coal shed or anywhere else with you."

She's actually sounded scared, and he peered at her face. "I'm not going to hurt you. I just want to help. Honest." He was a bit offended that she'd actually thought he'd try something.

"I'll take the bucket now, thank you." Lilly held out her hand. "You go indoors. Your supper is waiting."

"Well, all right, if you want to be like that." Charlie handed over the bucket and she practically snatched it from his hand.

Just then he heard footsteps on the frosty ground. He didn't need to see in the dark to know it was Henry, on his way back to the kitchen.

He felt a tug low in his stomach as he turned back toward the building. All thoughts of helping Lilly vanished as he headed for the kitchen door, his entire body aware of Henry following behind him. It was hunger attacking his gut, he assured himself as Henry caught up with him.

Something he didn't understand made him stop and signal to the boy to go ahead of him. Henry gave him a nervous smile as he slipped through the door, and Charlie swallowed. That boy was messing up his mind. It was driving him crazy going back and forth between wanting to turn Henry into a proper man and fancying him. This had to stop.

Like it or not, Lilly was going to succumb to his charms sooner or later. And it had better be sooner. He would win her over, or his name wasn't Charlie Muggins. Then he could get rid of his fascination with forbidden goods.

Right now, however, he needed to put some grub in his

belly. His stomach growled in approval, and heaving a sigh, he went in search of his supper.

Cecily laid her knife and fork on her plate and sat back with a sigh. "That was absolutely delicious. I swear we have the best chef in the entire country."

Seated opposite her in the privacy of their suite, Baxter smiled at his wife. "I always amazes me how much food you can devour in one sitting. You must have been ravenous."

Cecily patted her stomach. "I was, but I have to admit, I could eat twice as much of Michel's shepherd's pie. Just the smell of it has me swooning."

"I'm sure he'd be gratified to hear that." Baxter reached for his brandy and took a sip before adding, "So, you are convinced that Mazie is innocent of the crime?"

"I am." Having told him about her conversation with the housemaid, and her words with Albert, she was anxious now to learn his opinion. "What do you think about it?"

"About Mazie?" Baxter frowned. "I think you're right. I think someone else wrote that note to lure Farthingale to the laundry room."

"Precisely. Now I just have to convince Sam Northcott of that."

"That won't be easy. Once Northcott makes up his mind, he won't listen to anyone who contradicts him. He's a stubborn nitwit."

"What's worse, he could convince Inspector Cranshaw that Mazie is guilty."

Baxter snorted. "Another damn idiot."

Cecily was inclined to agree. "Which is why we really need to pursue this as quickly as possible and solve this murder."

Baxter heaved a sigh. "Very well. So, who do you think might have committed the dastardly deed? His wife?"

"Possibly. Or Edwin Coombs."

Baxter raised his eyebrows. "Coombs? What makes you think so?"

"He was angry with Lord Farthingale for accusing him of cheating."

"But would that be a strong enough motive to kill him?"

Cecily lifted her serviette from her lap and placed it on the table beside her plate. "I've been thinking about that. Lady Farthingale mentioned that her husband was celebrating a lucrative business transaction. That's why they were spending Christmas in Badgers End."

Baxter nodded. "I see. You think that Farthingale and Coombs had a business deal that went sour."

"Maybe. Mr. Coombs would not want to be labeled a cheat. It could affect any future business affairs for him."

"Ah, I see what you mean. Coombs would know that Farthingale had some kind of arrangement with Mazie. He most likely thought there was something nefarious going on, just as Charlotte surmised. He could have written the note, convinced that the man would run hotfoot to meet his paramour." He tapped the table with his fingers. "But wouldn't that rule out Farthingale's wife? She couldn't have known about Mazie. I doubt very much her husband would have told her about his illicit affair."

"Well, it wasn't an affair at all, if Mazie is to be believed."

"Obviously Farthingale thought it was, if he responded to a note from her inviting him to meet her in private at midnight."

"True, and you are right in that it's extremely unlikely that Lord Farthingale would mention the maid to his wife." Cecily frowned. "Unless we can find someone else with a motive to get rid of our victim, it would seem that Edwin Coombs is our only suspect."

"So, what do we do now?"

"I will have another word with Mr. Coombs." Cecily pushed her chair back from the table and stood, bringing her husband to his feet. "In the morning. It's too late to confront him now."

A look of alarm crossed Baxter's face. "If you're going to have it out with him, I want to be there."

"I'm not going to accuse him or anything. I will just ask a few questions, that's all. Now that everyone in the hotel presumably knows about the murder, it won't seem out of place for me to question the guests."

"That blasted fool Philip." Baxter grunted in disgust. "I hope you severely chastised him for spreading the bad news."

"I reprimanded him, yes." She wasn't sure that what she actually said to Philip could constitute a reprimand but she wasn't about to admit that. "But at least he also blurted out that the killer had been arrested, which should set our guests' minds at ease. As for Mr. Coombs, I don't want him to have an inkling that we suspect him. That will put him on guard. So, it's better if I talk to him alone. I shall be perfectly safe."

"I wonder how many times I've heard that before," Baxter

said grimly. "Just make certain you are within shouting distance of help if you should need it."

"I will, I promise." She moved closer and took his arm. "Now come and sit with me by the fire and enjoy the rest of your brandy."

His worried frown disappeared as he looked down at her. "That's the best suggestion I've heard all day."

With an answering smile she took a seat opposite him in front of the fireplace. This was the perfect end to a busy day, she thought, as she watched the flames lapping at the glowing coals. Now, if she could just solve the crime and bring Mazie home, her contentment would be complete.

CHAPTER
❀ 9 ❀

The following morning, immediately after enjoying breakfast with Baxter in the dining room, Cecily parted company with her husband and went in search of Edwin Coombs. She found him in the library, perusing the crowded shelves with such intensity, she felt obliged to enquire, "Are you looking for a specific title?"

He seemed startled to see her, and fumbled with his words. "No, er . . . thank you, I . . . er . . . I was just looking for something to pass the time. Eleanor, my . . . er . . . companion, wanted to go shopping alone, so I thought I'd catch up on some reading."

Cecily smiled. "A very worthwhile pursuit. What sort of books do you prefer?"

Edwin shrugged. "I'm not exactly an enthusiast. Something that moves along quickly, I suppose."

"Such as a good mystery novel?" Cecily peered at a shelf

and plucked a book from it. "Have you read a Sherlock Holmes story?"

The gentleman's face brightened. "Yes, I have actually. It was called *The Hound* of something. Most enjoyable."

"*The Hound of the Baskervilles.*" Cecily held out the book. "That is Sir Arthur Conan Doyle's third Sherlock Holmes novel. This is his second one. I think you will enjoy this one, too."

Edwin took the book from her and studied the spine. "*The Sign of the Four.* Hmmm. Sounds intriguing."

"It is a fascinating mystery, yes."

"Then I'm sure I shall enjoy it." He opened the book and started casually turning the pages. "By the way, I hear you have quite a mystery going on in the hotel."

"Oh?" Cecily made an effort to sound unconcerned. "And what is that?"

Edwin kept his gaze securely on the book, rapidly turning the pages without reading a word. "I heard that the gentleman we were discussing earlier had passed away."

"Yes," Cecily said cautiously, wondering how Edwin Coombs knew the identity of the victim. Philip had not mentioned Lord Farthingale's name in his startling announcement. "An unfortunate start to the holiday season, I'm afraid."

Edwin seemed to struggle with indecision for a moment before murmuring, "I don't know how much truth there is to the rumor, but I did hear that there was some question as to how he died."

Cecily studied him for a moment. Was he asking out of curiosity, or because he needed to know how much she actually knew about the murder, and how close she was to apprehending the killer?

Remembering her promise to her husband, she felt a stab of guilt. She wasn't exactly within shouting distance of help. Then again, the man surely wouldn't attack her here in the library in broad daylight, when anyone could walk in at any given moment. *Would he?*

Deciding that she was being overly cautious, she said carefully, "The police constable is investigating his death, but so far nothing has been established. It's the usual procedure when someone passes away unexpectedly."

"Wearing a woman's scarf about his neck?" Edwin murmured.

Cecily stared at him. "How did you come by all this information?"

Edwin shrugged. "I believe it was Sir Clarence who brought up the subject. A group of us were discussing it last night at the card table."

"Really. I wonder how Sir Clarence heard about it."

"There's a lot of chin wagging going on in the hotel. He could have heard it from anyone. After all, servants are notorious for spreading gossip."

Not my servants, Cecily assured herself, though she did wonder if perhaps Philip had been accommodating the guests by readily answering their questions. Reminding herself to have a sterner word with her desk clerk, she said lightly, "Well, I'm sure the news of Lord Farthingale's demise is not all that upsetting for you."

Edwin raised his eyebrows. "What makes you say that?"

Cecily ran a finger across the corner of the library table, pretending to check for dust. "I did hear that you were not the best of friends with the man."

Edwin's face darkened. "I assume you're referring to the confrontation I had with him the other night. News does get around fast in this place."

Cecily allowed a slight smile. "As you say, people will gossip."

"Well, if you're suggesting that I had something to do with Farthingale's death, I can assure you, I did not kill the man."

Realizing she had, perhaps, stepped over the line, Cecily hastened to contradict him. "Oh, no, not at all, Mr. Coombs. I was just wondering if, during the course of your argument, Lord Farthingale might have mentioned something that could help us in our enquiries."

After staring at her for a long, uncomfortable moment, Edwin said quietly, "I honestly don't remember what was said. We had both been indulging in a little too much scotch, and we were both overheated. I should have known better and held my tongue. As it was, we caused an unfortunate spectacle, and for that I apologize. I should have simply ignored the fool and continued with my game."

Cecily was sorely tempted to ask him for details of the argument, but decided she had gone far enough with her questions. Perhaps Sir Clarence could enlighten her, since he was also in the room and undoubtedly overheard the dispute. "Well, I appreciate your indulging me," she said with a smile. "I shan't trouble you any further. I hope you enjoy the book."

"I'm sure I shall." He actually looked relieved, and she took that impression along with her as she left the library.

Was Edwin Coombs's disagreement solely about Lord Farthingale's accusation of cheating, she asked herself as she made her way to her office, or was it about a more serious matter, such as a questionable business deal? Hopefully, Sir Clarence could give her the answer to that.

Promising herself to waylay that gentleman as soon as possible, she entered her office and sat down at her desk. There were tasks she had to take care of first, and the sooner she saw to them, the sooner she could continue her investigation. With luck, she could find the answers before the forbidding presence of Inspector Cranshaw descended upon her.

She reached for the pile of invoices waiting for her attention, but just then her telephone rang. After going through the tedious routine of answering Philip and the operator, she finally heard Sam Northcott's voice on the line.

"Albert said as how you wanted to speak with me," he said after a brief greeting.

"Yes, I did." Cecily paused, not sure what she could say to him without revealing her visit to her housemaid. "I wanted to tell you that I have strong reason to believe that Mazie did not kill Lord Farthingale."

The constable's pause on the end of the line warned her that he was not prepared to take her word for it. "Do you have proof, Mrs. B?"

She sighed. "Not exactly, but—"

"No buts, Mrs. B. Like I said before, all things point to her. I have to keep her here until Inspector Cranshaw gets here and he can question her. He already knows all about it.

He just has to finish up his case in Wellercombe before he can look into this one."

"Yes, but, Sam, perhaps you could release Mazie into my care until the inspector can arrive. I promise I will see that she doesn't run away again."

She wasn't really surprised when he answered, "I'm sorry, Mrs. Baxter, I 'ave to follow the law, and the law says I keep the suspect under lock and key until the inspector can talk to her. Good-bye, m'm."

The line clicked in her ear, and she hung up the receiver. There was only one way, she told herself, that she could obtain Mazie's freedom, and that was to find the real killer. And the sooner the better.

Kneeling in front of the massive fireplace in the ballroom, Gertie sat back on her heels. She held a can of blacklead in one hand and a cloth in the other as she inspected the grate for any smudges that might mar its shiny surface.

This wasn't normally her job, but with Mazie gone, it had left the housekeeper shorthanded, and she had asked her chief housemaid to fill in where she could.

Behind her, Gertie could hear Charlotte humming a tune she didn't recognize. Probably something the girl had heard down the pub, since that's where she seemed to spend a lot of her spare time.

Not that they had much spare time. One afternoon off a week and a rare whole day off for something really special. Still, it was enough. There wasn't much to do in Badgers End, especially in the winter. Nothing that she could afford anyway.

She flicked a glance over her shoulder at Charlotte, who stood at a table close by vigorously polishing a silver candlestick. "What's that you're humming?"

Charlotte grinned at her. "It's called 'Daisy Bell.' They sing it down the pub."

Gertie wrinkled her nose. "I don't know why you go down there. How'd you get in there anyway? They won't let women in the public bar, where all the fun is, and you have to have a man with you in the lounge bar."

Charlotte giggled. "I can usually find a gentleman to take me in. I just wait outside until I see one on his own, and ask him if I can join him."

Gertie almost choked. "*Wot!* You lost your mind or something? That's bleeding dangerous."

"I'm a big girl." Charlotte tossed her head. "I can look after myself. There's always people all around me and it's not rough in there like in the public bar."

"What about when you leave? How do you get home?"

"On my bicycle, of course. Same way as how I got down there."

Numb with disbelief, Gertie sat back on her heels. "You are playing with bloody fire, my girl. One of these days one of those blokes is going to be wanting more than a drink, and you won't be able to stop him."

"Then he'll get what's coming to him." Charlotte leaned forward. "I carry a knife in my pocket. Just in case."

Gertie groaned. "That's even worse. The bobbies will lock you up if you knife someone."

"Then I'll just have to make sure no one bothers me. They haven't so far."

"There's always a bleeding first time." Shaking her head, Gertie went back to polishing the grate. Charlotte was a grown woman, and there wasn't much Gertie could do to save her, but she was very much afraid that her friend would get herself into some serious trouble before too long.

"I'm taking the knife when we go to the Christmas parade in Wellercombe," Charlotte announced. "I'm not going to let no cop take us in."

Clutching the cloth to her chest, Gertie twisted around on her knees to face her. "Now, wait a blinking minute. Knifing a bugger what attacks you is one thing. You could plead self-defense. Knifing a bobby is something else. You could hang for that."

Charlotte shrugged. "It's the price we women have to pay for the vote."

"No, we don't." Gertie heaved herself off the floor. "That's too much to pay. And I'm not going to be part of it. So, unless you promise me on your mother's grave that you won't take a knife, I'm not going with you to the protest."

"My mum's not dead."

Gertie sighed. "You know what I flipping mean. Now promise me."

"All right." Looking disgruntled, Charlotte shrugged. "I promise. But don't blame me if we get hauled off to the clink."

"If we get hauled off to the clink," Gertie said grimly, "I'll blame you for the rest of my bloody life." With that, she stooped down to retrieve the can of blacklead.

"Does that mean you've got the time off to go with me?"

Gertie straightened. "It means I'm going to try. I haven't

asked yet. I'll tell Chubby I want to see the parade, and she'll probably let me go."

"Good."

"Just don't take a knife."

"All right, I said I won't." Charlotte ducked her hand into her pocket and drew out a small sheathed knife. "I'm going to carry it with me until then, though."

Gertie widened her eyes. "Wot? What for?"

"In case our murderer comes after me, that's what for." Charlotte dropped the knife back into her pocket. "I'm not taking any chances. Just in case it's not Mazie."

Gertie shot a look around the empty ballroom. "Shush! We're not supposed to talk about it."

Charlotte sighed. "Well, all right, but some of the guests are getting a bit jumpy about it. I've had a couple of 'em asking me if it's true the killer has been caught."

"What did you tell them?"

"I told them that's what I'd heard. I told Mr. Baxter and asked him what I should say, and he said it was all right to say that."

"Then keep saying that."

Just then a shrill voice rang out from the far end of the ballroom. "Come along, girls! Stop your dawdling! We have a rehearsal to conduct."

Gertie closed her eyes. Phoebe Carter Holmes Fortescue and her dance troupe. That was all she needed to make this a perfect morning. She still had the grate in the second fireplace to polish, and now she would have to listen to the awful caterwauling of Mrs. Fortescue's dancers, if she could call them that.

Opening her eyes again, she saw Phoebe marching across the floor like a suffragette on the warpath, with a bunch of silly women trailing behind her.

"You there! Gertie?" Phoebe's voice penetrated Gertie's skull like a dull sword. "Have you seen Archie? Where is that man? He was supposed to be working on my set this morning."

Before Gertie could answer, Charlotte sang out, "I can go and look for him for you, Mrs. Fortescue!"

"No need!" Archie's deep voice answered her, and Gertie looked over at the stage just in time to see him emerge from the wings. "Morning, Mrs. Fortescue! I've been backstage getting a few things together."

A chorus of murmurs and giggles erupted from the young women clustered in a group in front of the stage.

Gertie rolled her eyes. Those stupid girls acted like little kids instead of grown women.

"I've been waiting for a footman to come and help me," Archie explained as Phoebe advanced to the door that led to the wings. "Mrs. Baxter promised me some help but he hasn't got here yet."

"I'll help you!" Charlotte dropped the candlestick onto the table and rushed toward the stage.

Shaking her head, Gertie watched her dash past Phoebe and plunge through the door.

Phoebe halted with a cry of protest. "Really! Such manners. Is there no discipline with this hotel staff?"

Gertie folded her arms and leaned back against the table. This was going to be good.

Phoebe had now reached the door, and beckoned to her

unruly dance troupe with an imperious arm. "Get to your marks onstage, *now*. We don't have all day."

With a great deal of nudging and shoving, the dancers followed their director through the door.

Meanwhile, Charlotte had arrived onstage and was standing close to Archie, gazing up into his face as if he were a bloody king.

Gertie rolled her eyes. Talk about being obvious. It was a wonder the girl wasn't groveling at his blinking feet.

Even Archie seemed somewhat surprised by this show of aggression. He backed away a step or two, muttering something Gertie couldn't hear. She tried not to gloat about that. After all, it was none of her business if Charlotte wanted to chase after a man.

Phoebe sailed out onto the stage at that moment, screeching at the top of her voice. "Get off my stage this minute, you little hussy! I have a performance to rehearse."

Charlotte turned on her at once. "I was just trying to help."

Archie stepped forward. "It's all right, Mrs. Fortescue."

"No, it's not all right." Phoebe advanced on the girl. "I know what you're up to, and I won't have it. This man is here to build my set, and you will leave him alone to do it. I want no distractions to slow him down. Do I make myself clear?"

The dancers were now grouped at the edge of the stage, whispering and snickering among themselves. Gertie was beginning to feel sorry for Charlotte, then reminded herself that the girl could take care of herself. She'd made that very clear.

Charlotte folded her arms in a gesture Gertie knew well. Her friend was not going to give up without a fight.

Just then the ballroom doors opened and one of the footmen wandered in. Gertie recognized him as Wally, a quiet-spoken young man with a shock of ginger hair and a face full of freckles. He stood looking up at the stage, apparently wondering what was going on.

Not surprising, since Phoebe was now red in the face, waving her arms about as she screamed at Charlotte, while her faithful dancers stood cheering her on. Archie was quietly talking, obviously trying to defuse the situation, while Charlotte was mouthing off something Gertie mercifully couldn't understand.

The noise was deafening, and Wally seemed frozen to the spot. Thankfully, after several moments of chaos, Archie caught sight of him and waved to him to come up onstage.

Once up there, Wally had to push his way through the group of dancers, which intensified their giggling. The young man's cheeks burned by the time he reached Phoebe. He stood there for so long, Archie was forced to signal to her that the footman was standing behind her.

Phoebe stopped yelling and spun around to face the terrified young man. "Where have you been? We've all been waiting for you. I need work on this set to begin immediately. *This minute!* Do you understand?"

Wally backed away from her, mumbling his apologies. Charlotte must have felt sorry for him, as she snarled something at Phoebe and marched offstage.

Gertie watched as order was gradually restored. Archie took Wally's arm and led him back into the wings, while

Phoebe yelled commands to her dancers, finally getting their attention. Charlotte appeared in the doorway and tramped over to Gertie, still in a huff judging from her face.

"That old biddy," Charlotte muttered as she reached her friend. "Who the heck does she think she's talking to?"

"A housemaid," Gertie said, getting worried now that the fun was over. "You'll get it in the neck if she goes bleating to madam. You're not supposed to talk that way to your betters. Just keep your fingers crossed Chubby doesn't hear about it, or you could be out of a job."

Charlotte shrugged. "She attacked me for no reason."

"Well, you was interfering with her rehearsal."

"I was offering to help Archie." Charlotte's scowl disappeared. "I'd help that man do anything, anytime. He's a real corker, that one." She sighed, switching her gaze to the ceiling. "I can see myself married to him. I really can." With one hand at her throat, she wandered back to the tables and picked up another candlestick.

Gertie grabbed up her polish and cloth and headed over to the second fireplace. All this fuss and palaver had lost her time. Chubby would be gnashing her teeth by now, wondering why her chief housemaid wasn't in the dining room, helping to get the tables ready for lunchtime. She was all behind now, thanks to Charlotte and her chasing after Archie Docker.

Gertie dropped to her knees and slammed the tin of blacklead down on the hearth. She should be feeling happy for her friend, glad that Charlotte had found someone to cozy up to and have fun with, and instead of that, all she was feeling was resentment.

She didn't know why she was jealous of Charlotte. Gertie leaned forward and attacked the grate with vengeance. Maybe it was because she didn't have no one, like she had last year, and it didn't look like she ever would now. She was getting too old to meet someone new, even if she wanted to, which she didn't, she hastily assured herself.

It was just that this Christmas was going to be a whole lot different than the last one. And that was sad.

In the next instant, she chided herself. She had the twins, who loved her, she had a job she enjoyed, people she liked working with, a nice room to live in, and plenty to eat. Not many people like her could say the same thing.

Count your blessings, she told herself, *and stop wishing for stuff you know you can't have.* It was good advice, but she couldn't prevent a small sigh escaping for what might have been.

Cecily had to wait until the afternoon in order to speak with Sir Clarence. Apparently that gentleman had taken part in the game shooting that morning, and didn't arrive back until the midday meal was being served.

Cecily waited until he had left the dining room before accosting him in the foyer. He was alone, apparently having left his wife to her own pursuits.

At first, she thought he would decline to talk to her, but good manners held him in place when she approached him. "Sir Clarence, I shan't keep you a minute. I just have one question to ask you, if you have a moment?"

He sent a hunted look to the staircase, as if wishing he

could escape up them, then said, with a note of resignation, "How can I help you, Mrs. Baxter?"

"I was talking to Mr. Coombs this morning, and it appears he had a serious argument with Lord Farthingale during a card game. Since you were present, I was wondering if you could tell me what the argument was about."

Sir Clarence's jaw tightened as he glared at her. "I have not the slightest idea. I have to say, Mrs. Baxter, these questions seem entirely unnecessary. I was under the impression that Lord Farthingale's assailant has been arrested."

"One of my housemaids has been arrested, yes." Cecily drew a deep breath. "I am, however, convinced she did not kill the gentleman. I am trying to discover the true culprit, and I was hoping you could help me."

Sir Clarence nodded. "I wish I could help you, Mrs. Baxter, but I'm afraid I know little of what transpired between the gentlemen. Perhaps you should question Mr. Coombs?"

"Oh, I have." Cecily sighed. "Unfortunately, he wasn't entirely informative."

"You suspect him of the crime?"

"Oh, no," Cecily answered hastily. "I'm merely trying to find out exactly what happened leading up to the murder."

"Isn't that the work of the constabulary?"

"It is, but I have found very often that people are more forthcoming when speaking with me, rather than answering a constable's questions. I have had some success in the past in solving a crime, and I have high hopes of solving this one."

"I see." Sir Clarence stroked his chin. "Well, it seems obvious to me that whoever silenced Lord Farthingale tied a scarf around his neck to implicate a woman. Rather despicable if you ask me, but then, anyone who would take someone else's life would most likely be a person of inferior breeding. You might have to look among the male members of your staff to find your killer, Mrs. Baxter."

Bristling at the slur to her beloved household members, Cecily took a moment to answer. "You may well be right, Sir Clarence, though it pains me deeply to suspect any of my servants."

"Yes, well, one never knows these days whom we can trust." He turned his head to look at the grandfather clock in the corner. "Please excuse me. I have an appointment I must keep."

"Of course." Cecily still struggled to gather her thoughts. His comment had reminded her of Madeline's dire warning. *You will face danger from an unexpected source.* She would do well to remember that. "Thank you for taking the time to speak with me. You have been most helpful."

For a second he looked puzzled, then he twitched his lips in the semblance of a smile, turned sharply on his heel, and marched toward the stairs.

Cecily followed more slowly, her mind working over the conversation that had just taken place. Both Sir Clarence and Kevin Prestwick had put forth the idea that the killer had used the scarf in order to make everyone think a woman had committed the crime.

She had to confess, she had not once suspected a member of her staff guilty of the crime. Indeed, she had been determined to clear Mazie's name. Now that Sir Clarence had put the idea in her head, however, she could not dismiss it.

Was it possible that this was a crime of jealousy? Perhaps

one of her footmen, having become enamored of Mazie, saw her with Lord Farthingale and decided to rid himself of his competition?

It was a scenario she did not want to consider, yet she had to admit, she could not deny the possibility existed. She would have to make enquiries to find out if Mazie had an admirer, and that was something she was not happy about at all.

CHAPTER 10

Charlie took a last look into the cracked mirror hanging on the far wall of the stables. His hair could do with a comb, but since only sissies carried one, he would have to improvise. Raking his fingers through his dark curls, he rehearsed in his mind what he would say to Lilly. That is, if she stayed around long enough for him to say anything at all.

He frowned at his reflection. Granted, it had been a while since he had fancied a girl enough to chase after her, but normally he didn't have a lot of resistance to his advances. Lilly, on the other hand, seemed determined to give him the cold shoulder.

That bothered him. Either she was playing hard to get or he was losing his touch. Nah, that would never happen. Charlie Muggins was at the top of his game, and Lilly would come around if he dealt the right cards.

Having assured himself that he looked the best he could under the circumstances, he set off for the kitchen.

His timing was dead-on. He was halfway across the courtyard when the object of his affections appeared in the doorway, framed in the reflection of the kitchen's gas lamps. He knew that every evening, after the guests' dinners had been served, Lilly would bring out the milk churns and stand them by the kitchen door for the milkman to fill. He'd expected to have to wait for her, but here she was, bending over to set the churns on the ground, giving him the perfect opportunity to approach her.

"Good evening to you!" he sang out as he strode toward her. "Do you need a hand with those?"

Lilly straightened, peering into the darkness in his direction. "Is that you, Charlie?"

"It is, indeed. Charlie Muggins at your service." He walked into the light, his mouth stretched tight in a grin.

Lilly backed up a step, as if she were afraid he might attack her or something.

His grin faded as he stared at her. Most of the snow that had fallen the night before had thawed, but there was still enough on the ground to reflect the light back to her face. She actually looked scared.

All his bravado melted away and he softened his voice. "I was just wondering if you needed my help, that's all."

She shook her head. "Thanks, but I'm all right."

He half expected her to turn tail and disappear back into the kitchen, but she sort of hovered there as if trying to make up her mind about something.

Feeling a little more confident, he tried to sound offhand.

"I was thinking of going down the pub later tonight. I don't suppose you'd like to come along?"

Her eyes widened, looking huge in her pale face. "Are you asking me out?"

Aware that he had shocked her, he hurried to reassure her. "Only if you want to. I mean, I just thought you might like to join me, but if you don't, well, that's all right, I just—"

"Charlie."

She was almost smiling, and he relaxed. "What?"

She looked at him for a long moment, then said quietly, "I think there's something you should know. I promised not to tell, 'cos it's supposed to be a big secret, but it's going to come out sooner or later and you might as well know now."

Now his curiosity was at full throttle. "What is it, then?"

Lilly turned back to peer through the crack in the kitchen door. Apparently satisfied, she turned back to Charlie. "Before I tell you, you have to swear to me up and down that you won't tell another soul."

"I swear, I swear." Charlie was almost sweating with anticipation.

"Cross your heart, then."

Charlie drew his thumb over his chest. "There, crossed my heart. Now tell me."

Lilly leaned forward. "It's about Henry. He's really—"

A piercing voice sliced through the air, making them both jump. "Lilly? Where are you, girl? These dishes are not going to clean themselves. Get back in here this minute."

"Yes, Mrs. Chubb!" Lilly mouthed *Sorry* at him, leapt through the door, and slammed it shut behind her.

Charlie stared at the closed door for several seconds.

Henry's really what? What was it Lilly was going to tell him? Whatever it was, he had a strong feeling it was something important he should know.

Or maybe he already did know. Was Lilly trying to tell him that Henry was queer? Nah, how would she know that?

Maybe Henry was her boyfriend. He found that even more unbelievable.

He was sorely tempted to march into the kitchen and demand Lilly finish what she was going to tell him. Only he couldn't do that. For one thing, he didn't want to face Mrs. Chubb's wrath, and for another thing, whatever it was Lilly knew, she'd promised to keep it secret. She certainly wasn't going to spill the beans with everyone listening in.

No, he'd have to corner her again when she was alone. Until then, he'd just have to wait, even though he was busting to know the big secret. Either that, or he could ask Henry what it was all about.

Yeah, that was it. Henry should be back in the stables by now, waiting for the last motorcar to be returned. Henry would tell him what all this secret stuff was about.

Hunching his shoulders against the cold, Charlie headed back to the stables.

"I'm going down to the ballroom," Cecily announced to Baxter as Charlotte disappeared out the door of their suite with what remained of their evening meal. "I know Archie is working late on Phoebe's set and I want to have a word with him."

"That man must like working. I saw him the other night

walking across the bowling green to his cottage. It must have been past midnight."

Cecily raised her eyebrows. "What were you doing on the bowling green after midnight?"

Baxter smiled. "I wasn't outside. I saw him from the window. I couldn't sleep that night, so I went into my office to check on a report." He frowned. "Come to think of it, that was the same night as Farthingale's murder. Archie might have seen something useful. You should ask him."

"I will. Do you feel like accompanying me?"

Baxter got up from his chair and stretched his arms above his head. "I would, my dear, but I have a report I need to finish up that has to be sent up to London tomorrow. Unless this is something that requires my attention?"

"Oh, no, I can handle it." Cecily smiled up at him. "I just want Archie to look at the gas lamps above the staircase. He's supposed to be taking care of them, but I noticed on my way up here earlier that two of them were not functioning properly. The wicks must be low or something. I need him to replace them before he goes to bed. We don't want someone tripping in the darkness and falling down the stairs."

"No, indeed." Baxter hid a yawn behind his hand. "We have enough problems as it is. Some of the guests are apparently anxious about the murder. I understand they have been asking the maids about it. Mostly if it's true that the perpetrator has actually been apprehended."

"Well, the police have made an arrest, so that should calm their fears."

Baxter slid his arms out of his coat and reached for his

smoking jacket. "As long as they are not aware we believe in Mazie's innocence."

"I know." Cecily sighed. "I'm afraid I made a mistake this afternoon. I did mention to Sir Clarence that I wasn't convinced Mazie was guilty. I probably shouldn't have said that. From what I hear, Sir Clarence can be quite free with information he overhears."

"That's unfortunate, but I wouldn't fret too much over it. We've weathered these problems before and come through it unscathed. I'm sure we will do it again." He leaned forward and deposited a kiss on her cheek. "Now I must take care of that report."

She watched him cross the room to enter the boudoir, wishing she could share his optimism. If word got around that Mazie could be innocent of the crime, the guests would be peering in the corners for fear of confronting a murderer. Or worse, they could simply decide to cut short their visit. It had happened before.

Cursing herself for her slip of the tongue, Cecily left the suite and made her way to the staircase. All was quiet in the hotel now. The guests were most likely either enjoying a card game in the cellars, or perhaps gathered in the library for some conversation before retiring for the night. Some of them were apparently already returning to their rooms, as she thought she heard footsteps behind her.

When she glanced back over her shoulder, however, she could see nothing in the dim light from the gas lamps.

Reaching the top of the stairway, she looked over the banister to peer at the curving steps below her. The pool of darkness stretched halfway down the top flight of stairs. She would have to chastise Archie for neglecting his duty.

Which was a shame, since otherwise she was most satisfied with his work. The maintenance man he had replaced had been a disaster, and it had been a tremendous relief to find someone reliable. Until now.

Shaking her head, she started down the stairs.

She had just reached the shadowed part when she heard a soft sound behind her. She started to turn her head, but at that moment something nudged her back. Making a grab at the handrail, she uttered a cry of despair as her fingers slipped on the polished surface and she pitched forward.

She was falling, tumbling headfirst down the stairs.

A burst of pain exploded through her head as she smacked into the sharp curve of the railings, and then everything slowly turned black.

Charlie could see the yellow reflection of a lamp swinging back and forth as he approached the open door of the stable. Henry must be moving around, probably checking out the motorcars for mud splatters before he closed up for the night.

Now that he was about to confront the lad, Charlie felt decidedly uncomfortable. He could feel his heart beginning to thump, and in spite of the cold, his forehead felt damp with sweat.

He was coming down with something, he told himself, as he reached the doorway. A hot toddy when he got back to his room should take care of that.

An odd buzzing sound caught his attention. He stepped inside the musty-smelling barn, and abruptly halted. Hardly able to believe his eyes, he saw Henry halfway down the stalls, actually dancing—waltzing around and around with the lamp swinging to and fro in his hand. The buzzing sound he'd heard was Henry humming, his squeaky voice slightly out of tune.

Charlie felt mesmerized, part of him repelled by the sight, and a bigger part of him relishing the grace and elegance in the twirling vision in front of him. He stood there staring for far too long before he managed to pull himself together.

"What in the world are you doing?" he roared, angrier at himself than at the boy.

Henry let out a high-pitched shriek and dropped the lamp. It fluttered when it hit the ground, but thankfully the glass didn't shatter.

Charlie leapt forward and snatched it up. "Dammit, Henry, you could have set this whole place ablaze." He scrubbed the floor with his foot, making sure that no oil had spilled out. "Don't you know how bloody dangerous it is to drop an oil lamp on straw?"

Henry didn't answer, but just stood there, his chin resting on his chest.

His cap hid his face, and Charlie could swear he heard a sniff. Staring at the lad, he said harshly, "You're not crying, are you?"

Henry shook his head and sniffed again.

Now Charlie felt like a heel. The boy had obviously been enjoying cavorting around like that, and he had to barge in on him and spoil it. In the next instance he reminded himself of his mission to toughen up the lad. Dancing around like a girl was not what he had in mind.

"Here," he said gruffly, and thrust the lamp at Henry. "Finish up here and make sure you close up properly afterwards. We don't want the wolves wandering in here attacking the horses."

"Wolves?" Henry's face shot up in alarm and Charlie could see a tear glistening in the corner of his eye.

With a loud sigh, Charlie shook his head. "It's just an expression. There ain't no wolves in this country. They got wiped out donkey's years ago. Just close up everything and get to bed, all right?"

Henry nodded, and Charlie left, feeling only slightly better. As it was, the memory of Henry's woeful face stayed with him long after he'd snuggled under the eiderdown on his narrow cot that night. He was nodding off when he remembered he'd never asked Henry what the big secret was all about.

Tomorrow, he promised himself. Tomorrow either he'd ask Henry, or better still, he'd waylay Lilly when he could get her alone and find out what was going on. With that, he closed his eyes and let sleep take over.

Cecily groaned as she tried to open her eyes. A hammer inside her head pounded against her skull, and there was something wrong with her right knee. It pained her greatly to bend it.

"She's coming around," a familiar voice said, somewhere out there in the misty darkness.

Another voice, even more familiar, uttered a heartfelt "Thank God."

"Cecily," the first voice said with a soft urgency that warned her that something was awry.

She forced her eyelids to open, wincing as the light increased the hammering in her head. "Yes. I'm here." She was lying down, she realized. In her suite. On the couch. What was she doing lying on the couch, and why in the world was Kevin Prestwick bending over her with a stethoscope dangling around his neck?

This was most inappropriate. She started to raise her head, but the hammer in her skull turned into a knife and she groaned again, falling back on the pillow that cushioned her head.

"Lie still," the doctor ordered. "You've had a bad fall."

"Thank God," the second voice said again. "I thought you were dead."

She frowned as a white face swam in front of her. It had sounded familiar, yet there was a note in it she couldn't quite understand. Anxiety? Fear?

"Cecily, my love. How are you feeling? Tell me you are all right."

She blinked, finally recognizing the beloved face of her husband. Now she was beginning to remember. She was on the stairs. It was dark. She'd heard a sound behind her and . . .

"You tripped down the stairs," Kevin said. "You received a nasty crack on the head, and there's quite a swelling, which is going to be sore for a while."

"Those blasted lamps were out," Baxter said, sounding

furious. "Our maintenance man is responsible for this. You were concerned that someone might trip in the dark, and that's exactly what happened. He deserves to be sacked for this."

"No!" She'd intended to sound forceful, but it came out more as a croak. Clearing her throat, she tried again. "It was hard enough to find a decent maintenance man, I really don't want to go through that again. I'll speak with him. He's been terribly busy building Phoebe's set, and hasn't had the time to attend to everything."

Baxter swore under his breath. "That blasted pantomime. When are we going to put a stop to that nonsense? Look at all the time and effort our staff goes through for a two-hour performance that more often than not ends up with a total disaster."

Realizing that her husband's wrath stemmed more from his concern over her condition than Phoebe's feeble attempts at producing a masterpiece, Cecily managed a smile. "It's tradition, darling. The guests expect it. They look forward to it."

"I will never in a million years understand why."

"It's the anticipation of not knowing when the disaster will occur," Kevin said dryly. He peered down at his patient. "I imagine you have a massive headache."

"I do," Cecily assured him, resisting the inclination to nod.

"I will give you something for that." He held up his hand. "How many fingers do you see?"

She blinked. "Three, but why—"

"How many now?"

"One."

"Good. Now follow my finger."

He moved it slowly from side to side and she followed it with her eyes.

Seemingly satisfied, he straightened. "I don't think there's any serious concussion, but if the headache gets worse, or doesn't go away in a day or two, give me a ring. All right?"

Again she prevented a nod from increasing the pain. "All right."

"Do you hurt anywhere else? I did check you out pretty thoroughly. You don't seem to have any broken bones, which is good news."

She flexed her right knee. The pain had decreased somewhat, and since there didn't appear to be any serious damage to it, she murmured, "I have no doubt I'll make a full recovery."

"Well, you're bound to be sore for a day or two after a fall like that. If things don't improve considerably in a few days, then please let me know." With that, he tugged the stethoscope from his neck and tucked it in his black bag, then took out a small bottle of liquid.

Turning to Baxter, he added, "See that she rests up for at least a day or so. I'll leave this with you, and if you need more, send a footman to my office. The directions are on the bottle."

Baxter took the bottle from him and peered at it. "Thank you, Kevin. I appreciate you getting here so fast."

"Not at all. I'm just happy things turned out not to be as serious as we first thought." He looked back at Cecily. "Do not do anything strenuous for at least a week. You need to take care of that crack on the head."

"I will." She smiled up at him. "Don't worry, Kevin. I'm stronger than I look."

"And just as stubborn." He picked up his bag, muttering something to Baxter as he left the room.

"What did he say to you?" Cecily demanded when her husband returned to her side.

"He said he didn't envy me trying to keep you in check."

She eyed him with suspicion, not sure if he was telling the truth, or if he was reluctant to repeat whatever it was Kevin had said. "How amusing."

Baxter gave her one of his rare smiles. "Indubitably. Now, tell me what happened out there. You are usually so sure-footed and you've been up and down those stairs a million times."

She shrugged, flinching as the movement sent pain through her head again. "Accidents happen. It was dark, I was thinking about other things and wasn't paying attention. I was in too much of a hurry, I suppose. I will be sure to pay attention in the future."

He stared at her for so long, she was sure he was going to accuse her of keeping something from him, but then he twisted the cap off the bottle, poured a measure of the brown liquid into the cap, and leaned over to cradle her shoulders in his arm.

"Drink this," he said, "and then I'll go down and have a word with Archie. I'll have him take care of those lamps before he goes to bed. We certainly don't need anyone else taking a tumble down there."

Obediently, she sipped the bitter liquid, shuddering as it drained down her throat. "Thank you, darling, but please, be careful how you handle Archie. He's normally an excellent worker and I would really hate to lose him."

"Very well, my love." Baxter replaced the cap on the bottle and stood it on the sideboard. "I shall hold my temper as best I can. It won't be easy, however." He bent over. "For a dreadful moment or two, when Charlotte summoned me to the stairs and I saw you lying there, I thought I'd lost you. I felt such a terrible devastation. It was quite unbearable."

Cecily reached up and touched his cheek. "You will never lose me, my darling. I'm certain we will be together throughout eternity."

"I'll hold you to that." He dropped a quick kiss on her mouth then stood up. "I will be back shortly. Please, don't try to get up. You may not be steady on your feet and the last thing I want is for you to fall again."

She reached for his hand and squeezed it. "Don't worry. I'm quite drowsy. I'll probably doze until you return."

"Good. Then I will help you into bed." With a worried nod at her, he left the room.

Left alone, Cecily stared at the ceiling and struggled to replay those moments on the stairs. Everything was hazy at best. She thought she remembered hearing a sound behind her just before she tripped. Had she imagined it, or had someone behind her jolted her so that she missed her footing? Had someone wanted her to fall? Someone who was afraid she was getting close to the truth and was determined to put an end to her investigation?

Part of her had been tempted to tell Baxter about her suspicions. Had she done that, however, he would have panicked, and out of worry, he would no doubt have forbidden her to continue the investigation.

In which case, there would have been subterfuge and evasions between them, something she had always hated in the past. No, it was better that he not be made aware of her misgivings.

So far, none of the guests had departed from the hotel. So, if the killer was, indeed, one of her guests, he was still in the hotel. On the other hand, since, at least to her knowledge, none of her staff had left, if one of them were guilty of murder, he also remained in the hotel.

The missing link at the moment was motive. Just about anyone had opportunity and means. What she needed was to know who had a strong reason to kill Lord Farthingale.

Her thoughts immediately switched to Edwin Coombs. He had obviously held a deep dislike for Lord Farthingale, though she had to admit, the motive was somewhat thin. The victim had accused Coombs of cheating, but was that enough reason to kill a man? Was Coombs, perhaps, afraid that his reputation would be ruined if someone was allowed to broadcast far and wide that he was a cheat?

Then again, there remained the mysterious business matter to which Lady Farthingale referred. For a moment Cecily had forgotten about that. If only she could find out with what sort of transaction Lord Farthingale was involved, it might shed some light on the puzzle.

Her mind flashed back to her conversation with Lady Farthingale. It must have been frustrating for the widow to be celebrating something without knowing what it was. Why had her husband refused to tell her the details? Had there been something unsavory about the deal? Was that why Coombs had felt compelled to silence the man?

One thing seemed certain—if Lord Farthingale's killer had been responsible for her falling down the stairs, it couldn't have been Mazie, since she was locked up in jail.

Cecily sat up. Maybe she should inform Sam Northcott of her suspicions. Although she had no proof that it was more than a simple accident—it was merely a feeling of something not quite right about it all. She seriously doubted that Sam would accept that as a reason to release Mazie.

Her head ached with the effort to work it all out. She acknowledged that she could be simply overreacting—to nothing more than an unfortunate coincidence. On the other hand, it could mean that the killer was aware she was on his trail and had issued a warning. If that was so, she would have to be very much on her guard until the culprit was identified and arrested.

Madeline's warning flashed through her mind. *Beware of the beast that flies.* She still didn't know what it meant, and there was no use asking her friend to explain. Madeline never remembered anything she said while in a trance.

Cecily shifted her position, trying to make her knee feel more comfortable. She had faced danger many times before, and she had survived. She would do so again, she promised herself, and tried to ignore the little voice warning her that someday, if she didn't take care, her luck would finally run out.

CHAPTER
❋ 11 ❋

"I don't know why on earth you would want to go to the Wellercombe Parade," Mrs. Chubb exclaimed the following morning. She stepped back from the kitchen table and dusted her hands on her apron, sending a cloud of flour into the air. "It's noisy, crowded, and there'll be pickpockets everywhere."

Gertie tossed her head. "Well, they won't get nothing from me, as I ain't got nothing to give them."

"Well, just hope they don't bash you over the head out of frustration."

"They do and I'll bash them right back."

The housekeeper stared at her in alarm. "That's the best way to get hurt, Gertie. Stay away from that mess." The last words were spoken over her shoulder as she walked over to the sink.

Wondering what Chubby would say if she knew her chief

173

housemaid intended to join in a protest, Gertie said lightly, "I promised Charlotte I would go with her. She's never seen the parade. She's really excited about it and I don't want to disappoint her."

Mrs. Chubb turned on the tap and rinsed her hands in the icy water. "Well, the both of you do work hard, so I suppose you deserve a little fun now and then. It won't be easy, doing without you both on the same afternoon, but I suppose we can manage. Lilly will just have to do double duty, and I can spare one of the housemaids to help out."

Gertie grinned. "Ta, ever so! I'll tell Charlotte we're going to the parade this afternoon."

The housekeeper snatched a tea towel from a hook on the wall and briskly dried her hands. "Just be sure you're back here by dinnertime. Lilly will need help clearing the tables and washing the dishes."

"Course we will!" *If we're not in the clink*, Gertie silently added. In the next instant she scolded herself. That kind of thinking could get her into trouble. No matter what happened, she would see that she and Charlotte got back in time to clean up the dining room.

She kept reminding herself of that promise as Charlie drove them in the carriage to Wellercombe that afternoon. The snow had started to fall again, heavier this time and settling fast on the pavements.

Charlotte didn't have much to say on the way there. Gertie suspected the girl was worried about the possible outcome of their adventure, and she couldn't blame her. Protesting in such a visible and public display was taking an enormous risk of being attacked by the crowd or arrested by the constables.

Charlotte would never admit to having doubts, however, and Gertie told herself she could forget her hopes that her friend would change her mind. They were on their way to protest, and she would just have to do her best to see they got out of there safe and sound.

Charlie was prevented from driving too far into the town, his way barred by thick ropes slung across the High Street. He pulled over to the side of the road, and halted the carriage with a jerk that sent Charlotte tipping forward.

Her hat slipped over her eyes and she shoved it back with an impatient hand. "Why's he stopping?"

"He can't go any farther." Gertie peered out the window. "They've got a barrier across the street. We'll have to walk the rest of the way."

"In this?" Charlotte waved her hand at the fluffy snow-flakes drifting down outside the window. "It's cold out there."

Gertie grasped the faint hope. "You want to change your mind? We can get Charlie to turn around and take us back to the nice warm kitchen. I bet Mrs. Chubb would let us make a cup of hot cocoa."

For a second or two, Charlotte wavered, then she shook her head. "Nah. We came to join the protest. We suffrag-ettes have to suffer for the cause."

Charlie's voice floated down to them, sounding impa-tient. "Are you two going to get out or what?"

The horse stamped in agreement, jerking the carriage again. Gertie gave in to the inevitable and reached for the door handle. "Come on, if you're going. Charlie won't wait all day."

"He's not going to open the door for us?"

Gertie snorted. "Wot are you, royalty? We're bloody lucky he agreed to bring us here and fetch us after the parade. You upset him and we'll be walking all the way home."

Grumbling to herself, Charlotte opened the door and climbed down to the snow-frosted road.

Gertie tugged her coat collar up to shield her neck against the cold. It didn't look too glamorous, but then, she wasn't there to impress anyone. All she wanted was to get this over with and get back home.

They had to walk for what seemed like miles before they finally reached the edge of the crowd. People lined the streets on either side of the High Street—men in caps and scarves, women in cloaks and wide-brimmed hats, children jumping up and down with impatient excitement, their bare knees pink from the cold.

"Where are your mates?" Gertie asked as she pushed her way through the crowd.

Charlotte looked disgruntled and disheveled, her hat tilted on her head and one hand clutching the collar of her coat. "I dunno."

Gertie stopped so suddenly, her friend bumped into her. "Wot? You don't know where they're meeting?"

Charlotte raised her chin in defiance. "No, I only know they're going to be here."

Hardly able to believe her ears, Gertie folded her arms. "Are you telling me you're not part of their group? Do they bloody know you at all?"

Avoiding her incredulous gaze, Charlotte pretended to study the sky. "Not exactly."

"Have you met any of them?"

"Well, I did go to that one meeting, but I never got to really talk to anyone."

Gertie stared at her for a moment longer. "So, we're just going to plunge in there and join in the flipping fun, is that it?"

"Something like that."

Gertie felt her stomach churning and swallowed hard. "You do know that if something goes wrong, and it probably will, they won't give us no protection if they don't know who we are, right?"

Charlotte shrugged. "Maybe someone will remember me from the meeting. Anyway, women jump in off the street all the time to join in with the suffragettes."

"Not in a bloody public parade what the whole town is watching."

"Well, we're here now, so we might as well go through with it." Her words were echoed by the sound of music in the distance. "They're coming!" She grabbed Gertie's arm. "Come on, we have to get in there before they get too far."

Giving up, Gertie allowed herself to be dragged through the crowd. Something told her they were heading toward complete disaster, but it was too late to turn back now. She couldn't leave Charlotte to do it alone. *Just get us back safely*, she silently prayed. Her kids needed her, and the last thing she wanted to do was ruin their Christmas by being chucked into the clink.

With that frightening thought in mind, she surged forward toward her fate.

Cecily sat in front of her dressing table and studied her image in the mirror. Her cheeks looked rather pale, and she pinched them to bring some color back. Her husband was eagle-eyed, and he would raise strong objections to her leaving the hotel if he thought she was in any way under the weather.

It had taken every ounce of her willpower to refrain all morning from limping. Her knee was sore, and although the mixture Kevin had given her helped, it had not entirely masked the pain from it, nor the ache that still throbbed in her forehead.

Nevertheless, she had promised to meet both Phoebe and Madeline at Dolly's Tea Shop for afternoon tea, and she intended to keep the appointment. For one thing, she greatly enjoyed meeting with her friends in that warm, cozy place, and she would gladly walk through fire for one of Dolly's delicious scones or pastries.

For another thing, if she didn't go, Baxter would know she wasn't feeling up to par, and would insist she rest. She was in no mood for a battle of words. Indeed, she would much rather put up with a little ache here and there to spend a delightful hour or so in one of her favorite haunts.

"Henry has the carriage outside," Baxter said from behind her, making her jump. "If you're ready to leave, I'll accompany you downstairs."

She glanced up at his reflection in the mirror. "There's no

need. I'm perfectly capable of walking down them by myself."

His look told her he was not about to argue with her. "Indubitably, my dear, but I would very much like to escort my wife from the premises, so please don't give me an argument."

She managed to smother a grunt of pain as she rose from her chair. "Of course, darling. I shall be happy to take your arm. Nothing pleases me more than having my handsome husband at my side."

His mouth twitched, though lines of worry marred his brow. "Are you quite sure you feel up to going out?"

"Absolutely." She gave him a wide smile. "The medicine Kevin gave me worked miracles. I hardly feel any twinges at all."

He took her hand and tucked it under his elbow. "You will tell me if your headache returns?"

"Of course." She held her breath as he led her toward the door. The headache was easily masked, the pain shooting through her knee not so much.

Somehow, she managed to endure the climb down three flights of stairs, arriving in the lobby with a sigh of relief. She had clung rather hard to her husband's arm throughout the torture, and he looked down at her with deep creases in his forehead.

"Please take good care of yourself," he murmured as he opened the doors for her. "You know I shall worry until you return home. Perhaps I should come with you? I'm sure Phoebe and Madeline won't mind if I join you all."

Cecily uttered a light laugh. "Of course they would

mind! They adore you, darling, as I do, but this is a ladies-only outing, which unfortunately we don't manage to enjoy too often. Madeline has her daughter and her herbal cures to take care of, Phoebe has the colonel and all her pursuits to keep her busy, and I have my duties here so—"

Baxter held up his hand. "Enough! I know when I'm beaten."

He led her down the steps, and again she had to do her best to ignore the stabs of pain.

The moment Henry caught sight of them, he jumped down from the box and opened the carriage door for her.

Turning to her husband, Cecily offered her face up for his kiss.

He touched her cheek with his lips and squeezed her gloved hand. "Enjoy your ladies-only outing."

"I shall." She smiled up at him. "I shall enjoy returning to you even more."

That seemed to appease him, and he actually smiled back at her before handing her up into the carriage. Henry closed the door as she seated herself, and as the carriage pulled away from the curb, the last thing she saw was Baxter's face, once more creased in worry as he watched them leave.

Finally alone, she stretched out her leg and allowed herself a soft groan. The effort to hide the discomfort had left her feeling somewhat deflated. She needed this outing to restore her energy and incentive to continue this investigation.

The moment she entered the tea shop minutes later, she felt her resolve seeping back. Just the smell of freshly baked pastries was enough to stir the juices, and the sight of the roaring fire crackling in the brick fireplace warmed her throughout.

Dolly and her assistants had decorated the entire room. Brightly colored garlands and paper chains looped over the copper kettles, brass urns, and china teapots hanging from the rafters, while wreaths of fir filled the windows. On each table, sprigs of holly sat in silver vases, their red berries glowing above the crisp white tablecloths.

In one corner by the fireplace, a small fir tree nestled in a bright red container, its branches bowing beneath the weight of gleaming colored balls and bells, silver stars, and an assortment of figures of Father Christmas, reindeer, and carol singers.

In the corner, by the window, two women sat across from each other, holding what appeared to be a rather stilted conversation. Smiling, Cecily made her way over to them.

They looked up as she reached them. Phoebe spoke first, gushing as usual as she greeted her friend. "We were just wondering if something was holding you up," she said with a sly look at Madeline.

The other woman shook her head. "We well understand how busy you are this time of year. We're just happy you could join us."

"Of course." Phoebe looked put out, as if Madeline's comment was a jibe at her.

There had always been a certain amount of tension between Cecily's two best friends. Phoebe didn't approve of Madeline's casual attire, or the way she allowed her hair to fall loose about her shoulders, or her healing powers with herbs, or her unsettling ability to foretell the future.

Madeline, by the same token, considered Phoebe too concerned about appearances, a confirmed elitist, and far too emotional for her own good.

In spite of all that, Cecily knew quite well that they would defend and protect each other to the death if need be. Which was why she adored them both.

Seating herself on the empty chair, she let out a sigh of relief. Even those few steps from the carriage had tested her stamina.

Madeline, as always, was quick to detect something amiss. "You are looking a little pale, Cecily. You must be feeling the effects from your mishap yesterday."

Phoebe uttered a murmur of concern. "You're not ill, are you?"

Guessing that Kevin had told his wife about his visit to the Pennyfoot the night before, Cecily managed a light laugh. "No, Phoebe, I am quite well, thank you. I tripped on the stairs last night, but thankfully no real damage was done."

Phoebe's eyes, as always, were overshadowed by the brim of her hat, but Cecily could tell she was staring at her with a keen curiosity. "How awful for you, but I'm glad you escaped injury. You certainly don't need any more disasters, what with this dreadful business of your murdered guest and the arrest of your housemaid. Not that you're not accustomed to chasing after murderers. I declare, I don't understand why you put yourself in harm's way so many times. One would think that once would be far too much. Really, I—"

Cecily had tried throughout Phoebe's outburst to discreetly hush the woman, to no avail. It was Madeline who mercifully put an end to the flood of words.

"Phoebe!" Madeline reached for a scone and held it out to her. "Put this in your mouth this second and stop squawking about things that are best kept quiet."

Phoebe sputtered into silence, stared at the scone, then said in a tone as brittle as ice, "If you think that I'm going to touch that after you've mauled it about in your fingers, you are badly mistaken. I don't know why on earth you can't wear gloves, like the rest of us."

Madeline shrugged. "Fingers are easier to wash than gloves." She took a bite from the scone before dropping it on her plate.

Cecily sent her a glance of gratitude, then turned to Phoebe. "We would rather not broadcast the unfortunate incident, Phoebe. We don't want the reputation of the hotel to suffer."

"I shouldn't have said anything about it to her," Madeline murmured. "Kevin told me, of course, but I should have known better than to pass it along to someone who can't keep her mouth closed. I only mentioned it as a possible reason for you arriving late."

Phoebe raised her chin high enough to reveal her eyes and glared at Madeline. "You didn't say it was supposed to be a secret. After all, it's not the first time it's happened."

Cecily cleared her throat. "I would very much prefer that we change the subject."

Madeline sent a long look around the room. "Thankfully,

everyone seems too involved in their own conversations to pay attention to what Miss Chatterbox is saying."

Cecily quickly intervened as Phoebe began to protest. "Well, Phoebe," she said firmly, "tell us how the pantomime rehearsals are moving along. How is Archie managing the set? How does your dance group like performing *Aladdin?*"

To her relief, Phoebe snatched at the opportunity to gush about her Christmas presentation. As she listened with one ear to her friend's animated account of the mishaps of her wayward dancers, Cecily's thoughts kept wandering off to the question uppermost in her mind.

Who had reason to kill Lord Farthingale? There were a lot more questions to be answered before she could come close to the truth and rescue her housemaid, and time was running out. Any day now Inspector Cranshaw would arrive on the scene and begin his investigation. Once that happened, her hands would be severely tied. She had to find out more about Mazie's part in the mystery. Even if she hadn't been responsible for the death of Lord Farthingale, she could well be involved in some way.

"Don't you agree, Cecily?"

Phoebe's voice held a tinge of irritation, and Cecily forced her mind back to the conversation at the table. "I'm sorry. I'm afraid I was a little preoccupied. What were you saying?"

Phoebe tapped her fingers on her handbag—a sure sign she was annoyed. "Really, Cecily, if we can make the effort to meet you here, you can at least pay attention to what we say."

Cecily reached out and patted her arm. "You're quite

right, Phoebe, and I deeply apologize. Now, to what did you require my approval?"

"As I was saying, your new maintenance man is an absolute wizard. He has almost completed the set, and it is truly magnificent." She waved a gloved hand in the air to emphasize her point, narrowly missing the tiered pastry stand with its bounty of delicious treats. "I do declare, Cecily, this will be quite the most spectacular performance I have ever presented. Your guests will never forget it."

"That last part is most likely true," Madeline murmured, earning a suspicious glare from Phoebe.

Cecily could only pray that, this year, Phoebe would manage to provide an evening's entertainment without the usual chaos.

For once she was quite thankful when Madeline announced she had to return home. "My nanny has asked for the evening off," she explained, "and I need to make sure everything is in order before she leaves."

"Do give Angelina a hug from me." Cecily prepared to rise, testing her knee before she put weight on it. Although she had enjoyed the rendezvous, as always, the effort had tired her—a warning that she had not fully recovered from her fall.

As she led the way from the tea shop, it took all her fortitude to refrain from limping. She knew that if Madeline detected the slightest sign of discomfort, she would relay as much to her husband, who, in turn, would inform Baxter, and that would mean another round of protests.

Once outside on the busy street, she took a long, deep breath of the frigid air. The clouds had disappeared, and the setting sun cast shadows on the snow-covered pavements. The evening was drawing near and the darkness of night would be upon them before too long.

She drew her cloak closer about her and smiled at her friends. Both of them would be walking home, as neither lived too far from the town. Henry had returned as ordered, and her carriage awaited her, the horse impatiently snorting and stamping in the cold.

"Can I give either of you a lift?" she asked, knowing they would both refuse the offer, as they always did.

"No, thank you," Madeline said as she swept a thick wave of hair from her face. "I need the exercise to remove the pounds that I put on my hips this afternoon."

"Frederick is meeting me at the end of the street," Phoebe announced. "He's probably waiting there already, poor dear."

"Very well, if you're sure." Bidding them good-bye, she climbed up onto her seat and sank back against the soft leather with a sigh. Pain kept shooting through her knee and shinbone, and she wriggled her foot in an attempt to relieve it.

As the horse pulled the carriage away from the curb, she looked out the window. Harried-looking housewives hurried past the shops, their shopping baskets loaded to overflowing with vegetables, meats, and sundries.

Across from her a shop window glowed in the last rays of the sun, lighting up the display of evening gowns with their sparkling sequins and gold trimmings. As she watched, the door opened and a woman swept out onto the pavement. She stood on the curb, looking left and right, no doubt watching for a Hansom cab.

As the coach passed her, Cecily stared at the woman in startled surprise. She recognized that face beneath the sweeping gray hat. The woman was Lady Farthingale.

She was apparently enjoying a shopping spree, and now Cecily wanted very much to know the reason for the widow's return to Badgers End. As well as when, exactly, she had arrived.

CHAPTER
❊12❊

Gertie was already tired by the time she and Charlotte caught up with the parade, so she wasn't too chuffed about having to march along behind a bunch of shouting, chanting suffragettes waving their signs at a none-too-friendly crowd.

Not that she didn't sympathize with their cause. It wasn't that long ago when she'd done some protesting, too. She'd actually been chucked out of the Fox and Hounds for disrupting the public bar with her presence.

She had to smile when she thought about the faces of the enraged blokes trying to compete in a dart match while she and her mates stomped around the room chanting "Votes for women!"

They'd had beer and nuts thrown at them and had come out of there smelling like a dark alley on New Year's Eve, and once she'd been chased down the road by P.C. Northcott, who even back then had been too old and too fat to catch up with her.

Luckily, he hadn't recognized her, or she'd have ended up in the clink. It was that night that she'd decided she'd find some other way to support the cause. Which was why she was wondering right now why the heck she'd agreed to march in this stupid parade, in the bitter cold, with one eye out for the bobbies and the other watching in case someone in the crowd got fed up with them and threw something at them.

She cast a glance at Charlotte, who was marching along with her chin in the air like she was going to bloody war, shouting, "Deeds, not words!"

At that moment Charlotte turned her head to look at her. She said something that Gertie couldn't hear above the brass band farther down the road, the yelling of the suffragettes, and the cheers and howls from the onlookers.

Gertie shook her head and pointed to her ears.

Charlotte edged closer. "I can't hear you yelling!" she shouted.

"That's because I'm not!" Gertie bellowed back at her.

"Why not?"

Gertie was about to answer when she felt something smack hard into the middle of her back. Turning her head, she saw a bruised apple rolling away from her. She spun around, just in time to see a red-cheeked youth aiming another apple at her.

Without stopping to think, she stooped down, snatched up the apple, and threw it as hard as she could back at him.

It hit him square in the face, and he let out a howl of

pain. A roar went up from the crowd and a couple of young men surged forward.

"Cripes," Charlotte yelped. "You've gone and done it now."

"Come on!" Gertie grabbed Charlotte's hand and darted forward, plunging into the midst of the suffragettes.

There was a lot of jostling, pushing, and shoving, then a shout went up from somewhere in the group. "Bobbies! Run!"

The women scattered, and for a moment Gertie froze, trying to recognize where the biggest danger was coming from, while Charlotte stood like a statue, her eyes staring from her ashen face.

At that moment one of the young protestors grabbed hold of Gertie while her companion tugged Charlotte's arm and the two of them were dragged away from the belligerent crowd of spectators and down an alley.

Struggling to keep up with her savior, Gertie had no breath to ask where they were going. She was greatly relieved when their rescuers pulled them through a gate and down a long path that led to the doors of a church.

Once inside, Gertie could finally breathe again. After the turmoil of the streets, the heavenly silence was a welcome contrast. Sinking onto the nearest bench, she looked around her. The empty pews were decorated with wreaths of holly and bright red bows, and huge silver stars dangled from the rafters. Light streamed from the tall stained-glass windows, highlighting the altar with its red cloth and the beautiful display of holly, ivy, mistletoe, and fir.

She was still admiring the sight when one of the protestors sat down next to her. "You're new, aren't you."

"Yeah." Gertie nodded at Charlotte, who was deep in conversation with the other woman. "I came with her."

The young lady nodded. "So, what's your name?"

"I'm Gertie and that's Charlotte. She's the suffragette. I just came along to keep her company."

"Well, one thing you should always remember when you're protesting, Gertie. Never retaliate. It can get you and everyone else into a whole lot of trouble."

"I know." Gertie looked down at her hands. "I didn't think. I'm sorry. It's been a long time since I went on protests."

"It's all right. It happens now and then. I'm Rachel, by the way."

"Well, thank you, Rachel, for rescuing us. I can't believe I did such a stupid thing."

"It's hard not to hit back when you're taken by surprise."

"Don't I know it." Gertie eased her shoulders. "My back still hurts. I didn't mean to hit him, though. That was just bad luck. I only wanted to let him know what it felt like to have stuff thrown at you."

The woman grinned. "I think he got the message."

"Yeah." Gertie sighed. "Was that you calling out that the bobbies were coming?"

She nodded. "It's the fastest way to warn everybody that trouble's brewing."

"I'll have to remember that. Not that I plan on doing any more protesting."

Rachel's face fell in dismay. "Really? Why not? We need all the help we can get."

"I know, and I do agree with everything you are all trying to do. But I have twins to take care of, and a job that I love."

Sympathy crept across the woman's face. "Your children have no father?"

"Nope. I found out after we were married that he was already married to somebody else. By then the twins were on the way."

"Oh, I'm so sorry. That must have been hard."

"Yeah, it was. Luckily, I had my job at the Pennyfoot, and they looked after me and the babies, until I could afford to hire a nanny."

"The Pennyfoot?" Rachel looked surprised. "You mean the Pennyfoot Hotel in Badgers End?"

"Yeah, that's it. You know it?"

"Not personally, but a friend of mine is staying there. Harriet is a lady's maid to one of your guests, Lady Oakes."

"Oh, yeah, I know her." Gertie wrinkled her nose. "Stuck-up snob, she is. I accidentally bumped into her on the stairs, and she acted as if she'd been attacked by a gutter-snipe."

Her new friend snorted. "Well, she's got nothing to be snotty about, from what I heard."

Gertie ears pricked up. "Oh?"

"Yeah." Rachel leaned forward and lowered her voice. "I heard that her husband met her on the streets. You know, one of *them*."

Gertie stared at her. "One of what?"

Rachel sighed. "You know, a streetwalker. Someone that does it for money."

Understanding dawned, leaving Gertie speechless.

After a moment, Rachel said anxiously, "You can't tell anybody that I told you. I'd get my mate into trouble. The

Oakeses have gone to a lot trouble and even paid to keep it a secret. Harriet could lose her job if Lady Hoity-Toity found out her maid had been tattling. She only found out by accident when she heard Lady Oakes in a spat with her husband."

Gertie finally found her voice. "He knew she was one of them and he still married her?"

Rachel shrugged. "I don't think he knew at first. He thought she was just poor and alone. I suppose by the time he found out the truth, he was already in love with her." Rachel clasped her hands to her bosom and sighed. "It's so romantic when you think about it."

"Romantic" wasn't exactly the word Gertie would have used. It was hard to envision the elegant, disdainful woman as anything other than a woman of high breeding, and even harder to imagine the pompous Sir Clarence marrying someone so far beneath him.

She wasn't sure she entirely believed the story, but it was none of her business and she wasn't going to spread the gossip. Still, it was an awfully good story—too good to keep it all to herself. Maybe she'd share the news with Mrs. Chubb. Chubby knew how to keep her mouth shut.

Charlotte's sharp voice brought Gertie out of her reverie. "We need to get moving. Charlie will be waiting for us by now, and we still have to get through town."

"Be careful out there." Rachel stood up and brushed at her skirt with her hand. "Those hooligans might still be looking for you. Take the backstreets. That way you'll be harder to spot."

"Good idea." Gertie got up. "Thanks again for rescuing us."

Rachel grinned. "My pleasure. And if you change your mind, there's always a place for you in the WSPU." She looked at Charlotte. "You need to come to more meetings and get acquainted with some of the women."

Charlotte nodded, though she looked none too enthusiastic. "Maybe I will."

Which told Gertie that her friend was having second thoughts about being a suffragette. Not that she could blame her. Although infinitely worthwhile, it was a perilous path to take for little reward and a lot of grief.

She didn't breathe easy until they were safely inside the carriage and on their way back to the Pennyfoot. No matter where she went or how much she enjoyed the outing, she was always happiest when returning home to the hotel.

She was lucky, she told herself, to have a job she enjoyed and people she loved surrounding her. Who needed a bloody man when she had so much?

For an instant a vision of Archie hovered in her mind. Impatient with herself, she shut down the image and turned to Charlotte. "So, what did you think about your first protest?"

Charlotte shrugged. "It was all right, I s'pose, but I'd think twice about doing it again."

"If I were you," Gertie said, snuggling more comfortably on her seat, "I'd think a blinking dozen times about doing it again."

She didn't hear Charlotte's answer. Her mind was too busy sorting out what she needed to buy for the twins'

Christmas presents. After all, that was who was important in her life. And that was all she needed. Now all she wanted was to get home to the warm kitchen and get on with her life.

Using her knuckles, Cecily rapped on the carriage wall facing her. She wasn't sure that Henry would hear her above the clip-clopping of horses' hooves and the loud rattle and roar of the occasional motorcar. In fact, just as she rapped, one of the despised contraptions backfired, startling her horse and jerking the carriage forward.

Cecily rapped again, her irritation giving her hand more emphasis. Baxter had talked a lot lately about acquiring one of those monsters. Not only did she thoroughly dislike the idea of rattling along the street with all the noise and fumes, but she was very much afraid that her husband would get carried away and lose control of the dratted thing and cause an accident.

To her relief, Henry must have heard her, as a moment or two later, he pulled over to the curb and halted the carriage.

Without waiting for his assistance, Cecily scrambled out and onto the street. Looking back from whence they had come, she spotted the gray hat with its bright red ribbons bouncing along within the crowd.

"I shan't be a minute," Cecily said, turning to Henry. "I need to have a word with someone. Wait for me here."

"Yes, m'm." Henry looked surprised and just a little concerned, but offered no more comment, and ignoring the pain in her knee, she sped away toward the hat. Except she could no longer see it. Lady Farthingale must have entered another shop.

Reaching the spot where she had last seen the hat, Cecily glanced at the shop window. A male mannequin in plus fours stood brandishing a golf club amid a collection of cricket bats and tennis rackets. The cotton wool snow looked somewhat out of place considering the summer sports, and was the only nod to the season in the entire arrangement.

Cecily closed her mind to reimagining the display and concentrated on the matter at hand. She seriously doubted the graceful dowager would be purchasing anything from a gentleman's sports supplier, but one never knew these days.

She tried to peer through the glass aperture in the door, but it was too dark to see inside. Picking up the hem of her skirt, she pushed the door open.

One look inside told her that Lady Farthingale was not inside. Nor was anyone else by the look of it. A gruff voice from the shadowed interior growled at her, and she hastily backed out and closed the door again.

She had no better luck at any of the shops along the street, and she finally arrived back at the carriage.

Henry, who had apparently been watching her rather erratic progress in and out of doors, seemed even more concerned. "Were you looking for something, m'm?" he asked in his soft voice, which always triggered a question mark in Cecily's mind.

She smiled at him. "I thought I saw an acquaintance down the street, but I must have been mistaken. You can take me home now, Henry, though I would like to call in at the Regency Hotel on the way back.

"Yes, m'm."

Henry opened the carriage door for her and she climbed up onto her seat. If Lady Farthingale had returned to Badgers End, it was quite possible that she had also returned to the Regency. All of the other hotels in the area were most likely full for the Christmas season, and the room the widow had booked was probably still available. It was certainly worth a visit to find out if she was there.

Cecily stared out the window as the carriage jogged along the Esplanade. The dark gray sky looked ominous, but the air had warmed a little, and the wheels of the carriage made swishing noises as it plowed through the melting snow.

She jerked forward as the carriage abruptly slowed, then pulled to a stop. They had reached the Regency Hotel.

Once more Henry hopped down and opened her door, and she stepped outside, careful to raise her skirt above the wet slush. Limping up the steps, she kept her gaze on her boots, just in case a patch of ice still remained to trip her up.

An eager young man greeted her at the reception desk. Apparently, he was a recent addition to the staff, as he appeared not to recognize her. He gave her a wide smile as he asked, "May I help you, madam?"

"I am looking for an acquaintance of mine," Cecily said, casting a glance around the lobby. It wasn't the first time she had visited the hotel, but it was the first time she'd seen it decorated for Christmas.

The foyer looked somewhat drab compared to the lush arrangements Madeline had used in the Pennyfoot. A small Christmas tree stood in one corner, with a few baubles and ribbons hanging from its branches, and a single wreath clung to the railings of the staircase. The chandelier looked rather gaudy, Cecily thought, with all that silver tinsel draped over it. Still, there was no accounting for taste.

"Madam? What is the name of your friend?"

Catching sight of the gray hat, she quickly turned back to the clerk. "Never mind. I see her." Without waiting for his reply, she hurried over to where Lady Farthingale sat on a blue velvet chaise longue.

The widow seemed preoccupied, staring into space as if she were following a scene unfolding in her mind.

Cecily paused in front of her, saying quietly, "Lady Farthingale? I hope you remember me?"

The widow looked up, her entire body jerking in recognition. "Mrs. Baxter! This is a surprise!"

And not a particularly pleasant one, Cecily reflected, judging by the look on the dowager's face. "I'm sorry if I startled you. I happened to see you in the High Street and I thought you might have returned here." She sent a quick glance around her. "Would you mind if we talked in private?"

Lady Farthingale's expression registered a flash of apprehension, then she nodded. "Of course. We can go up to my room." She got up slowly, as if immensely weary, and started for the stairs.

Once inside her room, she gestured at one of the two chairs by the window. "Not terribly comfortable, I'm afraid," she murmured as she took the other seat.

Thankful to sit down, Cecily cleared her throat. "I must confess, I was surprised to see you back in Badgers End."

Lady Farthingale removed her hat pins, then took off her hat and laid it on the table at her side. "P.C. Northcott sent me a telegram yesterday morning. He wanted me to make arrangements for my husband's body. I arrived yesterday afternoon, too late to talk to the constable. Fortunately, my room here was still vacant, so I was able to stay the night. I spoke with P.C. Northcott this afternoon."

Watching Lady Farthingale's stony expression, Cecily couldn't be sure if the widow was being stoic about the ordeal with Sam Northcott, or if, perhaps, she was trying to hide the fact that she had been responsible for the attack on the stairs.

"I'm sorry," she said. "That must have been difficult."

"It was. Most upsetting."

But apparently not enough to prevent the dowager from enjoying a spot of shopping on the way back to the hotel.

Cecily was immediately ashamed of her uncharitable thought. It was quite possible the woman was telling the truth. Buying something frivolous for oneself was a common cure for a lady's distress. "So," she said brightly, "I assume you will be returning to London shortly."

"Actually, I shall be here for a day or two longer." The dowager sighed. "There are still some formalities that need to be taken care of, and I want to dispose of everything before I leave." She sent Cecily a brief glance. "Forgive me for saying so, but I have no desire to return to Badgers End. As you can imagine, this place has nothing but ugly memories for me."

"Of course. I quite understand." Cecily rose, and smoothed down her skirt. "I will leave you now, Lady Farthingale, and I wish you a more pleasing future ahead."

"Thank you." The widow also rose. "I hope you enjoy a very happy Christmas."

"And you." Cecily left her alone, uncomfortably aware that a joyful holiday was probably not in the cards for Lady Farthingale—a thought that would shortly come back to haunt her.

Climbing once more into the carriage, she made herself comfortable on the cold leather seat, her mind already revisiting her conversation with the dowager. Lady Farthingale's attitude had changed since their meeting in London.

Back then, the widow had been uncommonly blasé about the death of her husband. Now, however, she seemed despondent. It was likely that the reality of her situation had not transpired until she had actually viewed her husband's body. She could also be worried that her hand in it would be revealed and she would spend the rest of her life in prison. Or worse.

It didn't seem possible that the graceful dowager could have struck down her husband, even in anger. Then again, Cecily knew quite well that even the unlikeliest person was capable of murder if the motive was strong enough.

Lady Farthingale had obviously been unhappy in her marriage, and her husband's death gave her the escape she needed. Had she planned to rid herself of him by sending him the note, knowing that he would not be able to resist a midnight rendezvous with a pretty maid?

It would have been simple to raise the heavy flatiron and bring it down on his head as he entered the room. It would have been dark, unless he had been carrying an oil lamp. Then again, no lamp was found in the room, though the killer could have taken it away.

But if Lady Farthingale had killed her husband, why would she have tied her own scarf around his neck? Again, Sam's theory came to mind. *She thought he wasn't quite dead yet so she finished him off with her scarf.* Cecily closed her eyes as the memory of the night before came back to haunt her. Had Lady Farthingale somehow slipped into the hotel and waited for her on the stairs? Had she imagined that slight sound behind her and the nudge in the back just before she fell? Was her mind playing tricks on her?

She gave herself a mental shake. She was clutching at straws. Even if she was right about someone causing her fall last night, she couldn't imagine Lady Farthingale being that desperate.

What she needed, she told herself, was to go home, have a nice evening meal with her husband, and rest her aching knee.

Having settled that, she leaned back and glanced out the window. The carriage jerked as Henry pulled away from the curb, and she was just in time to see a gentleman hastily mounting the steps to the hotel. She recognized him instantly.

What, she wondered, was Sir Clarence Oakes doing at the Regency? Was he, perhaps, engaging in a liaison with a female companion, unbeknownst to his wife? If so, he was playing a dangerous game. She would not want to be in his shoes if his wife found out about his infidelity.

Arriving back at the hotel, she crossed the lobby to where Philip was dozing behind his desk. Baxter had been unable to locate Archie the night before, and she needed to know he had been successful today in talking to the maintenance man about replacing the wicks in the staircase lamps.

Tapping on the counter, she said loudly, "Philip, I need you to summon Archie to the lobby."

Philip started, stared at her for a moment, then mumbled, "Yes, m'm. Right away, m'm." He started to reach for the bellpull behind him, then turned back to her. "I believe he's in the ballroom, m'm. I shall have to summon one of the maids to fetch him."

"Never mind. I'll go to the ballroom myself." Wishing she had a cane to lean on, Cecily made her way slowly down the long hallway to the ballroom.

The sound of hammering reached her as she approached the doors. Pushing them open, she spotted her maintenance man on his knees on the stage in front of a façade of a palace. Archie had created a magnificent piece of scenery. The cream walls rose at least twelve feet high, and were topped with bright turquoise globular towers. The grand entrance was framed in gold, with steps leading up to the door.

As Cecily drew closer, she saw that the set actually sat on a large, round platform. Impressed, she could only stand and stare, until the hammering stopped and Archie climbed to his feet.

As he turned, he caught sight of her, and snatched off his cap. "Pardon me, m'm. I didn't see you there."

"It's all right, Archie. I didn't want to disturb you." She waved a hand at the set. "This is spectacular. Phoebe must be ecstatic."

Archie grinned. "Mrs. Fortescue is a hard one to please, if I may be so bold."

"But surely she must adore what you have done." Cecily studied the palace again. "Though I must confess, I don't understand why it's sitting on a platform."

"It's a turntable." Archie beamed with pride. "It's called the Shakespeare stage because they use it a lot in Shakespeare's plays that have a lot of different scenes. There are two other sets on it. We just have to move the whole thing around for the scenes. It saves a lot of time and effort."

"It revolves?" She moved closer. "How?"

Archie's grin grew wider. "With the help of a cartwheel and rope. I'll be backstage on the night hauling this thing around."

Cecily shook her head in awe. "Phoebe must be over the moon. She has never had such a spectacular set."

"Thank you, m'm. I'll tell her you said so. But it wasn't just me. Wally helped, and I couldn't have done all this without him."

"Then I commend Wally as well. I sincerely hope Mrs. Fortescue expresses her gratitude and gives you both all the praise you deserve. I shall advise her to mention your names at the conclusion of the performance."

"Thank you, m'm, but it's not necessary. We're just doing our job."

Impressed by his modesty, she stepped closer. "Has my husband stopped by today to have a word with you?"

"Mr. Baxter? Yes, m'm. I spoke to him this afternoon."

"Then he told you the lamps on the staircase needed attention?"

Archie pulled a rag from his pocket and wiped his hands. "Yes, m'm, he did. I looked at them, but the wicks are not burned out. Someone must have turned them down really low. I turned them back up again, so they should be nice and bright now."

Cecily stared at him, her mind racing. "I see," she said at last. "Well, thank you, Archie. Keep up the good work, and tell Mrs. Fortescue I consider her extremely fortunate to have such remarkable help with her pantomime."

"Yes, m'm. Thank you, m'm."

She was about to leave when she remembered something else. "Oh, by the way, I'm assuming you have heard about the unfortunate incident in the laundry room the other night?" She'd carefully worded her question, just in case the man hadn't heard the gossip.

She wasn't too surprised when he answered, "Yes, m'm. I heard it from one of the maids. Nasty business, that."

"Yes, very." Cecily paused, then added quickly, "Mr. Baxter happened to mention to me that he saw you crossing the bowling green on that night around midnight."

Archie's face seemed to close up. "Yes, m'm. I had to fix the plumbing in the ground floor WC and I had to wait for the guests to leave the library."

"Yes, I thought you might be working after hours." Cecily smiled to reassure him. "I was wondering if you happened to notice anything out of the ordinary as you left?"

Archie's gaze met hers. "No, m'm. I did not."

"Very well. If you should happen to think of something later, I trust you will tell me?"

"Yes, m'm. I will, indeed."

Leaving the ballroom, Cecily replayed Archie's comments about the gas lamps in her mind.

The wicks had been turned down low. By whom? And why? The answers seemed obvious. Someone had darkened the stairway, then waited for her to descend. She hadn't imagined it after all. Now that she thought about it, she remembered something else. Just before she'd reached the stairs, she'd thought she'd heard footsteps on the landing behind her.

Now there was no longer any doubt in her mind. Someone had waited for her to start down the stairs, and had given her a little push to make sure she fell.

Lord Farthingale's killer was still in the hotel and was either sending her a warning to abandon her investigation, or intended to put a halt to it permanently.

As she began the climb to her suite, she squared her shoulders. The revelation only strengthened her determination. Mazie was innocent, and the villain had to pay. Somehow, she would see to it, and soon.

CHAPTER

❁13❁

Standing just inside the stable doors, Charlie stuck his hands into the bucket of ice-cold water. Scooping up a pool in his palms, he sloshed it over his face, then reached for a grubby towel hanging from a hook on the wall.

After drying his face, he raked his fingers through his hair, took one last look into the cracked mirror, then headed out the doors. It was almost time for Lilly to put out the churns, and he didn't want to miss her.

The yard was empty when he approached the kitchen door, but there were no churns on the doorstep. Relaxing his shoulders, he leaned against the wall to wait.

After a few minutes his arm felt numb, and he pushed himself away from the wall. The cold was making his bones ache, and he contemplated going into the warm kitchen to confront Lilly. But that wouldn't work. She'd never tell him a secret with people around them.

Besides, he hadn't given up on the idea of courting her, and his chances would be close to nothing if he made a move in front of everybody. Stamping his feet, he rubbed his chilled hands together. He'd give her another few minutes. It was almost time to go in for his supper, and his chances of catching her alone after that would be shot.

At that moment the door opened and Lilly stepped outside, the milk churns in her hands. She spotted him instantly, and dropped the churns on the ground with a clatter. "Whatcha doing out here in the cold?" She turned back to the door, which stood ajar. "Trying to catch pneumonia?"

"I was waiting to see you." Charlie had a hard time stopping his teeth from chattering. "You're late tonight."

"Yeah. I got busy in the kitchen." She looked back at him. "What do you want?"

"I want to talk to you." He stepped toward her, then halted as he saw alarm flash in her eyes. "I just want to ask you what you were going to tell me the other night."

For a long moment she hesitated, then quietly closed the door. Turning back to him, she lowered her voice. "I shouldn't have said anything. It's not my secret, and I have no right to tell you. If you want to know what it is, you'll have to ask Henry."

Charlie shrugged. "He's not going to tell me anything. He's more tight-lipped than a priest in a brothel." Emboldened by the flicker of amusement he saw in her eyes, he added casually, "How about coming down the pub with me tomorrow night? It's your afternoon off, right? I'll treat you to a gin and orange."

"Sorry. I changed my time off to today."

"Well, we could go later, then. After you're finished for the day."

He wasn't really surprised when she turned away from him and opened the door again. "No, thanks. I've got letters to write." She slipped through the door, but before she closed it again, she stuck her face through the gap. "Maybe you should take Henry down the pub."

She shut the door before he could answer her. Frowning, he shoved his hands in his pockets. What the heck was she getting at? Surely, she didn't think he was . . . nah . . . he was much too virile for her to make that mistake.

That settled it. He needed a lady friend, and he needed one now. He would either have to step up his pursuit of Lilly, or find someone else to keep him company.

He reached out to open the kitchen door, just as footsteps crunched up behind him. All his senses went on alert. He knew who it was walking toward him, and he didn't like the way it made him feel. Somehow he had to get Henry Simmons out of his head, once and for all.

Without turning around, he shoved open the door and charged into the kitchen, startling Michel, who was reaching into a cupboard.

The chef uttered a fierce *"Mon Dieu!"* and leapt back, a bag of raisins flying from his hand to land on the floor. The bag split open, spilling the contents across the tiled floor.

Charlie pulled up short, muttering, "Sorry."

Michel stared down at the mess, straightened his tall chef's hat, then turned on his assailant. "Sorry? You are *sorry*? Do you know how much ze raisins cost? These are the only raisins I have for my puddings. Now they are on ze floor." He jerked his hand at his feet. "How you think I make my puddings now?"

"They're not all on the floor." Charlie squatted down, picked up the half-empty bag, and rose, handing the bag to the chef. "Here. There's still lots left."

Michel sniffed, and snatched the raisins from Charlie's fingers. "Now you pick up the rest of them, *oui?* You wash each one of them *très* carefully, and then you put them back in this bag."

He dropped the bag on the kitchen table and folded his arms. "And you do it *now.*"

Charlie winced, but before he could say anything, Henry's soft voice spoke from behind him.

"I'll help you." The lad stooped down and started picking up the dried fruit, one by one.

As Charlie stared down at him, he felt a warm feeling of gratitude spreading all over him. At least, he hoped it was gratitude and nothing more. Shaking his head, he muttered a terse "Thanks" and bent down beside his assistant to help.

Gertie slept badly that night, turning and tossing, drifting off only to dream about being chased by a gang of thugs brandishing swords. She awoke the next morning with a headache and a hearty wish that she had never agreed to go on a protest with Charlotte.

She only hoped that the girl had learned her lesson and had given up all ideas of being a suffragette. Some people, she told herself as she splashed her face and hands with chilly water, were gluttons for punishment.

Even herself once. That was before she grew up and got some bloody sense in her noggin. There were those what could take all that violence and suffering for the cause. She'd done her share, and although she was wholeheartedly with them in spirit, she was not going to risk life and limb when she had Lillian and James to worry about.

Charlotte was still snoring in bed, and Gertie leaned over to shake her awake. "Come on, lazybones, it's time to get up."

Charlotte groaned, and half opened her eyes. "I only just fell asleep a while ago."

"Then you must snore when you're awake. You'd better get moving or Chubby will be on the warpath."

"Chubby is always on the warpath."

Gertie walked over to the wardrobe and opened the door. "Yeah, well, she has to be to take charge of us lot. I wouldn't want to be in her shoes."

Charlotte struggled out of bed and yawned, stretching her arms above her head. "I wouldn't mind. I bet she gets paid three times what we do."

"She bloody earns it and all." Struggling into her corset, Gertie held her breath as she fastened the buttons. Another day closer to Christmas and she still hadn't done anything about shopping for the twins. Normally she would have bought their presents at the toy shop, but the last thing she wanted to do was run into Clive. She would have to go into Wellercombe on her next afternoon off to buy them.

Working out in her mind how she would get there and back, she pulled on her cap, frowned at her reflection, then said to Charlotte's back, "I'm going downstairs. Don't take too long getting down there. We've got to get breakfast served."

"I know, I know."

Charlotte sounded grumpy, and Gertie left her alone. The girl was probably still deciding whether or not to give up her membership in the WSPU. Not an easy decision, considering she'd been so excited about the whole thing.

Reaching the kitchen, she found the usual chaos that ensued every morning around that time. Michel crashing and banging pots and pans, Chubby yelling at the maids, and everyone dashing around the room bumping into one another. It was a bleeding miracle they managed to get everything done every morning in the proper way at the proper time.

The next three hours passed swiftly as Gertie laid tables, sliced bread, whisked eggs, washed and cut up fruit, peeled mushrooms, served the tables, cleaned them off again after the guests left, washed and dried dishes and silverware, put them all away in the cupboards and drawers, then got ready to begin on the next meal.

She was just stacking the last plates into a cupboard when Mrs. Chubb called out to her. "Gertie! Archie needs two white sheets for the pantomime set. Get two clean ones from the laundry room and take them to him in the ballroom."

Before Gertie could open her mouth, Charlotte swung around from the sink and called out, "I can take them, Mrs. Chubb! I'm finished here now." Giving Gertie a sly glance, she lowered her wet hands and dried them on her apron.

Mrs. Chubb folded her arms. "Did you hear me ask you to go, Charlotte?"

Charlotte's smile faded. "No, but—"

"No buts." The housekeeper held up her hand. "I asked Gertie to go, and Gertie will go." She turned and glared at her chief housemaid. "*Now.*"

Gertie caught Charlotte's resentful glare as she quickly dried her hands. She gave the girl a slight shrug before heading for the door. After all, it wasn't her fault if Chubby wanted her to go instead of Charlotte. Maybe Chubby knew Charlotte had a crush on Archie, and was trying to keep things on safe ground.

Seconds later Gertie stood in front of the laundry room, one hand frozen on the door handle. This was the first time she'd had to go in there since she'd found the dead body, and she wasn't looking forward to revisiting the memory.

She could still see him lying there, eyes open and staring into space, that ridiculous scarf wrapped around his neck. She turned the handle, then paused. She'd seen that scarf somewhere before, or at least, one exactly like it. She just couldn't remember where.

For a moment or two she struggled to recall the image, then dismissed it. It couldn't be all that important now. After all, Mazie was in jail for the murder, though it was hard to believe that little twerp was capable of losing her temper, much less killing someone. She'd heard that Mazie had bashed the bloke over the head with a flatiron. He was a big bugger. Like Charlotte had said, Mazie would have had to leap into the air to reach his head.

Still trying to picture the skinny maid dealing the death blow, she turned the handle and stepped inside the room. Making her way over to the linen closets, she avoided looking at the corner of the room where the dead man had lain.

It took her only a moment to pull two sheets from the pile, tuck them under her arm, and hurry back to the door. Goose bumps chased up her arms as she escaped into the hallway and slammed the door shut behind her. She would never be able to go into that room again without getting in all of a dither.

She was still feeling jittery when she entered the ballroom, though she couldn't entirely blame it on her visit to the laundry room. Suppressing the idea that it had something to do with talking to Archie, she headed for the stage door.

Archie was up on the stage, as were Phoebe Fortescue and a dozen bored-looking members of her dance group. The women were dressed in gaudy costumes in eye-popping colors that made Gertie blink.

Phoebe stood stage center, apparently arguing with Archie, who just stood there shaking his head at whatever she was saying.

Curious to know what the argument was about, Gertie drew closer to the stage as she walked by.

"But you have to do it!" Phoebe exclaimed in her shrill voice. "There isn't anyone else I can ask!"

Again Archie shook his head. "I'm not dressing up as a woman, no matter what you say. I'm just not going to do it. Sorry."

Gertie hid a grin as Phoebe answered with obvious irritation. "You're making an enormous fuss about nothing. You just have to put on a frock and apron, and a wig, some rouge on your cheeks, and we'll stuff your clothes with—"

Archie raised his voice—something Gertie had never heard him do before. "You are not going to stuff anything into my clothes, or put any of that junk on my cheeks. I'm sorry, Mrs. Fortescue, but you will have to find someone else to play your nutty Widow Trankey."

"It's Widow Twankey, and she's perfectly sane." Phoebe was now screeching, and her voice echoed throughout the ballroom. "For heaven's sake, Archie, this is a pantomime. It's tradition. Widow Twankey is Aladdin's mother, and she's always played by a man. There's nothing peculiar about it. People expect it."

"Yeah, well, people expect the king of England to come to tea, but it doesn't mean it's going to happen. Find someone else to play your widow. Besides, I'm here to build a set, not act in your play."

"Pantomime." Phoebe straightened her hat, a sure sign she wasn't about to give up. "You have a duty, young man, to help out where you can. I must insist—"

She got no further as at that moment Archie caught sight of Gertie. Leaping forward, he called out, "You've got my sheets. I'll be right down."

"I can bring them up," Gertie offered, but Archie shook his head.

"No, wait there. I'll be down in a sec."

Guessing that he wanted to get away from Phoebe's outrageous demands, Gertie walked away from the stage and laid the sheets on a table, then sat down on a chair to wait.

She didn't have much time to sit during her busy day, and she wasn't about to miss an opportunity to do so now.

She didn't have long to wait. Her heart started doing a weird dance as Archie burst through the door and came striding toward her. Hastily reminding herself that he was off limits, she stood up.

As he reached her, she thrust the sheets at him. "Here. Mrs. Chubb said you needed these."

"Yeah, I did." He smiled at her, revealing a row of perfect teeth. Tucking the linens under his arm, he added, "Thanks so much for bringing them for me."

"My pleasure. Though it wasn't much fun going back into that laundry room. I don't think I'll ever feel right about that room again."

His smile faded. "That must have been a shock for you, finding a dead man on the floor."

"It was." Gertie shuddered. "It wasn't a good way to start the day, I can tell you. That poor bloke—someone must have really hated him."

Archie sounded odd when he answered. "Yeah, well, from what I hear, he wasn't a very nice bloke. Someone like that makes a lot of enemies."

She looked at him in surprise. "You knew him?"

"I knew some things about him."

His voice had hardened even more, and the dark look on his face startled Gertie. "What things?"

Archie gave her a blank look, then seemed to shake off whatever was troubling him. "Never mind. Enough to say that Mazie got herself into a lot of trouble over that bugger."

216

She couldn't stop herself from asking, "Do you think she did it?"

She'd expected him to leap to Mazie's defense, but instead, he simply shrugged. "Who knows? The bobbies think she did it, and they must have good reason to suspect her."

"Yeah, I s'pose so." Uncomfortable now with the direction the conversation had turned, she made a move to pass by him, but he stopped her with a hand on her arm.

"What's your hurry? You've got a minute to chat, haven't you?"

Her own voice sounded funny now when she answered. "Well, they're really busy in the kitchen, so I should get back there."

He looked disappointed when he dropped his hand. "Okay, then. Don't let me keep you."

Now she felt a pang of guilt. He was just trying to be nice. She made an effort to sound normal. "I heard Fussy Fortescue up there." She jerked a thumb at the stage, where Phoebe was now shrieking at her dance group. "She wants you to play a woman in her pantomime?"

Archie uttered a loud sigh. "Yeah. That nut head will drive me crazy."

"She drives everyone crazy." Gertie's laugh didn't sound natural and she cleared her throat. "Don't take no notice of her. Just be firm with her. She respects that."

Archie looked unconvinced. "I don't think she respects anyone. She's an ogre."

Some force she couldn't resist made her reach out and pat

his arm. "She likes you. That's why she's paying you all this attention. Just keep on her right side and you'll be fine."

He looked down at her hand, which somehow seemed reluctant to lift itself off his arm. She flinched when he laid his own warm palm over it, saying softly, "Thanks. Gertie. I'll keep that in mind."

Snatching her hand away, she said gruffly, "I have to go now." She didn't wait for him to answer but, instead, dove past him and fled to the doors. She didn't breathe again until she was out in the hallway.

No, no, no, no, no! she scolded herself, stamping her feet as she marched down to the lobby. She'd learned her lesson with men. No matter how charming and gentle they seemed to be, once they had you in their grasp, they were monsters, treating women like slaves. Just like Clive. He'd been the sweetest, most caring man she'd ever met, but when it had come down to marrying him, he had become demanding and obstinate, issuing bloody orders and expecting her to obey.

She wasn't going to get caught in that web again. Not in a million years. Never. Ever. Having fully convinced herself, she hurried on her way to the kitchen.

Cecily was in her office, balancing the accounts, when the knock came on her door. Raising her head, she called out, "Come in!" and laid down her pen.

The door opened and Lilly edged into the room, coming to a halt just inside the door. "I'm sorry to disturb you, m'm, but the constable is here. He wants to talk to you."

Cecily's spirits lifted. Perhaps Sam had decided to release

Mazie after all. "Show him in, Lilly. Thank you." As the girl turned to go, Cecily felt compelled to ask, "How are you doing, Lilly? Is everything all right?"

Lilly turned back, her cheeks growing pink. "Yes, m'm, thank you. I'm very happy here."

"Mrs. Chubb seems to think the work may be too much for you."

Now alarm spread over Lilly's thin face. "Oh, no, m'm. I try very hard to get it all done, and sometimes I have to ask about things, but I like it here, I really do, and I—"

She sounded close to tears, and Cecily hurried to reassure her. "It's quite all right, Lilly. I'm not criticizing you. I just want to be sure we're not working you too hard."

Lilly shook her head so briskly, a strand of hair escaped from its pin and whipped her face. Tucking it back in place with a nervous hand, she said quietly, "I don't care how hard the work is, m'm. I'm grateful to be here, safe and sound, and not have to worry about someone coming after me."

Cecily straightened her back. "Rest assured, Lilly, we will never let that happen." Remembering something she needed to do, she added quietly, "By the way, I wonder if you could answer a rather delicate question for me."

Lilly's eyes opened wide in her startled face. "Yes, m'm?"

"You must know Mazie quite well, since you shared a room. Can you tell me if she had an admirer? Perhaps someone on the Pennyfoot staff?"

Lilly's cheeks glowed red. "Er . . . I'm not sure, m'm. I know she talked to Archie a lot, but I don't know if they were . . . you know . . ." Her voice trailed off, and she stared down at the floor.

"It's all right, Lilly. Thank you. Now go and tell P.C. Northcott he may come in."

"Yes, m'm. Thank you, m'm." Lilly slipped through the door and disappeared, leaving Cecily to stare thoughtfully at the ledger in front of her. Could Archie possibly be the killer? It was the last thing she wanted to believe. Phoebe was right. She certainly didn't have much luck with maintenance men.

Remembering Lilly's words of gratitude, she wondered how much she should worry about the girl's husband tracking her down to the Pennyfoot. She sincerely hoped that wouldn't happen. It could be most unpleasant for everyone concerned, not to mention a disruption to the guests.

Sighing, she closed the ledger with a snap. Yet another Christmas season filled with trials and tribulations. Hopefully this one would end as peacefully and enjoyably as the earlier ones.

Another brisk rap on the door disturbed her thoughts, and she raised her head again. "Come in!"

Sam Northcott marched into the room, his helmet tucked under his arm and wearing an air of importance as if he were about to be presented with the Victoria Cross. "Mrs. Baxter," he announced in the voice he always used when imparting vital information, "I hope your day is starting well?"

"Very well, thank you, Sam. And yours?"

"Well, it was, until something 'appened." He nudged a hand toward a chair facing the desk. "May I?"

"Of course." She waited while he seated himself, which entailed a lot of shifting and grunting until he was settled. "You have news for me?"

"I'm afraid I do, m'm. Not good news, I'm sad to say."

Cecily's thoughts immediately flew to Mazie. Her heart seemed to freeze as she envisioned that fragile face and terrified eyes. "Oh, no, please don't tell me that something's happened to Mazie?"

"Mazie?" The constable frowned, staring at her in confusion.

Feeling more than slightly exasperated, Cecily answered curtly, "My maid, who is in your custody at the moment."

"Oh!" Enlightenment dawned in his eyes, and to her immense relief, he shook his head. "No, it's not about Mazie. She's all right, though I do wish she'd eat a bit more. She doesn't seem to like the food we give her and—"

"Sam? If it's not Mazie we're talking about, then who, pray, is the subject of this news?"

"Ah, yes." The constable coughed behind his hand. "Well, I thought you should know, seeing as how this is connected to what happened here. Strange coincidence, that. I'm not happy about it at all. We've never had trouble with street crimes in Badgers End. They usually don't bother with us here, seeing as how we're such a small town. They usually hang around Wellercombe, where the pickings are a lot bigger."

Cecily fought to keep her irritation at bay. "Would you please tell me what has happened to bring you to my office on a busy day?"

Northcott opened his mouth, closed it again, then said in a rush, "It's about Lady Farthingale. She's the widow of the bloke we found dead in your laundry room the other morning."

Cecily curled her fingers into her palms. "Yes, Sam, I'm familiar with Lady Farthingale. So, what is this all about?"

"She's dead."

Cecily blinked. The sparse statement seemed to ring in her ears, repeating itself over and over. "Dead? But she can't be. I just spoke with her yesterday and she seemed perfectly well."

P.C. Northcott cleared his throat. "Yes, well, she was attacked and robbed this morning in the High Street. She must have been taking a shortcut through an alley, as that's where her body was found. We 'ave deduced that it were a mugger what stabbed her, though they usually don't kill. The widow must have put up a fight." He shook his head. "You should never do that. Hand over everything you have, then run like hell." He coughed. "Begging your pardon, m'm."

Cecily barely heard his last words. She was still trying to make sense of the news. Lady Farthingale dead. Just a few days after her husband had died a violent death. Too much of a coincidence? She had no doubt of that. The deaths were connected. Someone was being very thorough.

The constable spoke again, but she didn't hear what he said. She was too busy playing a memory back in her mind. The vision of Sir Clarence Oakes rapidly climbing the steps to Lady Farthingale's hotel.

Another coincidence? She didn't think so. For a brief moment she considered sharing her suspicions with the constable, then immediately decided against it. Sam would probably charge up to the aristocrat with his usual blunt accusations without considering the evidence, or lack thereof, thus destroying any chance of catching the man off-guard.

On the other hand, if Sir Clarence was innocent of the

crime, he would likely be so angered by Sam's questioning, he could very well be unresponsive to any of her questions.

No, better that she keep her thoughts to herself for the time being. Her quest to solve this case, however, had just become crucial. Obviously, the villain had no qualms about disposing of anyone who posed a threat. She had better uncover the perpetrator before he had a chance to kill again.

CHAPTER
❀ 14 ❀

Pulling herself together, Cecily focused on the constable. "I'm sorry, Sam, I didn't quite hear what you said."

Northcott raised his voice. "I said, I hope this isn't a sign of things to come. We don't need that kind of riffraff in Badgers End. No, sir." He shook his head with such a vehemence, Cecily would have smiled had it not been for the direness of the situation. It was obvious Sam did not relish the idea of having to work harder to enforce the law.

"Well, let us hope this is an isolated incident. Can you tell me any more details?"

He gave her a suspicious look. "You are not going to interfere, are you, Mrs. B? You know I can't have that. Inspector Cranshaw would have my hide if I allowed you to poke into our business again."

Cecily opened her eyes wide in feigned innocence. "Why, Sam! You know I would never do anything to get you into

trouble. Especially with Inspector Cranshaw. I was just curious, that's all. After all, I spoke to the poor woman just
hours before she died. I would like to know how it happened."

A long pause followed, during which the constable was
apparently torn between betraying his superior and boasting
about what he knew. Finally, his ego won. "All we know is
that it was a robbery that got out of hand. Lady Farthingale's
handbag was found beside her body. Emptied out, of course.
There was a hole torn in her coat lapel, like someone had
ripped her jewelry right off her clothes. She was stabbed
more than once, and the doctor believes she bled to death
before someone found her and reported it to us." He sighed,
staring down at his hands. "I can't believe it 'appened right
here in Badgers End. I shall have to send Albert out to patrol
the blooming streets until the Christmas shopping season is
over. I might even have to do a spot of patrolling myself once
the inspector gets wind of it."

Cecily gave him a sharp look. "You haven't reported it to
him yet?"

The constable fidgeted on his chair. "Not exactly. He's on
an important case and I didn't want to disturb him until he's
finished with it."

"More important than two murders in less than a week?"

"Well. I did tell him about the first one, and that I had
the suspect in custody." He looked defiant when he raised his
chin. "This one seemed cut and dried, so I don't see any
sense in bothering him now."

What he didn't want, Cecily reflected, was for Cranshaw
to come roaring back to town and ruining Sam's Christmas.

Nevertheless, she was happy to know she wouldn't have to deal with the crusty inspector for now. Hopefully, by the time he arrived in town, she would have solved these crimes and wouldn't have to be involved with him at all.

Charlie lifted the neck collar and eased it carefully over Majesty's head. The horse shifted impatiently, as if eager to be out in the fresh air and on the road. In the stall next to Charlie, Champion snorted and stamped his feet, making Charlie smile. "It'll be your turn later," he told the horse, then turned back to fasten Majesty's collar.

Just then, Henry's quiet voice spoke from behind him. "I'm done with Lord Melton's motorcar. What do you want me to do next?"

What he wanted the lad to do, Charlie thought viciously, was to get out of his life and stop tormenting him. A second later he was contradicting himself. He'd miss the boy. That thought did nothing to improve his temper. Without turning around, he answered, "You should probably take a look at Sir James's car. It hasn't been out since he's been here. It's the black and gray one at the end of the row. Just get it started up to make sure it's still running all right."

"Yes, sir."

Charlie waited until Henry's footsteps had faded before letting out his breath. He'd been awake half the night wondering how he could ask Henry about his big secret. He wasn't sure why it mattered so much to him, but he knew he couldn't rest until he learned what all the mystery was about.

After all, he'd told himself, he and Henry worked closely

together, taking care of the entire transportation services for the Pennyfoot Hotel. It was important to have each other's trust and confidence in each other. He could have neither if all the time he was wondering what it was his assistant was keeping from him.

Knowing Henry, demanding answers from him would only result in tearful denials. Politely asking wasn't likely to produce anything, either. The problem was, Charlie thought he knew what the secret was, and could understand why Henry didn't want to admit it.

If he were honest with himself, he'd rather not know that Henry walked on a different side of the road. Still, it was his duty to know everything there was to know about his assistant, and if Henry was a queer, then as his boss, Charlie wanted to know.

One way or another, he would have to make Lilly tell him what he had long suspected. Only then could he make up his mind how he wanted to deal with it.

Long after P.C. Northcott had departed for the kitchen, Cecily sat at her desk, going over in her mind the constable's account of Lady Farthingale's murder. She didn't believe for one second that it was a random attack by a street robber. Someone wanted to silence the widow. What was it Lady Farthingale knew that was so incriminating, it caused her to lose her life?

It seemed highly possible that it had something to do with the lucrative business deal her husband had bragged about.

Cecily stared at the window, and the patch of gray sky beyond. If she could find out what the business deal was and who it was with, she might be a lot closer to finding the killer. It seemed obvious that Sir Clarence Oakes was involved, since he had visited the dowager the day before.

Then again, there was that contentious exchange with Edwin Coombs, which could have been about more than an accusation of cheating. Maybe it was time to confront Mr. Coombs again.

She was just about to get up when she heard a tap on the door.

It opened immediately and Phoebe's face appeared, pink-cheeked beneath her enormous hat. "Cecily, dear," she sang out, "may I come in?"

Since she had already sailed into the room as she was speaking, Cecily didn't bother to give her permission. "Good afternoon, Phoebe. I trust the rehearsals are going well?"

"They are progressing spendidly." Phoebe plopped herself down on a chair and brushed a hand across her blue velvet skirt. "I was just on my way to the dining room for a spot of lunch, and I thought I'd pop in and see how things are with you."

Phoebe never simply "popped in" without good reason, but Cecily knew better than to ask. Her friend would say what was on her mind when she was ready, and not before. "Things are very well, thank you. The last of the guests have arrived for Christmas, and we are full to capacity."

"Good. I'm glad to hear it." Phoebe nodded, sending the blossoms on her hat dancing.

"I saw the set that Archie built for you. Most impressive. I hope you complimented him on it."

Phoebe beamed. "I did, of course. He created a miracle. I don't ever remember having such a beautiful and intricate set in my entire years of producing presentations. I am quite convinced that this year's pantomime will be the best ever."

Cecily hid a shudder, trying not to picture all the disasters of the years before. "I have no doubt. We are lucky to have such a talented maintenance man."

"And so accommodating! The man is a gem." Phoebe's hand fluttered in the air. "He is quite the gentleman, too. His manners are impeccable." Her expression sobered. "Though the footman helping him, er . . . I don't remember his name. . . ."

"Wally," Cecily reminded her.

"Oh, yes, of course. Wally. Anyway, he told me that Archie has quite a temper. Apparently, he saw him arguing with a gentleman, and he was quite volatile, from what I understand. I found that a little hard to believe. Archie has always been polite and helpful, though I must admit, he did balk quite vehemently at playing Widow Twankey."

Cecily frowned. "This argument with a gentleman happened here in the hotel?"

"I believe so, yes."

"Did Wally happen to mention the name of the other gentleman?"

"No, he did not." Phoebe frowned. "This isn't going to get Archie into trouble, is it? I wouldn't have said anything if I'd thought it would cause a problem."

Cecily quickly reassured her. "No, not at all. I was merely curious, that's all."

"Well, good." Phoebe folded her hands in her lap. "Anyway, as long as I'm here, perhaps I could ask a favor. I'm going to need some props for the cave scenes. I was wondering if you had some costume jewelry I could borrow. Madeline has been kind enough to lend me some of hers, but I could use some more to make a decent display."

"Of course. I'll sort some out this afternoon and have one of the maids bring it to the ballroom."

"Thank you, Cecily dear. I knew I could count on you." Phoebe rose, smoothing down her skirt again. "Now I must be off. There is still tons to do, and I need some sustenance before I continue. Freddie is in the bar, of course. I shall have to drag him out so that he can eat with me. That man would go all day without feeding himself if I wasn't there to take care of him."

With an airy wave of her hand, she swept out the door and closed it quietly behind her.

Cecily sat for a long moment staring at the closed door, Phoebe's words still resounding in her ears. *He saw him arguing with a gentleman, and he was quite volatile.* That didn't sound like the Archie she knew.

Making up her mind, she got up and swiftly left the room. She needed to have a word with her maintenance man while Phoebe was enjoying her lunch. Hopefully the dance troupe would be making the most of their lunch hour, and with any luck, she'd catch Archie alone, working on the set.

Much to her disappointment, when she entered the ballroom, the maintenance man was nowhere to be seen. He was most likely down in the kitchen sampling Michel's cooking. Her talk with him would have to wait.

Feeling decidedly unsettled, she went in search of Edwin Coombs.

She eventually found him in the library, seated by the window, his nose deep in a book. A group of guests was seated in front of the fireplace, exchanging jokes and laughing uproariously.

Madeline had decorated the mantel with boughs of holly and fir. Sparkling red and gold balls nestled inside the dark green foliage, accompanied by white lace angels and gold and silver miniature crowns. The centerpiece was a thick red candle, draped in red and gold ribbons.

In spite of the glorious Christmas tree in the lobby, and the more modest tree in the library, Cecily considered this room's fireplace to be the most impressive display in the hotel. As she passed by the group, she recognized a couple who had stayed at the hotel on earlier occasions, and exchanged polite nods with them before walking over to Edwin Coombs's chair.

"I see you are enjoying the adventures of Sherlock Holmes," she said as she paused in front of him.

Edwin looked up, smiling when he recognized her. "Good afternoon, Mrs. Baxter." He politely rose to his feet and held up the book. "Jolly good story. This Doyle chap is an excellent writer."

"He is, indeed." She glanced over at the fireside group, assuring herself that they were all focused on one another. Turning back to the gentleman at her side, she said quietly,

"I hope you don't mind me asking, but I understand Lord Farthingale was involved in a lucrative business deal, which was the reason for his presence here in Badgers End. I was wondering if perhaps you were involved and, if so, if you would mind telling me what the deal was all about."

As she'd been talking, Edwin's eyes had been gradually narrowing until they were mere slits. "As I believe I have already told you, Mrs. Baxter, I was not familiar with the gentleman, other than at the card tables the other night, where I met him for the first time. I know nothing of a business deal. If I were you, I would ask Sir Clarence Oakes to enlighten you, since he was deep in conversation with Farthingale on more than one occasion."

Cecily stared at him for a moment, then smiled. "I shan't bother you any longer, Mr. Coombs. Enjoy the book. I do believe we have another Sherlock Holmes mystery on the shelves. Feel free to borrow it if you like."

With that, she turned and hurried out of the library. She had some deep thinking to do, and her office was the only place she wanted to be.

Once inside the room, she closed the door and sat down at her desk. It seemed that whichever way she turned, all roads led to Sir Clarence Oakes. When she had first asked him about Lord Farthingale, he had professed not to know him, yet according to Edwin Coombs, the aristocrat had engaged in several conversations with the victim.

It seemed almost certain that Lord Farthingale's business deal had something to do with Sir Clarence.

Then there was the matter of the scarf. How did Sir

Clarence learn about that? Had he heard it from the grapevine, as Edwin Coombs had suggested? Or had he known about it from the start, because he had placed it around the man's neck himself?

What was the purpose of his visit to Lady Farthingale? If he'd intended to murder her, why hadn't he done so while he was at her hotel? Why wait until the next day?

Unless he was worried he'd be recognized as being at the scene of the crime.

Cecily absently turned the pages of her ledger. What if her suspicions were wrong, and Lady Farthingale's death was, as Sam had surmised, a simple matter of a street crime?

No, it was too much of a coincidence. She was convinced that Lord and Lady Farthingale's deaths were connected somehow to Sir Clarence Oakes. Now she had to prove it.

Thinking about the austere gentleman, she found it difficult to imagine him going to all the trouble of writing a note to lure his victim to the laundry room in order to kill him. She could more easily visualize Sir Clarence waylaying Percy outside somewhere and making the deed simple and quick.

On the other hand, if Sir Clarence was the killer, he could simply have engineered the meeting in the laundry room in an attempt to settle whatever the mysterious business matter was about. She had no doubt that, once provoked, the man would be swift to retaliate. Perhaps the meeting didn't go the way he'd hoped and he'd lost his temper, snatching up the nearest weapon and striking his victim in a fit of rage.

But then why attack Lady Farthingale? Unless she suspected that he had killed her husband and threatened to expose him. That would give the gentleman a motive to be rid of her.

Cecily withdrew her pen from its stand, though she made no move to dip it in the inkwell. What she really needed to know, she told herself, was the nature of the business deal. It was highly unlikely that Sir Clarence would enlighten her. Her only hope at this point was to approach Lady Oakes. Surely she would know of any significant transactions in which her husband was involved.

Making up her mind, Cecily replaced her pen and rose from her chair. Somehow, she had to find a way to speak to Lady Oakes alone. The likeliest time was that evening. The guests had been invited to meet in the library in order to enjoy carol singing around the Christmas tree. Hopefully, Sir Clarence would prefer to play cards, and she would have a chance to approach Lady Oakes.

Meanwhile, she would have another stern word with Philip about passing along secrets to people who had no right to hear them.

Once more Charlie had to sweat through another long day before he had a chance to talk to Lilly. The last of the guests were arriving at the Pennyfoot, and he was kept busy ferrying them from the station to the hotel, hauling heavy trunks, bags, and hat boxes up the steps, then going back for more visitors and doing it all over again.

Then he had to unharness, groom, and feed the horses.

Henry did his share, but he was better with cars than with horses, and Charlie did most of the work. Not that he minded that. He loved his job, working with the horses. They were his friends, and he looked forward to greeting them every morning.

His greatest reward was when one of them gave him a friendly nudge on the back, or snuffled his ear when he was putting on the harness. That sign of affection could keep him warm all day.

Nevertheless, he had to admit, he was ready to take a break when he closed the last gate on the stalls and walked over to the water pail to wash his hands and face.

Henry had already left, and after calling out to his charges a cheerful "Good night! Sleep tight!" Charlie closed the stable doors and headed across the courtyard to the kitchen.

To his dismay, as he drew close to the building, he spotted the milk churns already out on the doorstep. He'd missed Lilly. Now he'd either have to wait another day, or try to get her alone somewhere in the hotel—an almost impossible chance of that.

Shrugging, he walked toward the door, trying to work out just how he was going to confront the girl alone. He was still a few steps away when the door suddenly opened, spilling light across the paved ground.

Charlie halted, hope beginning to spring anew. To his immense delight, Lilly appeared in the doorway, a coal bucket in each hand. Hoping she hadn't seen him, he ducked out of sight behind a rain barrel.

Apparently Lilly had missed seeing him in the dark, as

she walked briskly toward the coal shed. Reaching the door, she set the buckets down, opened the door, and stretched out her hand for the oil lamp that hung just inside on the wall.

Charlie could see her fumbling to light it and fought the temptation to go over there to help her. Instead, he watched her while she finally lit the lamp, hung it back on the wall, and picked up the buckets before vanishing inside.

He waited just a few more seconds, listening to the sound of coal being shoveled into the buckets, and then crept across the ground to the shed. Reaching the door, he found it ajar and peeked inside.

Lilly had her back to him, bending over the coal pile as she loaded the shovel with the gleaming black coal. He wrinkled his nose against the sooty odor. He could smell the stink of something else that was probably a deposit from some wild animal. Not a pleasant place to have a chat, but then, beggars couldn't be choosers.

Carefully he edged inside and gently closed the door behind him. The flickering glow from the oil lamp made shadows dance across the walls. As he stepped forward, his own shadow appeared on the wall opposite him.

At that moment Lilly straightened, the shovel in her hand. She must have caught sight of the shadow, as she let out an earsplitting scream, startling something hiding in the corner. Charlie heard the scuffling and, suspecting a rat, turned his head just as Lilly raised the shovel and brought it down hard on his shoulder.

"Ow!" He leapt backward, bumping his back against the door. One hand clutching his bruised shoulder, he demanded, "Watcha go and do that for?"

Lilly's white face stared at him, her eyes looking huge. "I thought you was someone else."

"Who? Who else do you hate enough to clobber them with a shovel?"

"Never you mind." Much to his relief, she lowered the shovel. "What are you doing in here anyway, scaring me half to death?"

Still nursing his shoulder, Charlie muttered, "I wanted to talk to you."

"In the coal shed? Couldn't it have waited until I got back in the kitchen?"

"No, it's private. It's about Henry."

Lilly's lips thinned, and she turned back to shovel another load of coal. "I already told you, it's Henry's secret to tell. I'm not going to tell you, so you might as well get lost."

Charlie stared at her back for a moment, then blurted out, "I think I know what it is. Henry's a queer, isn't he?"

For a long moment Lilly didn't answer, then he saw her shoulders shaking and realized she was quietly laughing.

"What's so bloody funny?" Charlie demanded. "It's no joke for me, I can tell you. I have a responsibility, and if I'm right about Henry, then I should know and madam should know."

At that, Lilly dropped the shovel and spun around. "You can't tell madam anything. Henry could lose her job." The second the words were out, she smacked a hand over her mouth. "I meant *his* job," she mumbled, her words muffled by her hand.

Charlie's mind was in a whirl. No, it couldn't be. How could he possibly have worked so closely with the lad and not noticed? Visions of Henry danced before his eyes—the soft voice, the small steps, those, oh, so inviting lips . . .

He shook his head, remembering the moment he'd seen Henry waltzing around the stable, humming in a lilting voice that echoed in his gut. It would explain a lot. Much as he hated the idea, he had to accept the undeniable fact.

Henry was a girl. And he was sweet on her.

CHAPTER

❋ 15 ❋

It was quite late in the evening when Cecily finally had a chance to speak with Lady Oakes. She had arrived on the arm of Sir Clarence, and Cecily had resigned herself to forgoing her chat with the woman. She had concentrated, instead, on enjoying the festivities.

Madeline had lit the candles on the Christmas tree, with strict instructions to blow them all out as soon as the celebration was over. Ever since Cecily had almost lost her life in that very room when a Christmas tree burned to ashes, she had been extremely uneasy about lit candles on the tree.

She had to admit, though, that the effect of those shimmering flames reflecting off the red and silver baubles was extremely heartwarming. The choirboys, in their white surplices over red cassocks, added an extra touch to the ambience of the room. Their soaring voices, celebrating the birth of Jesus, brought a lump to her throat and total silence from the onlookers gathered around them.

Once the glorious sounds had ceased, however, and the candles on the tree extinguished, the guests broke out into enthused chattering and laughter. Two of the maids circulated among them, offering trays of delicious sausage rolls, miniature mince pies, maids of honor, and bakewell tarts. Some of the gentlemen left the room, and Cecily kept a hopeful eye on Sir Clarence in case he should decide to join them.

It wasn't long before he apparently made to leave, arousing his wife's anger. Whatever it was she said to him, he attempted to placate her by placing his hand on her shoulder. She twisted away from him, snatching her arm to her chest as if he'd hurt her.

Sir Clarence hesitated for a moment, staring at his wife's back, then he turned on his heel and strode from the room.

Lady Oakes stood quite still for several seconds, nursing her arm, making Cecily wonder if Sir Clarence had hurt the woman earlier. If so, the man was a brute, abusing his wife in that manner.

A group of deserted wives had gathered together in front of the crackling fire, and continued their conversation. Cecily watched Lady Oakes wander over to the shelves, pluck a book, and turn the pages before carrying it over to a seat across the room.

Cecily crossed the floor and pulled a chair up close to her. "May I join you?" she asked as she seated herself.

Lady Oakes's expression warned Cecily she would have preferred otherwise, but she merely answered with a reluctant nod.

"I hope you enjoyed the singing this evening. Our choir-boys have quite remarkable voices, do they not?"

"Agreed," Lady Oakes murmured, keeping her eyes on her book.

Deciding to come straight to the point, Cecily leaned forward and lowered her voice. "I was wondering if you could tell me something. It has come to my attention that your husband and Sir Farthingale were engaged in a significant business matter. It's rather important that I know what this entailed. I'm hoping you can enlighten me."

Lady Oakes's sharp features grew rigid as she stared at Cecily. "I have not the slightest idea what you mean. You will have to ask him, though as far as I know, my husband has never had any business dealings with Lord Farthingale."

"Really?" Cecily raised her eyebrows in feigned surprise. "I was assured that the transaction had taken place."

"Assured by whom?"

"I'd rather not say."

Lady Oakes's face darkened. "Allow me to guess. It was Lady Farthingale who fostered this story, was it not?"

"She may have mentioned it," Cecily admitted.

The other woman slapped her book down on her lap. "I might have known. That woman was an outrageous hypocrite. According to her, her husband was an avid gambler who threw away his entire fortune, leaving her practically destitute, yet she paraded around wearing expensive jewelry and silk scarves soaked in extravagant French perfume as though she were still one of us."

This time Cecily's eyebrows rose of their own accord. "I had no idea you knew the woman that well."

Lady Oakes tossed her head. "I passed by her upon occasion."

"I see." Cecily rose. "Well, I will leave you now to enjoy your book. I wish you a pleasant evening."

"Likewise," the other woman muttered.

Cecily's mind raced as she walked over to the door. The persistent notion that had tormented her earlier prodded at her, though she still couldn't quite grasp it. This happened to her often—an idea that she knew more than she was aware of, and all she needed to do was pin it down and she'd have her answers.

Somewhere deep in her mind, she had the information she needed to unmask a killer. She just needed to unearth it.

Charlie stared at Lilly, his voice hoarse as he asked, "How long have you known?"

Lilly's eyes widened in concern. "Please don't tell madam or Mr. Baxter. I swore to Henry I'd keep it a secret."

Charlie shook his head, trying frantically to clear his mind. "Why? Why is she pretending to be a lad?"

"She's always wanted to be a mechanic. Her father was one and he taught Henry everything he knew. Then her mother died and her father got sick and couldn't work anymore. Henry had to go to work to pay the bills. She knew she could earn good money taking care of cars, and when she heard that Mr. Baxter was looking for a mechanic, she asked for the job. She knew that he wouldn't hire a girl to work on cars, so she pretended to be a boy. She's been pretending ever since."

Charlie swore quietly under his breath. "She did a good job of deceiving everyone."

Lilly put out a hand to touch his arm. "Please, Charlie, don't say anything to anyone. If Henry loses this job, she and her father could lose everything, even their home. Besides, she loves working here. It would break her heart if she had to go."

It was those last few words that settled Charlie's mind. Whatever else was at stake, including his own job if all this came to light, he could not be responsible for breaking Henry's heart. "I'll say naught for now, but if things get too messy, I might have to say something later on."

"Things won't get messy." Lilly turned around and picked up the shovel. "Henry's an excellent mechanic and does her job. As long as nobody says anything, nothing's going to change."

"Someone's going to notice sooner or later," Charlie said grimly. "Where did she get the name 'Henry'? Did she just make it up?"

Lilly turned her head to look at him. "Her parents thought she was going to be a boy and were going to call her Henry. When she was born, they changed it to Henrietta."

"Henrietta." Just saying the name gave him squiggles in his stomach. He coughed, then said gruffly, "I'll give you a hand with those coal buckets if you like."

For a moment or two it seemed as if Lilly would refuse his offer, but then she nodded. "Ta, ever so."

"Okay." Reaching for a second shovel leaning against the wall, Charlie hoped fervently that he'd be able to keep his thoughts to himself when he was around Henry. It wouldn't be easy, and he would have to do his best to avoid her as much as possible. Just the thought of that made him miserable. What a mess.

On the one hand, he should be over the moon to discover Henry was really a girl, but on the other hand, knowing that now and not being able to do anything about it just about killed him.

With a deep sigh he dug the shovel into the pile of dusty, smelly coal and heaved the load into the empty bucket. The important thing was that Henry keep her job, and to do that he'd walk through fire for her. Heaven help them both.

Cecily slept fitfully that night, tossing around with her head full of scenarios, none of which made sense. She finally awoke the next morning to find her husband gone and daylight flooding the room. Baxter had drawn back the curtains, no doubt hoping to rouse her from her deep slumber.

One of the maids had brought in a china washbowl full of cold water. After sluicing her face and hands, she quickly dressed in a blue serge pleated skirt and a cream lace-trimmed shirtwaist. The room was chilly, and she drew a pale blue shawl about her shoulders before leaving the suite and carefully descending the stairs.

As she reached the lobby, she saw Mrs. Chubb striding toward her, a frown creasing her face.

"Good morning, m'm." The housekeeper paused in front of Cecily and peered into her face. "Are you feeling all right?"

Taken by surprise, Cecily took a moment to answer. "Why, yes, thank you, Altheda. I'm perfectly well."

Mrs. Chubb's features relaxed. "Thank goodness. I saw you limping yesterday and now you're late getting up this morning. Mr. Baxter said to take breakfast up to your room if you weren't down here by nine, but he wouldn't tell me if you were ill or not, and I was worried."

Cecily smiled. "That's very kind of you, but as you can see, I am quite well. I had a slight accident on the stairs the other night, but my knee is healing now."

"I'm very glad to hear that, m'm." The housekeeper glanced at a spot behind Cecily. "Good morning, your ladyship."

Cecily turned just in time to see Lady Oakes reach the bottom stair. Before she could greet the woman, however, the aristocrat swept a haughty glance across both of them, nodded at Cecily, and headed at a fast pace for the hallway.

Mrs. Chubb shook her head. "I don't know what she has to be so stuck up about. If people knew the truth about her, she'd soon be brought down a peg or two."

Her attention alerted, Cecily stared at the housekeeper. "What do you mean? What is this truth you're talking about?"

Mrs. Chubb shook her head. "I'm sorry, m'm. It just slipped out. I shouldn't have said anything. I'm not one to pass on gossip. Especially about the guests."

Cecily drew closer to her. "Mrs. Chubb, I need to know what you meant by the truth about Lady Oakes. It's important."

Curiosity flooded the housekeeper's face. "Important?"

"Yes." Cecily crossed her arms. "Never mind that. Just tell me what you meant."

Now looking deflated, Mrs. Chubb shrugged her shoulders.

"It was just something that Gertie heard when she was at the suffragettes' protest in Wellercombe."

Shocked, Cecily's voice rose. "Gertie was at a protest?"

"Yes, m'm. She went to keep Charlotte company."

Cecily groaned. "How long has this been going on?"

"I think it was the first time for Charlotte, and the first in a long time for Gertie." The housekeeper smiled. "I think it will be the last for both of them. They didn't know I was in the pantry and I overheard them talking about it. Apparently they got chased into a church by an angry mob."

"Heaven help us." Cecily threw up her hands. "Talk some sense into those two women, Altheda. Explain to them in great detail what could happen to them if they are caught by anti-protestors, or arrested by the constabulary."

"I already have, m'm. The minute I came out of that pantry. Don't you worry. I don't think they'll be doing any protesting for a while."

"Well, good. Now tell me what you know about Lady Oakes."

Mrs. Chubb fidgeted with the ribbons of her apron. "Well, one of the suffragettes helped rescue the girls and took them to the church. She told Gertie that a friend of hers was lady's maid to Lady Oakes. She said that the maid overheard Lady Oakes arguing with her husband."

The housekeeper hesitated, forcing Cecily to give her a nudge. "Do go on, Altheda. I haven't got all day."

"Yes, m'm. Well, it seems that before Lady Oakes met her husband, she was a woman of ill repute."

It took Cecily a moment or two to interpret her housekeeper's statement. "You mean she was . . . ?" She couldn't quite bring herself to say it.

"Yes, m'm," Mrs. Chubb said cheerfully. "She was a lady of the night, or a—"

"Yes, yes, I understand." Cecily held up her hand to stop the flow of words.

Mrs. Chubb nodded. "Yes, m'm. Anyway, according to what Gertie heard, Sir Clarence rescued her off the streets and fell in love with her. He's gone to great lengths to keep it a secret ever since."

"I imagine he has," Cecily murmured, her mind still grappling with what she'd heard. Lady Oakes, that beautiful, elegant, sophisticated woman, had once been a prostitute. It was difficult to believe.

"Well, m'm, I'll be off then. The maids will be clearing off the breakfast tables by now, and if I'm not down there to organize everything, there will be a holy mess. I can have breakfast sent up to your office, if you like?"

"That would be very nice, Altheda. Thank you."

"Yes, m'm. My pleasure." With that, she nodded, smiled, and trotted off for the stairs.

Cecily stood for a long moment staring after her, the housekeeper's words still ringing in her ears. *He's gone to great lengths to keep it a secret ever since.*

So, could that have been the lucrative business deal that Lord Farthingale was celebrating? Could he have been blackmailing Sir Clarence, having found out the truth about his wife? It certainly seemed feasible, and a sound motive for silencing the man forever.

Walking slowly down the hallway to her office, she mulled over her options. Talking to either Lady Oakes or her husband would be a waste of time and would undoubtedly alert him that she suspected him. She had already had one brush with death. She didn't need another.

She reached the door of her office and opened it. Lady Farthingale must have learned of the secret from her husband and perhaps, suspecting Sir Clarence, had threatened to carry on with the blackmail. Which could be why she was disposed of as well.

Frowning, Cecily walked over to her desk, and sat down. Now she was fairly confident that she had identified the killer of both Lord Farthingale and his wife. The problem remained, however, of how she could prove it.

Sam Northcott would never take her word for it. Especially since he already had Mazie in custody and was convinced she was the perpetrator of the crime. Sam did not like to be proven mistaken.

Perhaps she could discover something helpful in the aristocrats' suite. It wouldn't be the first time she'd searched a suspect's room for clues. She would have to do it when she was certain not to be disturbed.

She shuffled the papers in front of her, and stared at the next day's menu that Michel had provided. Roast pork and applesauce appeared on there for tomorrow's evening meal. Baxter's favorite. He would be delighted.

Forcing her mind back to the problem at hand, she tried to concentrate. Sir Clarence would be no problem, as he spent most evenings in the card rooms. Lady Oakes, on the other hand, was unpredictable. Some evenings she spent in the library, others in her room.

Cecily tapped her fingers on the surface of her desk. Maybe she could spot them leaving the hotel together during the day. But then other people would be wandering around and could possibly notice her entering Sir Clarence's suite.

No, that would not do. She was instantly recognizable. Better to attempt the search at night, when most of the guests would be occupied.

She curled her fingers into her palm as she remembered something. The pantomime was to be presented tomorrow night. As long as Sir Clarence and his wife attended the performance together, she could be assured of plenty of time to search the rooms.

Baxter would not be happy if she left him alone to suffer through Phoebe's masterpiece, and would certainly object if he knew why she was deserting him. He would probably insist on accompanying her on the search.

She could not allow that. On her own, she could most likely sneak out of there without being noticed. The two of them leaving together would certainly attract attention. She would have to come up with a really pressing excuse for deserting him and pray that, for once, he remained where he was until she returned.

With any luck at all, she just might find something to connect Sir Clarence to the murders. Then Inspector Cranshaw could take it from there.

Having settled that, she turned her attention to the

accounts ledger, and tried not to think about what might happen should her luck run out.

Alone in the stable that afternoon, Charlie led Champion out of his stall and backed him between the shafts of the carriage. "Come on, boy," he said as he lifted the carriage shafts and threaded them through the togs. "It's time to go to work. Some of the toffs want to go into town to spend their money in the shops, and we want to give them all the help they need."

Champion nodded his head as if he understood, and Charlie fondled the horse's ear. "You're a good boy, Champion. Too bad you're not a dog."

"You like dogs?"

The soft voice behind him made Charlie jump. Recognizing Henry's tantalizing tones, he stiffened his back. "Yeah, I like dogs. Don't you?"

"Yes, sir. I love them."

Charlie briefly closed his eyes as the tingling started again in his neck. "Well, good."

"Lilly says you used to have a dog."

Bracing himself, Charlie turned around. He could see it now, plain as the nose on his face. The gentle smile, the warm eyes, the smooth cheeks—he must have been blind not to realize it before. Henry was all girl, and oh, how he wanted to tell her he knew it.

"Yeah," he said gruffly, "there used to be a dog around here, but it wasn't mine. It belonged to Samuel, the stable manager before me."

Henry nodded. "I know about Samuel. His wife, Pansy, comes into the kitchen sometimes to see Gertie."

"Yeah, well, they took Tess with them when they got married and Pansy left the Pennyfoot."

Henry's soft blue eyes gazed into his, prompting his heart to start thumping like a bass drum. "You must miss her dreadfully."

Confused, he stared at her. "Pansy?"

Henry laughed—a high, lilting sound that seemed to echo in Charlie's ears. He must have shown something in his face, as she quickly changed the laugh to a cough. "I meant the dog." She turned away, muttering, "I have to get back to work."

Cursing under his breath, Charlie spun around and buckled the breeching around the shaft. From now on, he promised himself, he'd stay out of Henry's way. No more chitchat, just orders when he had to give them and nothing else.

Finishing up the harnessing, he grabbed the traces and started to lead Champion out of the stables. He'd gone only one step when the horse whinnied and reared up, sending the carriage twisting sideways. One of the shafts struck the door of the stall with a resounding clatter.

Henry's voice floated down to Charlie as he stared at the quivering horse. "What was that? Are you all right?"

Seeing Henry heading his way, Charlie yelled, "I'm okay. Get back to work."

He must have sounded a bit harsh, as Henry halted, then without a word, turned around and marched back to the motorcar she'd been working on.

Cursing again, Charlie sped around the carriage to inspect

the damage. The shaft was slightly chipped on the end, and the stall door had a dent in it. Otherwise there didn't seem to be any serious damage.

When he examined the harness, he saw that he had forgotten to buckle one of the traces. The shaft had slipped out of the tog when Champion stepped forward.

The horse was still quivering, and it took him a few moments to calm him. By the time he'd fastened everything securely and made sure Champion was relaxed again, Henry had disappeared.

Charlie stared into the empty space where Henry had been working. He owed the lad . . . girl . . . an apology. That would have to wait now. Turning back to the horse, he whispered, "I'm a mess, Champion. Well and truly buggered. I'll have to do something about this, or I'll be causing an accident."

Champion turned his head and nudged Charlie on the shoulder. It didn't solve his problem, but it did make Charlie feel a little better. And he'd have to make do with that. For now.

CHAPTER
❀16❀

Alone in her office the next morning, Cecily found it difficult to concentrate. Gertie had delivered the orders for supplies and the list lay on the desk, but when Cecily looked at it, all she could see was a blur of her housekeeper's scrawl on the paper.

Every instinct she had told her that Sir Clarence Oakes had killed Lord Farthingale. Yet, for some reason, a lingering doubt kept intruding on her thoughts. That annoying little voice in the back of her mind kept trying to tell her something, and no matter how hard she concentrated, she just couldn't quite grasp it.

The shrill jingling of the telephone made her jump. She snatched up the receiver and pressed it to her ear. "Yes, Philip. What is it?"

"I have the telephone operator on the line, m'm," Philip said, sounding bored. "Shall I put her through?"

"Yes, of course. Thank you."

"Yes, m'm." There followed a click, then silence.

"Hello?" Cecily shook the receiver, glared at it, then spoke into it again. "Hello? Are you there?" How she hated all these newfangled inventions. The dratted motorcar was bad enough, but now inventors were creating machines to do everything. There were even machines that sewed and ones that could write. Not that she'd ever use one. What was wrong with good old-fashioned handwriting, she'd like to know?

As for the telephone, true, it was a lot more convenient than having to wait for a carriage to visit the constabulary, but it annoyed her considerably when the dratted thing didn't work the way it was supposed to. She raised her voice. "Hello! Are you there?"

A series of clicks answered her, then Philip's voice followed, now sounding only slightly less bored. "Sorry, m'm. I pulled the wrong plug. I'll put you through now."

Shaking her head, Cecily waited through another two or three clicks, until the sharp voice of the operator spoke in her ear.

"Mrs. Baxter?"

"I am Mrs. Baxter," Cecily said, trying not to sound testy.

"I have Police Constable Northcott on the line for you."

Cecily straightened her back. Sam never rang her unless it was something vitally important.

After a moment of silence, Sam's voice echoed down the line. "Mrs. B? Is that you?"

"Yes, Sam." Cecily let out her breath. "What's happened? Is Mazie all right?"

"Yes, m'm. Your maid is fine. She's not eating much and she cries a lot, but otherwise she is fine."

"So, why are you ringing me?"

"I wanted to let you know, m'm . . ." Sam cleared his throat. "The inspector will be returning to Badgers End tomorrow. I expect he will transfer Mazie to the jail while she awaits trial."

Cecily uttered a cry of protest. The thought of her terrified maid being thrust into a crowded cell with criminals was too much to bear. "He can't do that! He has no proof."

"That'll be up to the courts to decide. All the evidence points to the maid. I'm sorry, m'm. There's nothing I can do about it."

"You can find out who really killed Lord Farthingale instead of sitting on your rear end, doing nothing," Cecily snapped, and was immediately ashamed of her outburst. "I'm sorry, Sam," she quickly added, "I am out of sorts this morning. I will speak with you later. Thank you for warning me about Inspector Cranshaw."

She dropped the receiver back onto the hook and glared at it for several moments, as if it might give her some idea of how to prove Sir Clarence guilty of murder. Her only hope, she decided, was to stick to her plan and search the Oakeses' suite. She just prayed that Phoebe's pantomime would be riveting enough to keep the aristocrats in their seats long enough for her to conduct a thorough inspection.

Glancing up at the clock, she hoped the next few hours would pass by quickly. She wanted this crisis over and done with, so that a vicious killer could be punished for his crime and Mazie could be free to enjoy the Christmas festivities.

• • •

It was almost noon, and the typical midday uproar in the kitchen had reached its peak. Michel's saucepan lids crashed and clattered as he inspected the contents of his pots and pans, Mrs. Chubb yelled orders to the maids, doors slammed as people raced in and out, and an ache was threatening in Gertie's head.

She'd had the sniffles all morning, and hoped fervently that she wasn't coming down with a cold. Not now, when they were so busy and Christmas was right around the corner. She was taking the twins to the pantomime tonight, and looking forward to it. More for what could go wrong than for what went right.

Her hands, buried in ice-cold water as she rinsed soil off the cabbages, felt numb. She pulled them from the sink and dried them on her apron. She would have liked to warm them in front of the stove, but Michel would have a pink fit if she got in his way.

As if in answer to her thoughts, Michel's raspy voice roared above the din. "*Zut alors!* Where eez my Brussels sprouts, huh?"

Mrs. Chubb smacked her knife down on the cutting board, which held the remains of a ham. "For goodness' sake, Michel! Do you have to yell like that? I almost cut my hand off."

Michel glared at her, his tall chef's hat bobbing as he shook his fist at her. "I order the Brussels sprouts, *non?* I say I need them this morning. They are not here." He waved a hand at the counter next to him. "Gertie! You have them in the sink, *oui?*"

"*Non.*" Gertie blew on her icy fingers. "I'm washing cabbages."

"Cabbages?" Michel threw up his hands. "How can I make the steak and kidney pie without the Brussels sprouts?"

Mrs. Chubb folded her arms. "Use the cabbage instead and stop acting like an imbecile."

Michel's cheeks glowed red. "*Imbecile?* It is you that is the imbecile. You ruin my cooking with your cabbage. I need my Brussels sprouts, and I need them *now*. Or there will be no lunch for anyone."

"Oh, for heaven's sake." Raising her voice, she called out, "Gertie!"

Hearing her name, Gertie twisted her head to look at the housekeeper.

"Go and find Archie," Mrs. Chubb said, flicking her hand at the door. "Ask him to pick two buckets of sprouts and bring them here to the kitchen as fast as possible."

Out of the corner of her eye Gertie could see Charlotte glaring at her. Too bleeding bad. Charlotte could wash the cabbages now. Giving her friend a triumphant grin, Gertie hurried over to the door.

"Five minutes!" Michel roared. "Not a second later!"

Rolling her eyes, Gertie dragged the door open and charged into the hallway, almost knocking Lilly flying as they came face-to-face.

"Sorry," Gertie muttered and fled to the stairs. She had five minutes, and she was going to make the most of them.

It took her four times that long to find Archie. He wasn't in the ballroom, which was the most obvious place to look, nor was he in the courtyard. After questioning Philip, which was, as usual, a complete waste of time, and a couple of foot-men, she learned that Archie had gone back to his cottage to fetch some tools.

Icy pellets of hail spattered down on her head as she rounded the side of the building and headed for the cottage. She wished now that she'd grabbed her shawl on the way out. Just as she reached the gravel path leading up to the front steps, the door opened and Archie stepped outside, carrying a box of tools in one hand and a broom in the other.

He seemed shocked to see her and halted, his face wearing a wary look as if expecting bad news.

Gertie slowed her step as she walked toward him. Without waiting to reach him, she called out, "I have a message from Mrs. Chubb."

Archie kept his gaze on her face as she drew closer. "What is it?"

Gertie pressed a hand to her throat. "Wait while I get my breath."

"You're puffing a bit. Were you running?"

"Sort of." She drew in a deep breath and let it out again. "Okay. Mrs. Chubb wants you to pick two buckets of Brussels sprouts and bring them to the kitchen right away. Michel's waiting for them."

Archie looked relieved. "Is that all? I thought something bad had happened again."

"What? No! But it might if you don't get those sprouts back to Michel. He needed them ages ago."

"Yes, madam. Right away." Archie thrust the tools and the broom at her. "Take those to the courtyard for me, there's a love. Just leave them by the coal shed. I'll pick them up later."

Gertie grabbed hold of the heavy tool box. "Who do you think I am? Your bloody lackey?"

Archie grinned. "No, sir. You're nobody's lackey. I can tell that. Just a good friend doing me a favor. Right? I promise I'll return it someday soon."

"I'll keep you to that." She took the broom from him. "You know we have brooms in the hallway closets, don't you?"

"Not like this one." Archie gave it a pat. "This one's special. Are you coming to the pantomime tonight?"

Startled by the abrupt change of subject, she stared at him. "I hope so. Dinner is being served early tonight, so if we can get everything cleared away in time, we should be able to see most of it."

"Good." He nodded. "See you there, then." With a saucy wink at her, he sprinted off in the direction of the vegetable gardens.

She stood staring after him for several seconds before she finally pulled herself together and headed back to the kitchen. She had to keep reminding herself that he was soft on Mazie, and if Mazie never came back, there was Charlotte waiting in the wings. Too much competition for her, she told herself, as she stomped across the courtyard. Not that she was interested anyway.

All she wanted to do now was drop the tools by the coal shed and get back into the nice warm kitchen. Even if it meant washing cabbages in ice-cold water.

Phoebe stood behind the drawn curtains, listening to the hum of voices from the audience. The rows were filling up, and she was anxious to see if she had a full house. Drawing the edge of one curtain aside just enough to peer through the opening, she quicky scanned the seats.

They were about half-full, but it was early yet. Still twenty minutes or so before the orchestra played the introduction. Actually, the orchestra was a quartet, consisting of piano, drums, bass, and clarinet. Not exactly what she'd had in mind when she'd planned her masterpiece, but all she could afford within her budget.

Still, they were adequate, and the dress rehearsal had gone better than she'd expected. If the actual performance went as well, she would be ecstatic. She firmly believed that Madeline had put a curse on her presentations, since not one of them had been performed without some kind of disruption.

Letting go of the curtain, she took a last look around the stage, then trotted off to the wings to look in on her performers. They should all be dressed by now and ready to go. She wanted to make quite sure every one of them was clothed to perfection. This was an ambitious project for her, and the journey had not been without headaches.

She didn't exactly have the cream of the crop to work with, but she had done her best with what she had, and the result had been satisfactory.

Reaching the dressing room door, she threw it open. The babble of voices ceased the moment she stepped into the room. Several of the young women sat in chairs in various stages of dressing. Adelaide Lewis, the young woman playing Aladdin, stood in front of the full-length mirror, frowning at her image.

Catching sight of Phoebe's reflection, Adelaide spun around. "Look at these!" She tugged at her baggy white trousers, which were actually ladies' bloomers with the frills cut off. "They make me look fat. Why can't I wear tights, like they do on the London stage?"

Phoebe stared at her in shock. "*Tights?* I would never let my ladies appear onstage in such revealing attire. Besides, Aladdin is an Arab. That's what they wear. Billowing trousers and a waistcoat over a shirt." Phoebe examined her star with a keen eye. She was rather proud of the blue satin waistcoat. She'd found it in the secondhand shop in the High Street, and had snapped it up.

She'd spent hours sewing all those sequins and gold braid onto it, and she had to admit, the result was spectacular. Her Aladdin was going to sparkle and shine in the footlights.

Phoebe felt a surge of excitement at the thought. She had the most incredible sets she'd ever had, the costumes looked magnificent, and everyone knew their lines. This performance was going to be a roaring success and she couldn't be happier.

Her elation subsided a little when she noticed her Widow Twankey in the corner. True, Rachel was rather plump to begin with, but Phoebe had ordered her to pad her costume to make her look even more portly. Obviously, the girl had not understood, as her costume hung loose on her.

Phoebe marched over to her, prompting a look of dismay on the girl's face. "Where is your padding? I specifically told you to tuck pillows under your clothes."

Tears appeared in Rachel's eyes. "They made me look enormous, so I took them out."

"You are *supposed* to look enormous," Phoebe snapped, ignoring the tears. "Put those pillows back at once. They are right over there, on that table." She stood there, waiting with arms crossed, until the sniffling performer had bulges all over her body. "That's better."

She turned away, wishing fervently that she had been able to persuade Archie to play the widow. That would have been quite a triumph. Widow Twankey was always played by a man in *Aladdin* on the London stage. Having a girl play the part was the only flaw in an otherwise perfect presentation.

Brushing off her irritation, she called out to the group. "It's almost time to take your places. Do your best, everyone, and here's to another memorable performance at the Pennyfoot Hotel."

She thought she heard someone mutter, "It'll be bloody memorable all right," as she rushed out the door, but she decided to disregard it. It was curtain time, and she couldn't wait to see and hear the audience's approval when they caught their first glimpse of the amazing sets.

Meanwhile, seated close to the back row, Cecily cast a glance over the audience. She couldn't spot Sir Clarence and Lady Oakes anywhere, and she grew anxious wondering if perhaps they had decided to forgo the performance. If so, then her plan would have to be revised.

Baxter had yet to join her, but then he always waited until the very last minute. She spotted Madeline and Kevin in the second row. They had their heads together, seemingly in earnest conversation. Madeline, as usual, allowed her dark hair to flow freely about her shoulders. She had tucked sprigs of holly and mistletoe behind her ear, which on anyone else would have looked ridiculous. On Madeline, however, they looked festive and endearing.

Staring at her friend, Cecily remembered Madeline's warning. *Beware of the beast that flies.* It still made no sense to her, and she made a mental note to catch Madeline alone at the earliest opportunity and ask her if perhaps she could decipher the meaning of her enigmatic words.

Just then another group wandered through the doors. Cecily's pulse quickened as she caught sight of Sir Clarence and his wife. Lady Oakes looked majestic in a blue and silver gown, and a brilliant diamond tiara sparkling on her head.

They took their seats in the front row on the side closest to the door. Cecily wondered if they planned to beat a hasty retreat if the performance wasn't to their liking.

She turned her gaze back to the stage as the quartet began the overture. The pantomime was about to begin, and Baxter still hadn't made an appearance. Anxious now, she looked back at the door, her body relaxing in relief as her husband appeared in the doorway. He paused long enough to scan the back rows until he saw her raised hand, then quickly made his way over to her.

She had chosen the chair at the end of the row, and stood aside to allow him to pass to the one next to her. "You're late," she murmured as she sat down again. "I was beginning to worry."

"I ran into Fortescue. The fool kept spouting one of his convoluted tales about his stint in the army until I finally had to walk away from him. He was still talking to himself when I left him alone."

Cecily frowned. "He's supposed to be sitting in the front row right now, waiting for the curtains to open."

Baxter uttered a dry laugh. "Not much chance of that. The last I saw of him, he was ordering another brandy at the bar."

"Phoebe is going to kill him if he doesn't come to her presentation."

"I'd say that's preferable to sitting through the dratted thing."

Cecily dug into his arm with her elbow. "You know you enjoy watching Phoebe's dance group make fools of themselves."

"Well, I suppose it's more entertaining than listening to Fortescue's war memories."

Cecily smothered a laugh as the lights dimmed, and the curtains drew apart to reveal a street scene where Aladdin first meets the villain, Mustapha. Unfortunately, since Phoebe's dance group was all female, the villain was being played by a young woman who was much shorter than Aladdin and visibly nervous. Although she did her best to keep her voice deep and gruff, she simply sounded as if she had a bad cold.

By the time it came to the part where Mustapha trapped Aladdin in the cave, the illusion of the evil sorcerer had long disappeared. Titters of quiet laughter arose from the audience as Mustapha pointed a trembling finger at Aladdin and uttered what was supposed to be a dire threat. Aladdin tried to portray a victim recoiling in terror, but succeeded only in arousing more sniggering from the audience.

Cecily thought she heard her husband snoring and quickly turned her head to look at him. He sat bolt upright with a slightly glazed look on his face, but his eyes were open, and she turned back to the stage.

She was too tense to enjoy the show. So far, she hadn't found an excuse to leave, and she was very much afraid that Sir Clarence and his wife might decide not to stay for the second act. It wouldn't be the first time some of the audience had fled during the intermission and failed to return. In fact, it happened more often than not.

She would just have to come up with something that would not arouse Baxter's suspicion. If she pretended she didn't feel well, he would insist on accompanying her, welcoming the excuse to leave.

Mustapha had now exited the stage, and Aladdin was alone in the cave. Her mind furiously seeking a reason to exit herself, Cecily watched as Aladdin poked among the various pots, pans, and kettles that had been borrowed from the kitchen.

After lamenting some time about being unable to escape, Aladdin withdrew the magic lamp from the pile of kitchenware. After examining it for a moment or two, she announced that it looked dirty. "I need to clean it and make it shine," she declared, whereupon she produced a handkerchief from her bloomers and rubbed it on the lamp.

A loud bang erupted, and some of the ladies in the audience uttered a startled yelp as a cloud of smoke rose up in front of Aladdin. Alarmed, Cecily sat up, wondering if Phoebe had set fire to the stage.

The smoke cleared, however, leaving Aladdin staring at the space where it had been. "I need to clean it and make it shine," she repeated, her voice raised. She rubbed the lamp again and Cecily braced for the next explosion, but it never came.

Aladdin stood in the middle of the stage, looking helpless, until Phoebe's voice could be heard from the wings screeching, "Where in heaven's name is that blasted genie?"

"I need to clean it and——" Aladdin shouted, and got no further as a dancer dressed in flowing robes leapt from behind a cardboard rock. The woman's elbow caught the side of the rock and sent it crashing to the ground.

Phoebe screeched again from the wings and the curtains began to close, while the audience cheered and clapped their approval.

Seizing the moment, Cecily leaned toward Baxter. "I had better go and see if I can help. I'll be back right away."

"I'll come, too," he began, but she shook her head at him.

"No, wait for me here. I shall only be a few moments." Before he could argue, she rose from her chair and headed for the stage door.

No doubt, when he found out later that she had deceived him, he would be upset with her. She hoped by then she would have found something to confirm her suspicions.

To her relief, Sir Clarence and Lady Oakes remained in their seats, though neither of them looked as if they were enjoying the performance. She may not have much time, Cecily warned herself, as she slipped through the door and closed it behind her.

Instead of turning into the wings, she headed straight for the dressing room. From there she could exit the back door and run around the building to the front door. It would mean passing by the ballroom windows, but thankfully it was pitch black outside. Everyone's attention was on the stage, with most of the audience no doubt eagerly awaiting the next calamity.

As she stepped outside into the cold night, she felt snow-flakes brushing her cheek. Shivers shook her body, and she wished she'd worn something warmer. Her violet silk gown bared her throat and a third of her back, and the flimsy material did little to protect her from the icy wind.

Light spilled from the windows, and she caught a glimpse of her husband. He sat with a grim expression on his face that made her wish now that she'd allowed him to accompany her on her mission.

Then common sense assured her that she was far more inconspicuous on her own. The last thing she wanted to do was draw attention to the fact that she was about to go snooping in a revered guest's suite.

She reached the front door without encountering anyone, and quickly dived into the warmth of the lobby. The crackling fire in the fireplace was so welcoming, she almost rushed over there to warm her shivering body. Time, however, was precious, and she couldn't spare a single second. Sir Clarence and his wife could return at any moment.

As she climbed the stairs, her knee reminded her that it was not quite healed. Ignoring the pain, she sped around the landing and hurried up the second flight. Reaching the top hallway, she cautiously looked left and right to ensure she was alone.

The fluttering gas lamps caused the shadows to leap across the walls, giving her a moment's concern, until she assured herself that no one was in the hallway. She had borrowed the master key from Mrs. Chubb earlier, who had known better than to ask questions.

It took her only a few seconds to reach Sir Clarence's suite, open the door, and step inside. An oil lamp sat on the bedside table, a bright flame covering the turned-up wick. Coal embers burned in the fireplace, casting a soft glow over the room.

Without knowing exactly what she was looking for, Cecily crossed the floor and flung open the wardrobe door. Suits and gowns hung from the rack, and several pairs of shoes sat beneath them. After examining everything, she could find nothing of interest.

Her next target was the wastebasket, but all she could find in there were the remains of train tickets, a crumpled invitation to a Christmas bazaar, and a single gray glove. Examining the glove, Cecily could find no mark on it anywhere. The luxurious soft suede would have warmed a hand in the coldest of weathers, and she wondered if Lady Oakes had perhaps accidentally dropped it in the basket.

Cecily was tempted to place the glove in a drawer, then reminded herself she was there to find some kind of proof that Sir Clarence was a vicious killer. Leaving the contents of the wastebasket alone, she walked over to the dressing table.

After searching through piles of undergarments in the drawers, she turned her attention to a gorgeous jewelry box fashioned in exquisite inlaid wood. Lifting the lid, she caught her breath at the sight of the glittering diamonds, glossy pearls, and gold chains. A beautiful emerald ring caught her attention, and feeling somewhat guilty about her prying, she picked it up for a closer look.

As she did so, a heavy gold necklace slipped to the side, revealing something beneath it that looked familiar. Her pulse quickened as she drew aside the necklace to have a better look.

With trembling fingers, she withdrew the sparkling object, Madeline's warning echoing in her mind. *Beware the beast that flies.* Now she knew what her friend had meant by those words. She was looking at Lady Farthingale's dragonfly brooch.

As she stared at it, her mind racing with the implications of finding it in Lady Oakes's jewelry box, she heard a sound behind her.

The distinct click of a key in the lock.

CHAPTER
❋ 17 ❋

Charlie sat at the kitchen table, munching on a ham sandwich. He'd forgotten that supper was being served earlier that evening, and by the time he'd arrived in the kitchen, everyone had gone upstairs to watch the pantomime.

Charlie did not like pantomimes. He had been to only one of Phoebe's presentations, and it had been enough to turn him off stage productions entirely. Especially pantomimes.

So, he was quite content to sit in the quiet, empty kitchen and enjoy his sandwich in peace, without the boisterous conversation and laughter that usually accompanied his meals.

He was still struggling with indecision about his dilemma with Henry. On the one hand, he desperately wanted to tell her he knew her secret, for his own peace of mind. On the other hand, he was worried that if he did so, it could lead to other people realizing the truth. If Mr. Baxter found out that his mechanic was a girl, he'd probably sack her on the spot.

The last thing Charlie wanted was for Henry to lose her job. Not only for the girl's sake, but because he would miss her more than he'd missed Tess. A lot more. Perhaps if he went to Mr. Baxter himself and explained the whole story, adding lots of praise for Henry's work, the boss might consider keeping her.

He started composing in his mind the speech he would give to Mr. Baxter, and took a large bite out of the sandwich to help him concentrate. Just then the door opened and in walked the girl of his dreams.

He gulped down the mouthful of bread and ham, choked, then started coughing and spluttering like an old codger.

Henry took one startled look at him, then leapt over to his chair and proceeded to thump him on the back.

Struggling to get his breath, Charlie gasped out, "Hold on! Hold on! You're killing me!"

Henry stopped the merciless pounding, stammering, "I'm sorry, sir. I was just trying to help."

Tears running down his cheeks, Charlie nodded. He tried to speak again but it came out as a hoarse croak. "Water?"

Henry leapt over to the sink, snatched a glass from a cupboard, and filled it with water. Carrying it back to Charlie, she asked anxiously, "Are you all right? Shall I tell someone? Dr. Prestwick is upstairs watching the pantomime. I can fetch him if you like."

Still trying to breathe normally, Charlie shook his head. "I'll be fine." The words sounded a little less hoarse, and he relaxed his shoulders. "Thank you." He took a sip of water and, finding it went down all right, drank half the glass before putting it down.

Henry sat down at the table, still watching him with an anxious expression that warmed his heart. "You look a little red in the face. Are you sure you're all right?"

Charlie nodded again. "I'm sure." He sounded a bit closer to his usual voice, and risked asking, "Why aren't you watching the pantomime?"

"I was." Henry shrugged. "It wasn't very good. I got bored and came down here for something to eat."

"You didn't have supper?"

"No, everyone was gone by the time I got here. I didn't know they were going to have it early."

"Me neither." He held up what was left of his sandwich. "This is my supper."

Henry shook her head. "There's got to be something better than that." She got up and went over to the counter. Lifting the lid of a cauldron, she sniffed at the contents. "Do you like beef stew?"

"I do." He watched her lift the cauldron and carry it over to the stove. After putting it down, she bent over to open the stove's belly, then shoveled coal into it and closed the door. He hastily looked away as she turned and walked back to the table.

"It was still warm, so it shouldn't take long," she said as she sat down again.

Charlie nodded.

Henry picked up a spoon and studied it for a moment before putting it down again. "They have stoves that are run by gas now. I wonder why Mrs. Baxter doesn't have one for the kitchen. They say it works a lot faster than a coal stove."

"It would cost too much to change it over." Charlie reached for his water. Now was the perfect opportunity to let her know that he knew her secret. Only, how did he tell her?

"But they already have gas lamps here. It would just mean a new stove and hooking it up, wouldn't it?"

He couldn't just blurt out that he knew the truth. He had to lead up to it somehow. Realizing that she'd asked a question, he looked at her. "What?"

That was a mistake, as he melted as soon as she looked into his eyes. He saw her frown, and quickly tried to make amends. "I'm sorry. I was trying to work out something in my mind. Actually, there's something I need to tell you—"

He broke off as the door opened and Gertie marched into the room. She seemed agitated, flapping her hand back and forth at them, as if warding off some evil spirit. "Did you see that pantomime? Have you ever seen such bloody rubbish in all your life?"

She stomped over to the stove, lifted the lid of the cauldron, dropped it again, and stomped back to the table. "At least my twins are enjoying it. I left them up there and came down for something to eat." She stared at Henry, who looked as if she was about to run from the room. "Have you ate yet?"

Sensing Henry's reluctance to answer, Charlie spoke for her. "We're waiting for the stew to heat up."

"All right. I'll wait with you." Gertie plonked herself down on a chair with a sigh.

At the same time, Henry shot up, muttering, "I'll have something later. Good night." With that, she rushed out the door.

Gertie stared after her. "What's got into his bloody hair?"

Charlie didn't answer. He was too busy cursing himself for not speaking up sooner. Now he'd lost a golden opportunity. Then again, this could be fate stepping in, warning him not to say a word to Henry or anyone else. Maybe it was for the best.

He picked up the glass and drank some more water. All right. No more agonizing over it. No matter how hard it might be, he would just keep the secret to himself and not say a word to Henry or anyone else. For everyone's sake.

Cecily turned around, the brooch still in her hand, and stared at the door as it slowly opened to reveal a familiar figure.

"What are you doing in here?" Lady Oakes stepped inside the room and closed the door behind her. Her gaze switched to the open jewelry box on the dresser. "You are stealing my jewels! I shall have you arrested."

"I don't think so," Cecily said, keeping her voice calm. She held up the brooch. "After all, you stole this from Lady Farthingale, did you not?"

Shock registered on the aristocrat's face, then she raised her chin. "I certainly did not. My husband purchased that brooch for me last Christmas."

"Indeed. Yet I saw Lady Farthingale wearing it just a few days ago." Cecily moved away from the dresser. "Perhaps I should ask your husband where he bought it."

"No!" Lady Oakes held up her hand. "There is no need to bother him with this. I didn't steal it from Lady Farthingale. She gave it to me. As a gift."

"I believe you told me you had never met the lady."

Lady Oakes sank onto the side of the bed. "I didn't want my husband to know that I was that well acquainted with her. He had a fierce feud with her husband."

Cecily stared at her, doubts creeping into her mind. Now that she thought about it, she didn't remember seeing the brooch when she had visited Lady Farthingale in her hotel. Could she possibly be wrong in her deductions of the crime? Or was Lady Oakes more of an accomplished liar than she'd realized?

There was only one way to find out. "Lady Oakes," she said as she sat down next to the woman on the bed, "I'm afraid I have some rather startling news about your husband."

The woman's eyes narrowed. "Clarence? What the devil are you saying?"

"I'm sure you will have trouble accepting this," Cecily said, "but I'm convinced that your husband was being black-mailed by Lord Percival, and Sir Clarence had to dispose of him."

Lady Oakes sat for a long moment in silence. When she spoke again, her voice sounded flat and unemotional. "Why would Lord Percival blackmail my husband?"

"I believe that somehow the gentleman found out about your past. Your husband must have been desperate to keep it a secret, since he is responsible for two deaths."

For an instant, raw anger blazed in the aristocrat's eyes, then she dropped her gaze to her hands. "I see," she said quietly.

Cecily cleared her throat. "I'm so sorry."

Lady Oakes looked up again. "How do you know about my past?"

"From one of my staff. She heard it from someone else while at a protest."

"A protest," Lady Oakes repeated, as if trying to work out something in her mind. After a moment or two, she added, "You said my husband was responsible for two deaths?"

"Yes. He was seen paying a visit to Lady Farthingale at her hotel. She was attacked later in the street. I believe your husband was responsible."

Lady Oakes shook her head. "Unbelievable."

"I feel confident enough in my suspicions to contact the constable. I wanted to warn you before I did so."

Cecily began to rise, but just then the aristocrat suddenly broke into a storm of weeping.

"I can't . . . believe . . . my husband would do such a thing," she managed between sobs. "I just can't understand."

Cecily sat down again and put out a tentative hand, but Lady Oakes surged to her feet.

"Excuse me. I need to fetch a handkerchief." Still sniffing and gulping, she hurried over to the dressing table and opened a drawer.

Cecily stared down at her hands. She was playing a dangerous game. If her hunches were wrong, she would be in all sorts of trouble. Not only with Sir Clarence, but also her husband and, no doubt, Inspector Cranshaw.

Lady Oakes returned to the bed and blew her nose on the white lace-edged handkerchief. "Please excuse me," she muttered. "This is all so overwhelming."

"I'm sure it must be." Cecily tried to sound sympathetic. "Is there anything I can do? Anyone I can call?"

"I think you've done quite enough."

Taken aback by the woman's sudden harsh tone, Cecily stared at her. "I beg your pardon?"

"Your prying into affairs that don't concern you are causing me a great deal of trouble."

So, she was right after all. Staring into the cold eyes of the aristocrat, Cecily could hear again the soft footstep behind her just before she fell down the stairs. She was right about everything. Lady Oakes standing by the Christmas tree, nursing a sore arm that must have been injured when she'd attacked Lady Farthingale. The single glove in the wastebasket—the other one no doubt covered in blood and had perhaps been disposed of immediately.

Her last conversation with Lady Oakes. The aristocrat had used the past tense when speaking of Lady Farthingale, though she couldn't have known the woman was dead.

At the time Cecily had not noticed the mistake. Now it all made sense.

Lady Oakes smiled, though without a trace of humor. "Ah, I see you are beginning to understand. Let me enlighten you. Yes, Sir Percival was blackmailing my husband. We have paid dearly to ensure his silence, but I just couldn't trust him to keep his mouth closed. When he drank too much, which was practically every night, he became careless with his conversation. I was afraid he'd unintentionally reveal our secret."

"So you decided to get rid of him."

Lady Oakes's gaze flickered for a moment. "I had no choice."

Cecily struggled to control her rising anger. "You let an innocent young girl take the blame for your despicable deed. Had I not intervened, that child would have spent most of her life in prison."

"I'm sorry about that." She actually sounded regretful. "I thought she would have an alibi, or that no one would believe she was capable of the crime. I only used her name on the note because I saw her with Percy and I knew he would come running if he thought she was inviting him to a midnight rendezvous."

"Well, you were mistaken. Mazie was arrested and she is still behind bars, quite terrified to be there, I might add."

Lady Oakes's face hardened again. "I did what I had to do. Not just for me, but for my husband's reputation. We would have been ruined if the truth had come out."

"What about Lady Farthingale?"

Lady Oakes shrugged. "She knew about the blackmail. I saw her leave her scarf at the reception desk, and I picked it up. I intended to keep it for myself, but then I decided to tie it around her husband's neck, hoping to cast suspicion on her. Her husband had left her close to destitute. It was feasible that she would want to get rid of him."

"You hated her that much?"

"She suspected my husband of killing Percy and demanded a large sum of money to keep her silence."

Cecily shook her head. All this scheming and destroying lives made her sick. "I saw your husband going into her hotel."

"He went to pay her. I couldn't trust her to keep silent about everything, so I followed her the next morning and took back the money."

"Stealing her brooch and killing her in the process."

"Again, I had no choice."

"Does your husband know you are responsible for these deaths?"

Lady Oakes's smile was far from pleasant. "If he does, he hasn't said as much. He's probably grateful to me for solving his problems."

"I would think they were more your problems than his."

Cecily started to rise, her blood chilling when a knife appeared in Lady Oakes's hand. Apparently, the woman had drawn it from its hiding place when she went to fetch her handkerchief. Given a few more minutes, Cecily told herself, she would have found the knife and the proof she'd sought.

Now she was faced with a woman who was obviously unbalanced if she thought she could get away with a third murder.

"You're not going anywhere." Lady Oakes surged to her feet and stood over her, the knife poised to strike. "I will silence anyone who threatens to reveal my secret."

Cecily struggled to remain calm. "How are you going to explain a dead body in your suite?"

Lady Oakes shrugged. "I came in here and found you lying dead on my bed. You must have learned the identity of Lord Farthingale's killer and he silenced you."

Cecily nodded. "In which case, since the body is in your suite, your husband will be an immediate suspect."

"He is in the card rooms with a dozen or more witnesses."

"Then you will be a suspect. If I were you, I'd find a better place to do your silencing."

The aristocrat stared at her for so long, Cecily began to

hope she'd made her point, but then, with a howl of rage, Lady Oakes raised her hand higher.

Just as she began the downward thrust, Cecily drove the open pin of the dragonfly brooch deep into the woman's upper arm.

Lady Oakes let out a shriek of pain and dropped the knife. Before she could bend down to retrieve it, Cecily thrust both her hands forward and shoved the woman hard.

As Lady Oakes toppled backward into the wardrobe behind her, Cecily scrambled to retrieve the knife.

Just then the door burst open and Sir Clarence bounded into the room. He stopped short at the sight of his wife cowering in front of the wardrobe and Cecily standing over her holding the knife.

"What the devil—" he began, but his wife's frantic outburst interrupted him.

"Stop her! She's trying to kill me!"

Sir Clarence turned to Cecily and she quickly held up her hand. "I'm not trying to kill anyone. It's your wife who has committed two murders. She has just confessed to the crimes."

The gentleman's face turned white and he staggered back a step or two.

"Don't believe her!" Lady Oakes screamed. "She's the one who killed them. Now she's trying to kill me."

Before Cecily could answer, the door opened once more. She let out a long sigh of relief when she saw the worried face of her husband.

"What the blue blazes is going on in here?" Baxter thundered.

"Lady Oakes has confessed to the murders of Lord and Lady Farthingale." Cecily held up the pearl-handled knife. "She attempted to kill me, too."

Sir Clarence groaned. "That is my wife's knife. I bought it for her long ago to protect herself if she was attacked by a pickpocket."

"She stole it from me!" Lady Oakes started weeping again. "I didn't kill anyone."

Sir Clarence put an arm around his wife. "It's all right, Penelope. We'll get this sorted out."

Worried that he believed in his wife's innocence, Cecily said quietly, "I must send for the constable. This has to be reported."

To her relief, there was only sorrow in Sir Clarence's eyes when he looked at her. "I know. We will wait here for him."

Baxter strode to his wife's side. "Are you all right?"

Cecily smiled up at him. "I'm perfectly fine. Thanks to a beast that flies."

Baxter shook his head. "What does that mean?"

"I'll tell you later." She turned to Sir Clarence, who still held his weeping wife. "I trust you will keep your wife here until the constable arrives?"

The gentleman gave her a solemn nod. "You have my word."

She met his gaze for a moment. "I'm so sorry."

His face was bleak as he answered, "As I am."

She left the room with her husband following close on her heels.

Outside in the hallway, Baxter drew her to a stop. His face was set in grim lines, and she braced herself for his anger.

"What in heaven's name possessed you to go after that woman alone?"

"I didn't go after her. I went to search her room and she surprised me." She laid a hand over his. "Can we discuss this in our room? We must ring the constabulary right away."

"Very well." He let her go and followed her to their suite.

Once inside, he made his way directly to his desk and reached for the telephone. After dialing for the night clerk at the main desk, he waited, his face a stern mask, for several long seconds before barking into the receiver, "Put me through to the police."

Seconds ticked by while he waited yet again, giving Cecily time to prepare her speech. She had promised him once that she would never again put herself in a dangerous position without him by her side. Then again, she had actually not been in danger when she entered the room. She just hadn't expected Lady Oakes to return to her suite quite so soon.

Obviously, the woman had not appreciated Phoebe's efforts at entertaining.

Baxter's voice brought Cecily back to attention. "Albert? Hugh Baxter here. We need a constable here at the Pennyfoot right away. Yes. I know. Yes, it is necessary. We have a murderer here waiting to be arrested. No, I will tell Northcott when he gets here. Or shall I ring Inspector Cranshaw? Yes, I thought so." Muttering an oath under his breath, Baxter replaced the receiver on its hook, and sat down behind his desk. After opening a drawer, he withdrew a small bottle of brandy, muttering, "I need some sustenance."

She watched him tip the bottle to his lips, her heart

racing with anxiety. Baxter rarely drank spirits, and when he did, it was always from a glass, a sip at a time. She had never before seen him drink straight from a bottle.

She sat down on her chair and folded her hands in her lap. Whatever happened next, she promised herself, she would remain calm. After a few moments of uncomfortable silence, she said quietly, "I'm sorry, Bax. I just wanted to take a look around the room. I thought Lady Oakes would be watching the pantomime."

"Why didn't you tell me that's where you were going?"

"Because you would have insisted on coming with me, and that would have attracted too much attention. As it was, I managed to slip away among all that confusion onstage. What prompted you to come to Lady Oakes's suite?"

"Phoebe managed to restore order onstage. When the curtains opened again and you didn't return, I became worried. I saw Sir Clarence and his wife get up and leave, and I decided to go and look for you. You weren't backstage and I thought you might have come back here for some reason. I reached the top of the stairs just in time to hear a scream and saw Sir Clarence burst into his suite. I heard your voice, and rushed in after him."

"Lady Oakes said her husband was in the card rooms. He must have changed his mind and decided to join his wife instead."

"There were no games tonight. I canceled them so the maids could see the pantomime if they were so inclined."

Cecily looked at him in surprise. "That was most thoughtful of you."

He gave her an accusing look. "When you left, you told me you were going to help Phoebe."

She shrugged. "I had to say something."

"You lied to me."

She looked down at her hands. "Yes, I did. And I'm sorry. Sometimes it is necessary."

"It should never be necessary to lie to your husband."

"You're right." She looked up at him and gave him her sweetest smile. "I'm so sorry. I did what I thought was best for the situation. I didn't think for one minute that I would be in danger."

Baxter leaned his elbows on the desk and ran his hands through his hair. "Cecily Sinclair Baxter, you will one day be the death of me. My heart can't take much more of this worrying about you."

She widened her smile. "But you love me, do you not?"

A reluctant glimmer of a smile tugged at his lips. "Indubitably."

"Then that's all that matters." She got up and walked around the desk. Bending over, she dropped a kiss on his cheek. "I love you, too."

P.C. Northcott arrived a short time later, out of breath and obviously annoyed at being dragged away from a family party. "I hope you didn't get me here on a wild-goose chase, Mrs. B," he said when Cecily met him in the lobby. "I'm confident I already have your murderer in custody."

"And I'm just as confident the real murderer is upstairs in

room number three. The lady has confessed to me that she killed Lord Farthingale to prevent him revealing a secret that would have destroyed not only her life but that of her husband, as well." She held out the knife she had taken with her from the room. "Here is what I believe is the murder weapon that killed Lady Farthingale. Lady Oakes also used it to attack me."

Judging from the pained expression on his face, P.C. Northcott wrestled for several moments with the desire to do his duty and his reluctance to admit he was wrong before slowly nodding. "Very well. I shall go up there and make an arrest. I may need you as a witness when Inspector Cranshaw gets here. That's unless the lady confesses to me." He took the knife from her and carefully wrapped it in his handkerchief before sliding it into his pocket.

Cecily wasn't too thrilled at the prospect of having to deal with the wretched inspector, but if it meant freeing Mazie from prison, she would match wits with the devil himself. "You can count on it," she told the constable, then watched him climb the stairs with a certain amount of misgivings.

Lady Oakes was an accomplished liar. Cecily had no actual proof of anything she had told Northcott. At least Sir Clarence appeared to believe her. She could only hope that he would persuade his wife to admit the truth.

It was not until the next morning that Cecily received the news for which she had been anxiously awaiting. Mrs. Chubb brought the message herself. "Mazie has been released!" she joyfully exclaimed the minute she entered Cecily's suite. "She's spending a day or two with her mother, but she'll be back here in time for Christmas."

"That is good news!" Cecily felt like hugging her house-keeper, but managed to restrain herself.

She was somewhat disappointed that Mrs. Chubb had no further news of the case, but her questions were answered when she arrived downstairs to find Sir Clarence about to leave the hotel.

"I must apologize for my wife," he told her when she walked over to him to bid him farewell. "She is not well. I suspected she might be involved in Lord Farthingale's demise when she told me his wife's scarf had been tied around his neck. I had to wonder how she knew that. I just couldn't make myself believe her capable of such a ghastly crime."

Looking into his agonized face, Cecily's heart went out to him. "I'm so terribly sorry. It must have been a shock for you."

"It was." He glanced around the lobby, apparently making sure they were out of earshot before adding, "I found her on a London street a few years ago. She had been beaten and was near death. I felt sorry for her and brought her home, intending only to keep her safe until she had recovered." He paused, obviously struggling to continue.

"But you fell in love with her," Cecily said, her heart aching for both of them. She could never condone the terrible deeds that Lady Oakes had committed, but she could certainly understand her desperation. The woman had been rescued from the worst kind of degradation and granted a magical life of love and security. The thought of losing it all again must have been unbearable. How sad that it had to end this way.

"Yes. I loved her." Sir Clarence raised his chin to gaze at

the ceiling. "I didn't find out until after we had married about her true past. I promised her I would keep it a secret, but somehow Lord Farthingale found out about it. He threatened to expose her unless I paid him."

"Yes, your wife told me as much."

Sir Clarence shook his head. "I was in the card rooms until after midnight the night the man died. When I returned to my room, my wife was still up and dressed. Normally, when I returned that late, she would be in bed and asleep. I thought nothing of it at the time, but when I heard Lord Farthingale had been murdered, I began to suspect my wife."

"That must have been hard."

"It was. I fought against my suspicions, but then Lady Farthingale met us as were leaving the hotel, and accused me of killing her husband. She said she would go to the police if we didn't keep up the payments." He shrugged. "What could I do? I agreed to pay her, although Penelope swore to me that she wasn't responsible for Percy's death."

"But she didn't trust the woman to keep silent."

Sir Clarence's face creased in pain. "No, she didn't. As I mentioned, my wife is not well. The stress of her past life affected her mind. She wasn't thinking as a normal person."

"She confessed to you?"

"Yes." He uttered a loud sigh. "After you left, she told me everything. When the constable arrested her, she just gave up and became, once more, the helpless, pitiful creature I'd found on the street. I would have done anything to keep her secret, but I would never have resorted to murder. I find that wholly unforgivable."

Cecily cleared her throat, fending off the tears that

threatened. "I'm so very sorry, Sir Clarence. If there's anything we can do for you, please don't hesitate to ask."

"Thank you, but no." He touched his forehead with his fingers in a brief farewell. "I'm returning to London and I'll do my best to put this part of my life behind me."

She watched him leave, wishing she could have found the words to give him some hope.

"So, it's all over?"

Hearing her husband's voice behind her, she turned, smiling through her threatening tears. "Hugh, my love. I am so lucky to have you. "

His face lit up as he smiled at her. "I am the lucky one." He reached for her hand and tucked it under his elbow. "Would you care to join me for breakfast?"

"I can't think of anything I would like more." She squeezed his arm. "I'm just so happy that all is well with our world again and now we can enjoy our Christmas."

Baxter covered her hand with his. "Amen to that."

Ready to find
your next great read?

Let us help.

Visit prh.com/nextread

Penguin
Random
House